74052928

W9-BFE-368

Michael
Recycle

Michael Recycle

Become our fan on Facebook **facebook.com/idwpublishing**
Follow us on Twitter **@idwpublishing**
Subscribe to us on YouTube **youtube.com/idwpublishing**
See what's new on Tumblr **tumblr.idwpublishing.com**
Check us out on Instagram **instagram.com/idwpublishing**

www.IDWPUBLISHING.com

Ted Adams, CEO & Publisher
Greg Goldstein, President & COO
Robbie Robbins, EVP/Sr. Graphic Artist
Chris Ryall, Chief Creative Officer
David Hedgecock, Editor-in-Chief
Laurie Windrow, Sr. VP of Sales & Marketing
Matthew Ruzicka, CPA, Chief Financial Officer
Lorelei Bunjes, VP of Digital Services
Jerry Bennington, VP of New Product Development

ISBN: 978-1-63140-985-1   20 19 18 17   1 2 3 4

Originally published as MICHAEL RECYCLE issues #1–4.

WRITER
ELLIE WHARTON

ARTIST
ALEXANDRA COLOMBO

LAYOUTS
THOM ZAHLER

LETTERER
SHAWN LEE

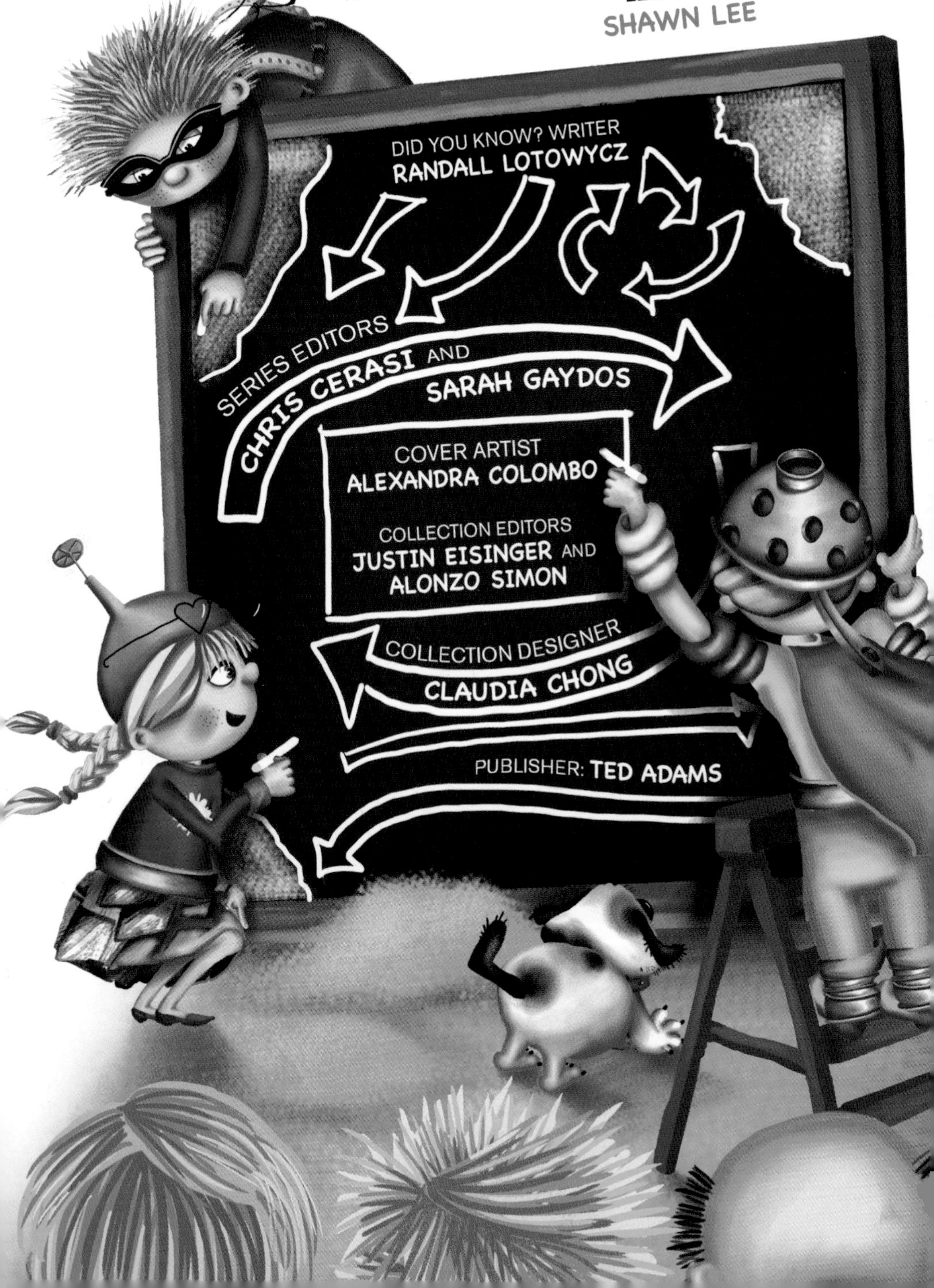

DID YOU KNOW? WRITER
RANDALL LOTOWYCZ
SERIES EDITORS
CHRIS CERASI AND
SARAH GAYDOS
COVER ARTIST
ALEXANDRA COLOMBO
COLLECTION EDITORS
JUSTIN EISINGER AND
ALONZO SIMON
COLLECTION DESIGNER
CLAUDIA CHONG
PUBLISHER: TED ADAMS

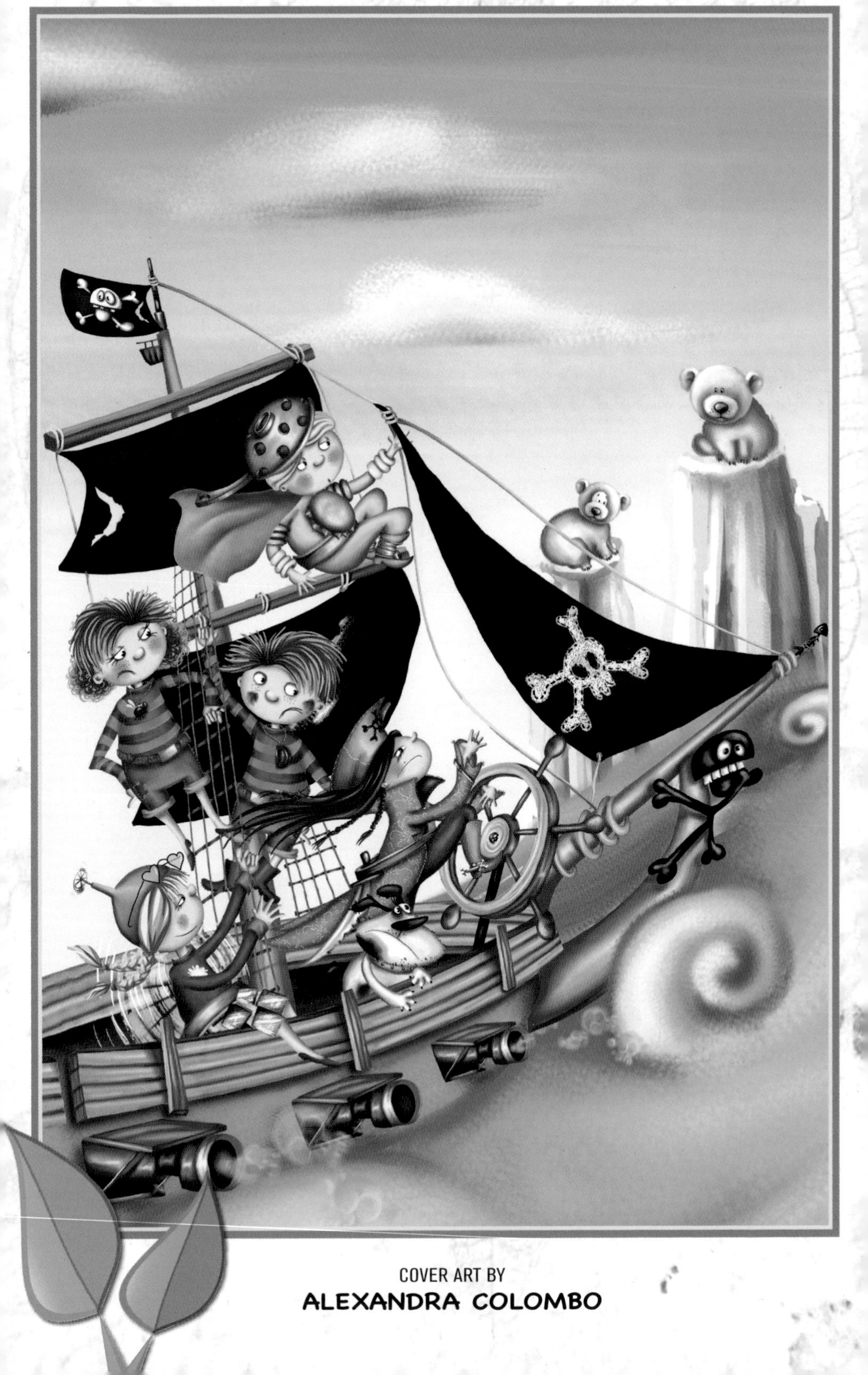

COVER ART BY
ALEXANDRA COLOMBO

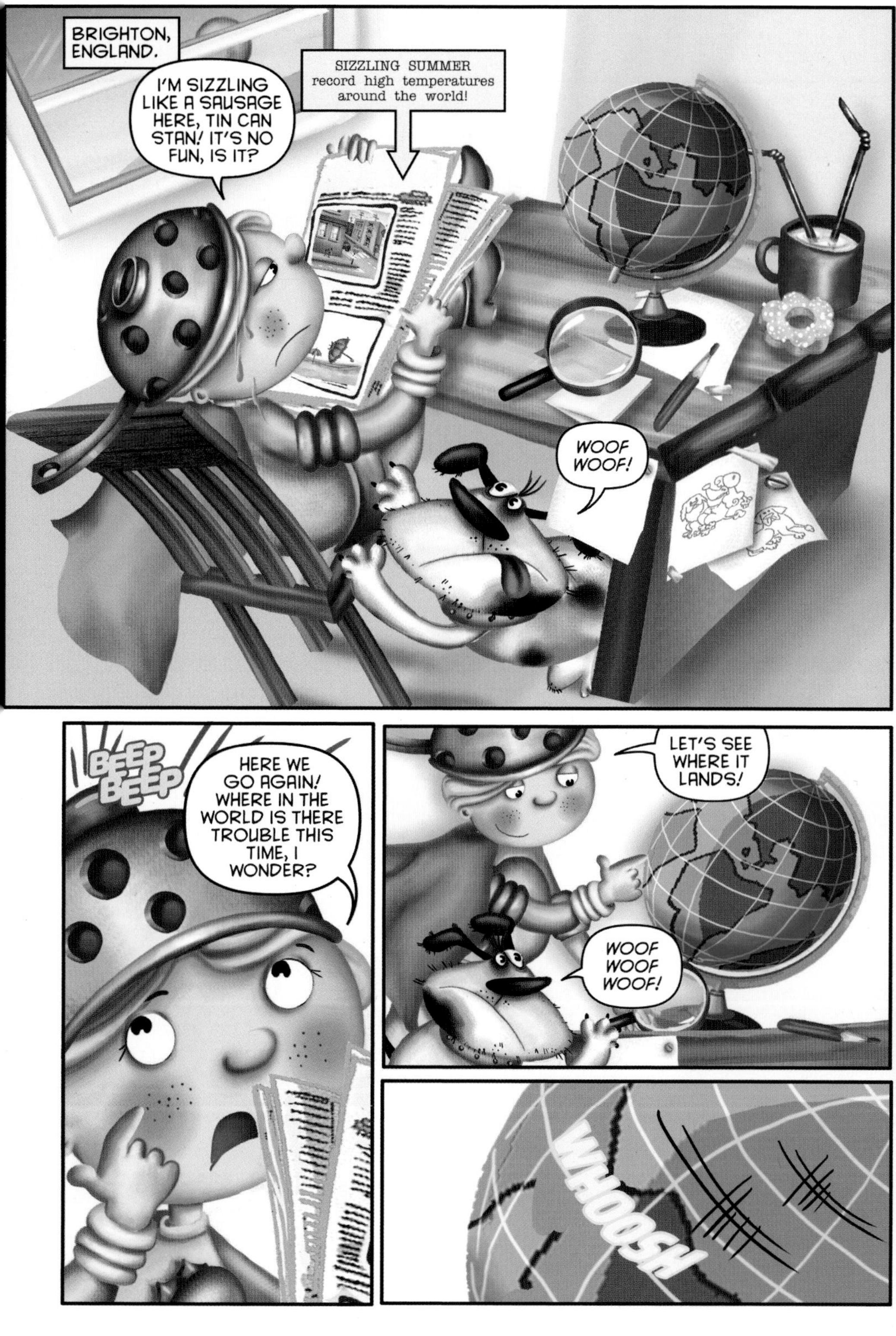
BRIGHTON, ENGLAND.
I'M SIZZLING LIKE A SAUSAGE HERE, TIN CAN STAN! IT'S NO FUN, IS IT?
SIZZLING SUMMER record high temperatures around the world!
WOOF WOOF!
BEEP BEEP
HERE WE GO AGAIN! WHERE IN THE WORLD IS THERE TROUBLE THIS TIME, I WONDER?
LET'S SEE WHERE IT LANDS!
WOOF WOOF WOOF!
WHOOSH

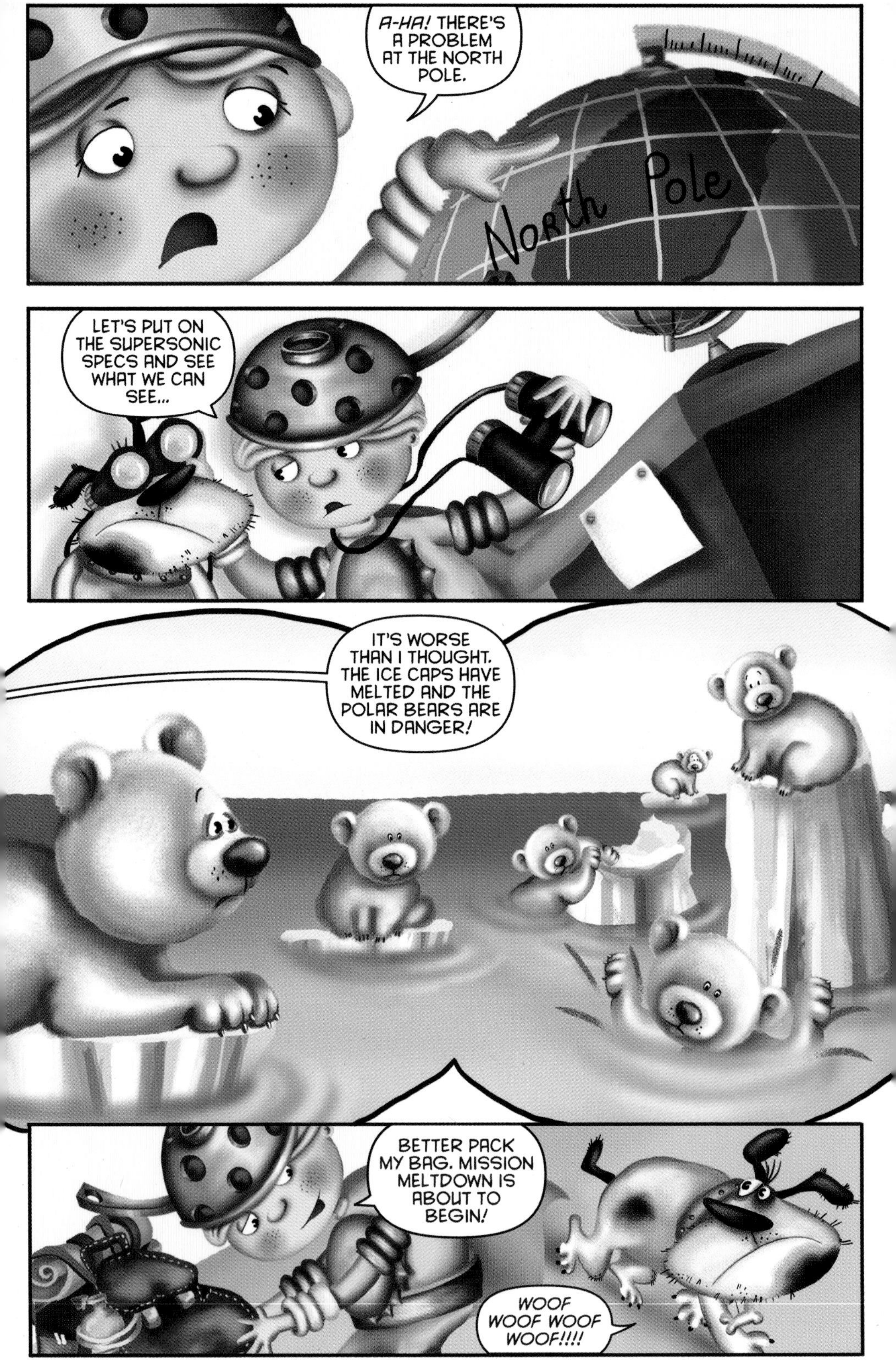
A-HA! THERE'S A PROBLEM AT THE NORTH POLE.
North Pole
LET'S PUT ON THE SUPERSONIC SPECS AND SEE WHAT WE CAN SEE...
IT'S WORSE THAN I THOUGHT. THE ICE CAPS HAVE MELTED AND THE POLAR BEARS ARE IN DANGER!
BETTER PACK MY BAG. MISSION MELTDOWN IS ABOUT TO BEGIN!
WOOF WOOF WOOF WOOF!!!!

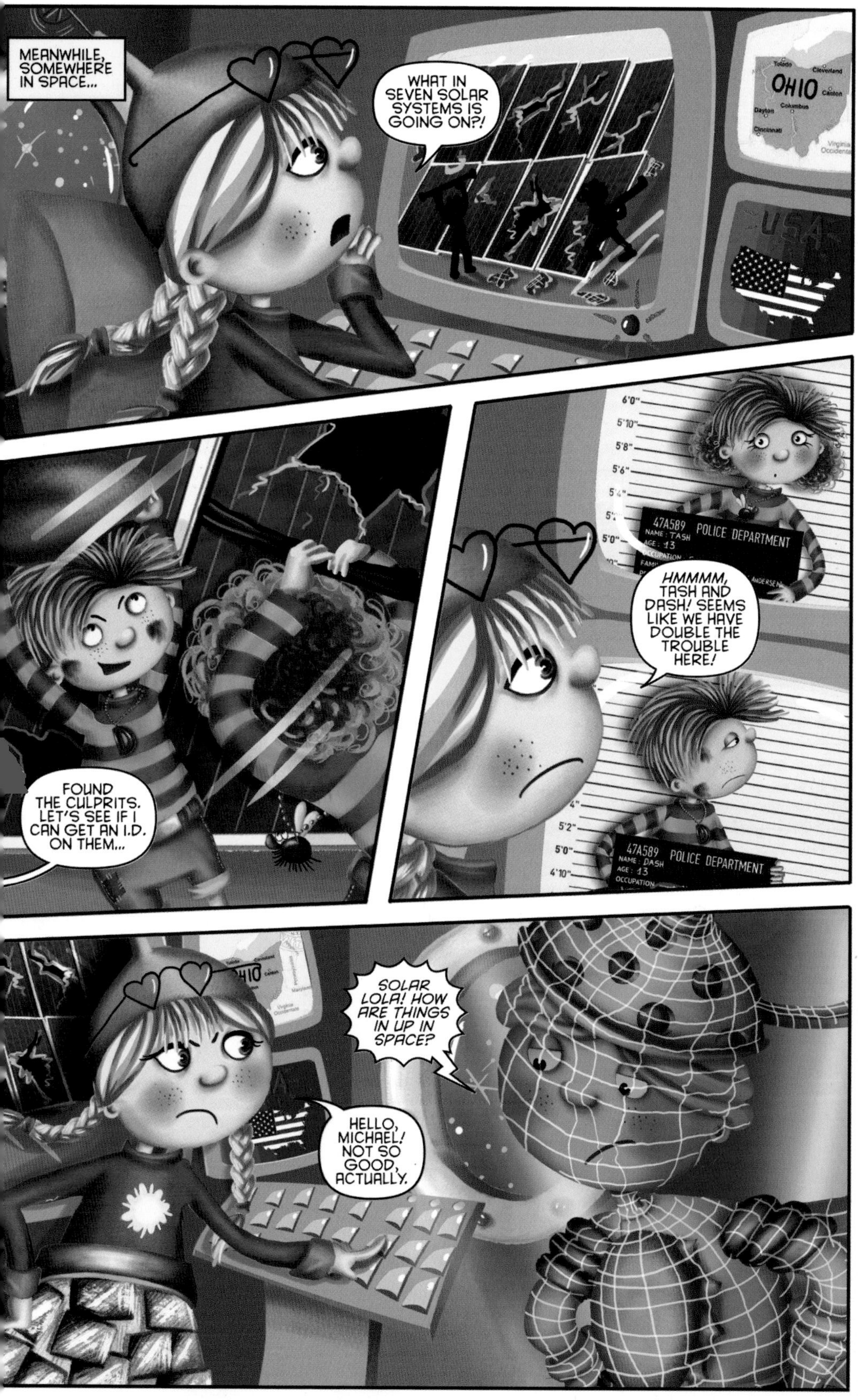

MEANWHILE, SOMEWHERE IN SPACE...
WHAT IN SEVEN SOLAR SYSTEMS IS GOING ON?!
OHIO
USA
FOUND THE CULPRITS. LET'S SEE IF I CAN GET AN I.D. ON THEM...
47A589 POLICE DEPARTMENT
NAME: TASH
AGE: 13
HMMMM, TASH AND DASH! SEEMS LIKE WE HAVE DOUBLE THE TROUBLE HERE!
47A589 POLICE DEPARTMENT
NAME: DASH
AGE: 13
SOLAR LOLA! HOW ARE THINGS IN UP IN SPACE?
HELLO, MICHAEL! NOT SO GOOD, ACTUALLY.

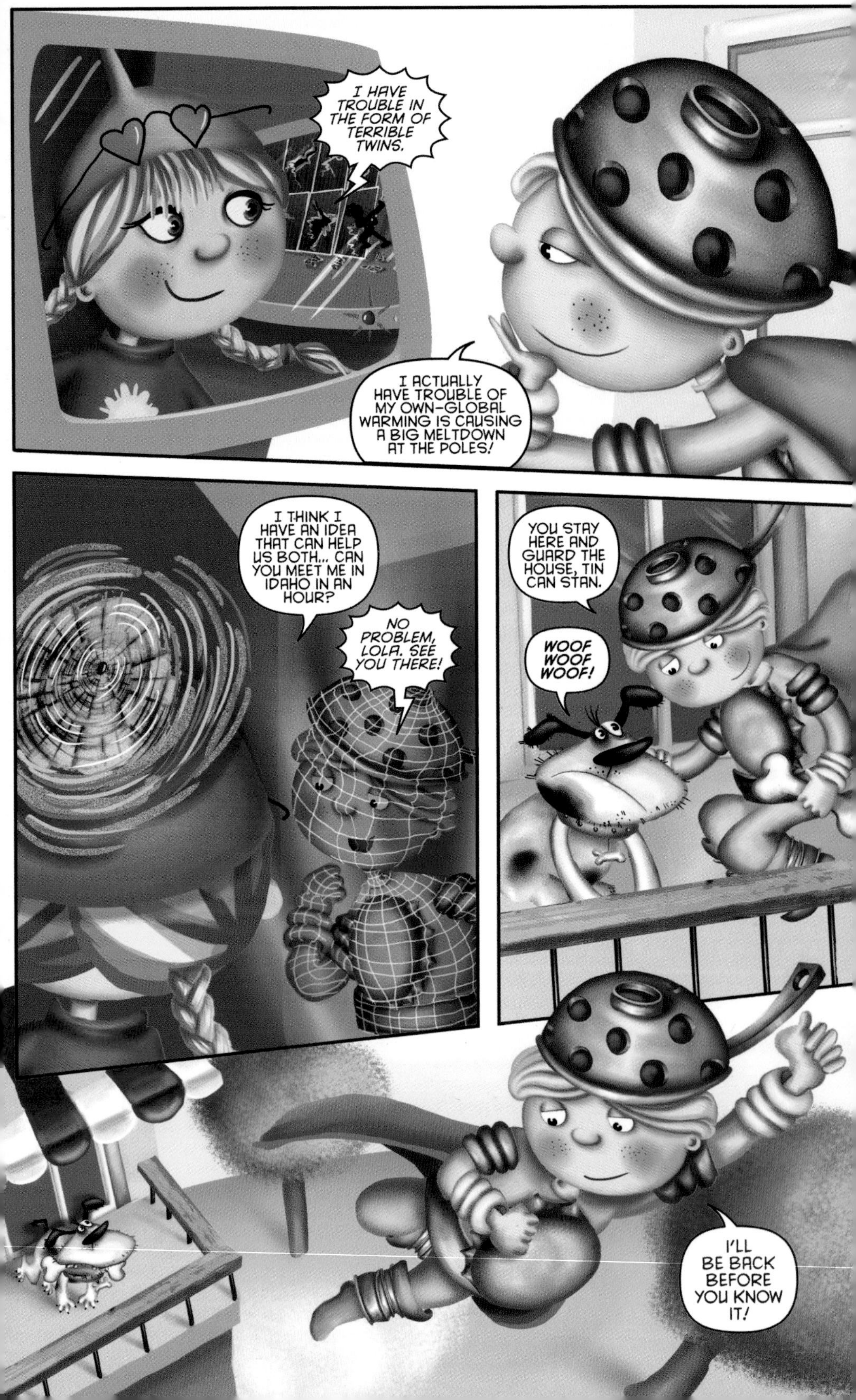
I HAVE TROUBLE IN THE FORM OF TERRIBLE TWINS.
I ACTUALLY HAVE TROUBLE OF MY OWN–GLOBAL WARMING IS CAUSING A BIG MELTDOWN AT THE POLES!
I THINK I HAVE AN IDEA THAT CAN HELP US BOTH... CAN YOU MEET ME IN IDAHO IN AN HOUR?
NO PROBLEM, LOLA. SEE YOU THERE!
YOU STAY HERE AND GUARD THE HOUSE, TIN CAN STAN.
WOOF WOOF WOOF!
I'LL BE BACK BEFORE YOU KNOW IT!

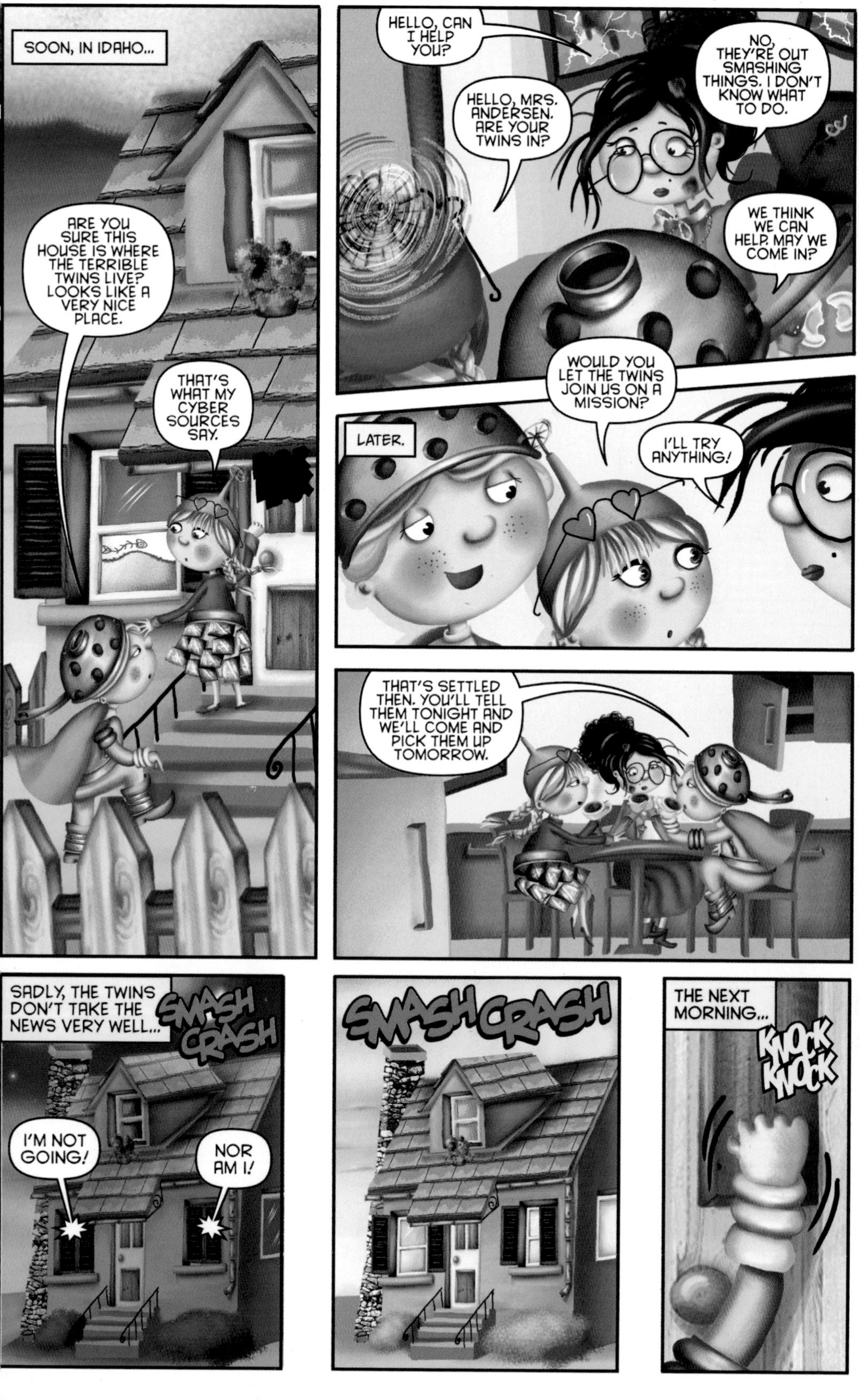
SOON, IN IDAHO...
ARE YOU SURE THIS HOUSE IS WHERE THE TERRIBLE TWINS LIVE? LOOKS LIKE A VERY NICE PLACE.
THAT'S WHAT MY CYBER SOURCES SAY.
HELLO, CAN I HELP YOU?
HELLO, MRS. ANDERSEN. ARE YOUR TWINS IN?
NO, THEY'RE OUT SMASHING THINGS. I DON'T KNOW WHAT TO DO.
WE THINK WE CAN HELP. MAY WE COME IN?
LATER.
WOULD YOU LET THE TWINS JOIN US ON A MISSION?
I'LL TRY ANYTHING!
THAT'S SETTLED THEN. YOU'LL TELL THEM TONIGHT AND WE'LL COME AND PICK THEM UP TOMORROW.
SADLY, THE TWINS DON'T TAKE THE NEWS VERY WELL...
SMASH
CRASH
I'M NOT GOING!
NOR AM I!
SMASH
CRASH
THE NEXT MORNING...
KNOCK
KNOCK

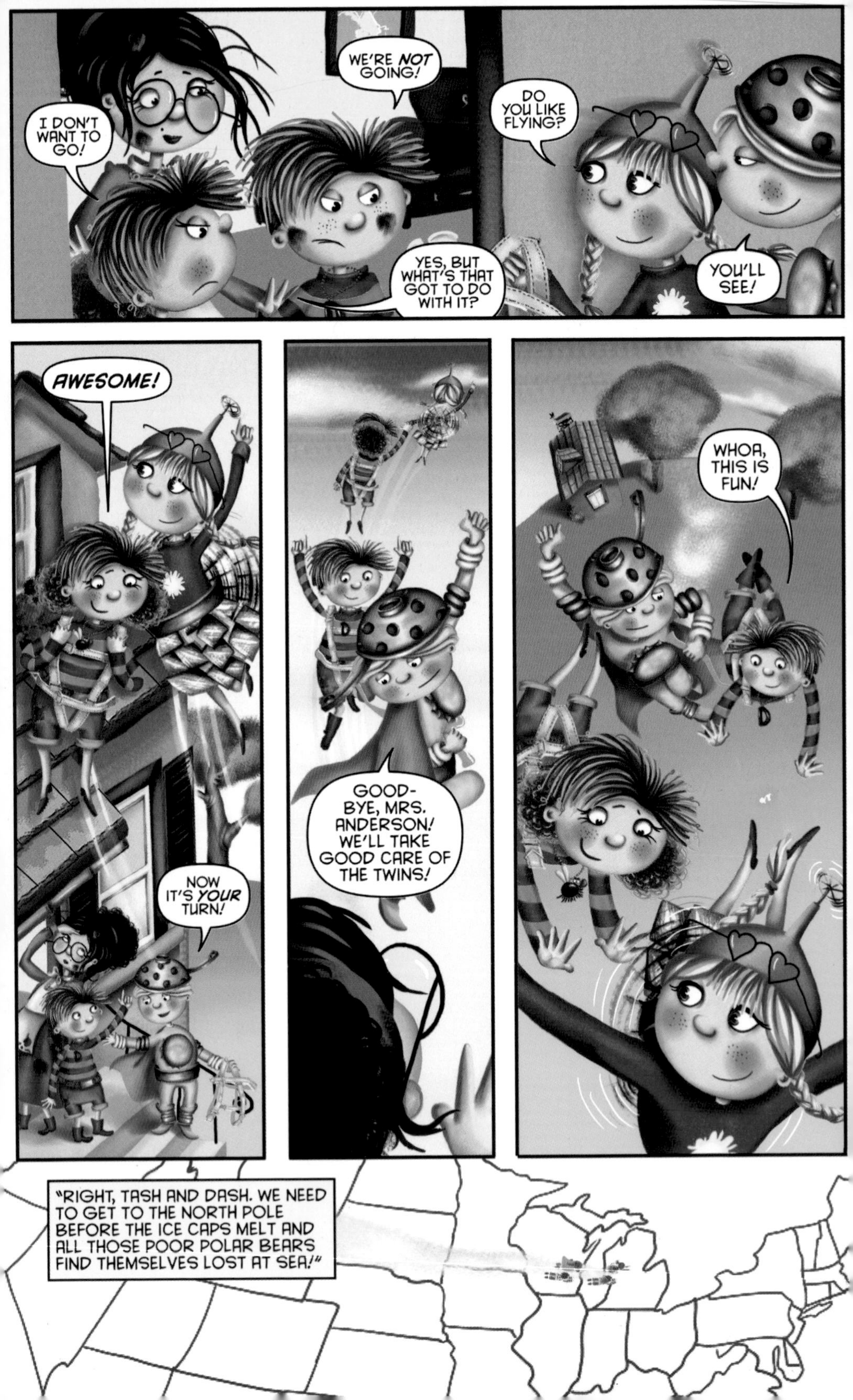
I DON'T WANT TO GO!
WE'RE NOT GOING!
DO YOU LIKE FLYING?
YES, BUT WHAT'S THAT GOT TO DO WITH IT?
YOU'LL SEE!
AWESOME!
NOW IT'S YOUR TURN!
GOOD-BYE, MRS. ANDERSON! WE'LL TAKE GOOD CARE OF THE TWINS!
WHOA, THIS IS FUN!
"RIGHT, TASH AND DASH. WE NEED TO GET TO THE NORTH POLE BEFORE THE ICE CAPS MELT AND ALL THOSE POOR POLAR BEARS FIND THEMSELVES LOST AT SEA!"

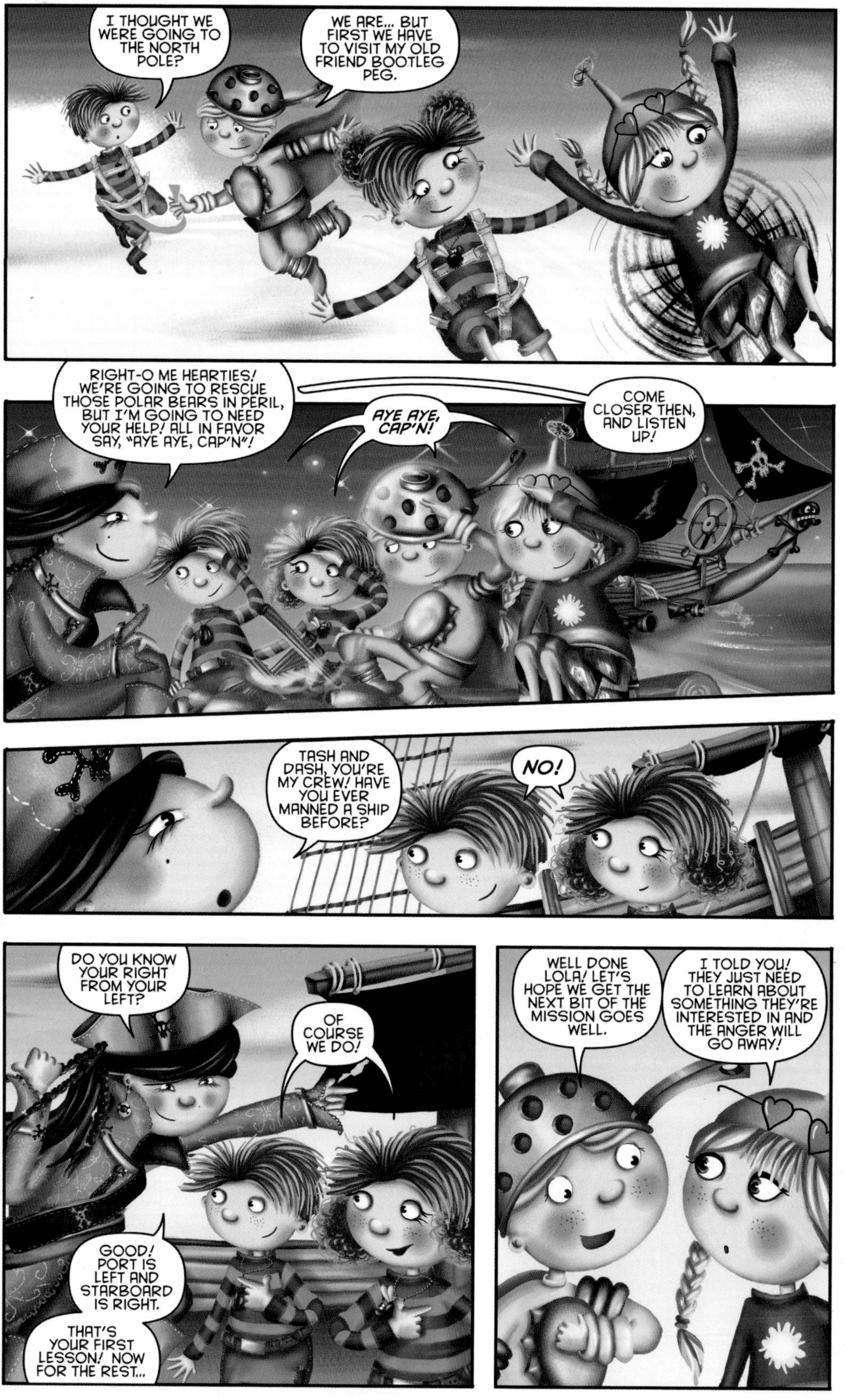
I THOUGHT WE WERE GOING TO THE NORTH POLE?
WE ARE... BUT FIRST WE HAVE TO VISIT MY OLD FRIEND BOOTLEG PEG.
RIGHT-O ME HEARTIES! WE'RE GOING TO RESCUE THOSE POLAR BEARS IN PERIL, BUT I'M GOING TO NEED YOUR HELP! ALL IN FAVOR SAY, "AYE AYE, CAP'N"!
AYE AYE, CAP'N!
COME CLOSER THEN, AND LISTEN UP!
TASH AND DASH, YOU'RE MY CREW! HAVE YOU EVER MANNED A SHIP BEFORE?
NO!
DO YOU KNOW YOUR RIGHT FROM YOUR LEFT?
OF COURSE WE DO!
GOOD! PORT IS LEFT AND STARBOARD IS RIGHT.
THAT'S YOUR FIRST LESSON! NOW FOR THE REST...
WELL DONE LOLA! LET'S HOPE WE GET THE NEXT BIT OF THE MISSION GOES WELL.
I TOLD YOU! THEY JUST NEED TO LEARN ABOUT SOMETHING THEY'RE INTERESTED IN AND THE ANGER WILL GO AWAY!

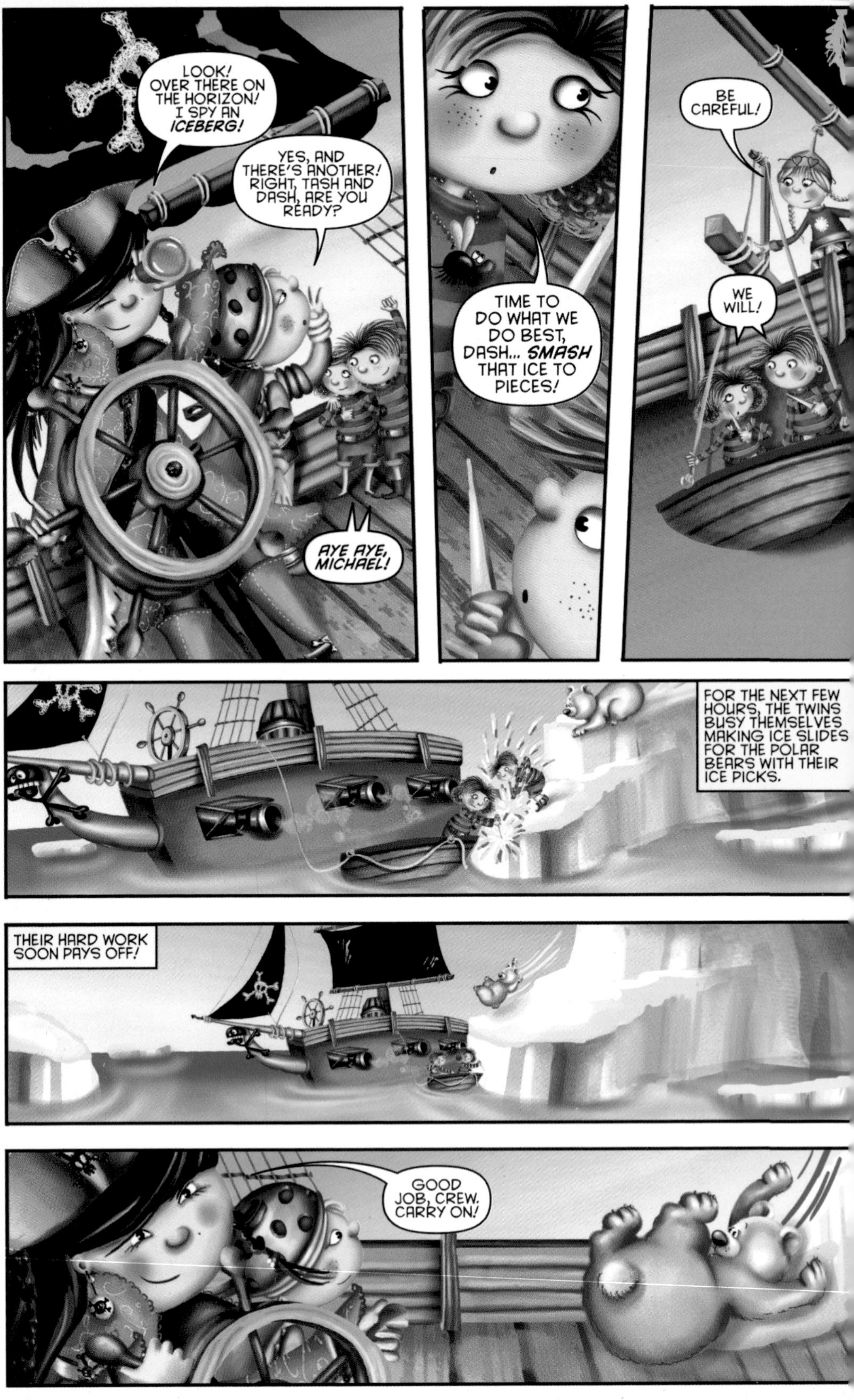

LOOK! OVER THERE ON THE HORIZON! I SPY AN ICEBERG!
YES, AND THERE'S ANOTHER! RIGHT, TASH AND DASH, ARE YOU READY?
AYE AYE, MICHAEL!
TIME TO DO WHAT WE DO BEST, DASH... SMASH THAT ICE TO PIECES!
BE CAREFUL!
WE WILL!
FOR THE NEXT FEW HOURS, THE TWINS BUSY THEMSELVES MAKING ICE SLIDES FOR THE POLAR BEARS WITH THEIR ICE PICKS.
THEIR HARD WORK SOON PAYS OFF!
GOOD JOB, CREW. CARRY ON!

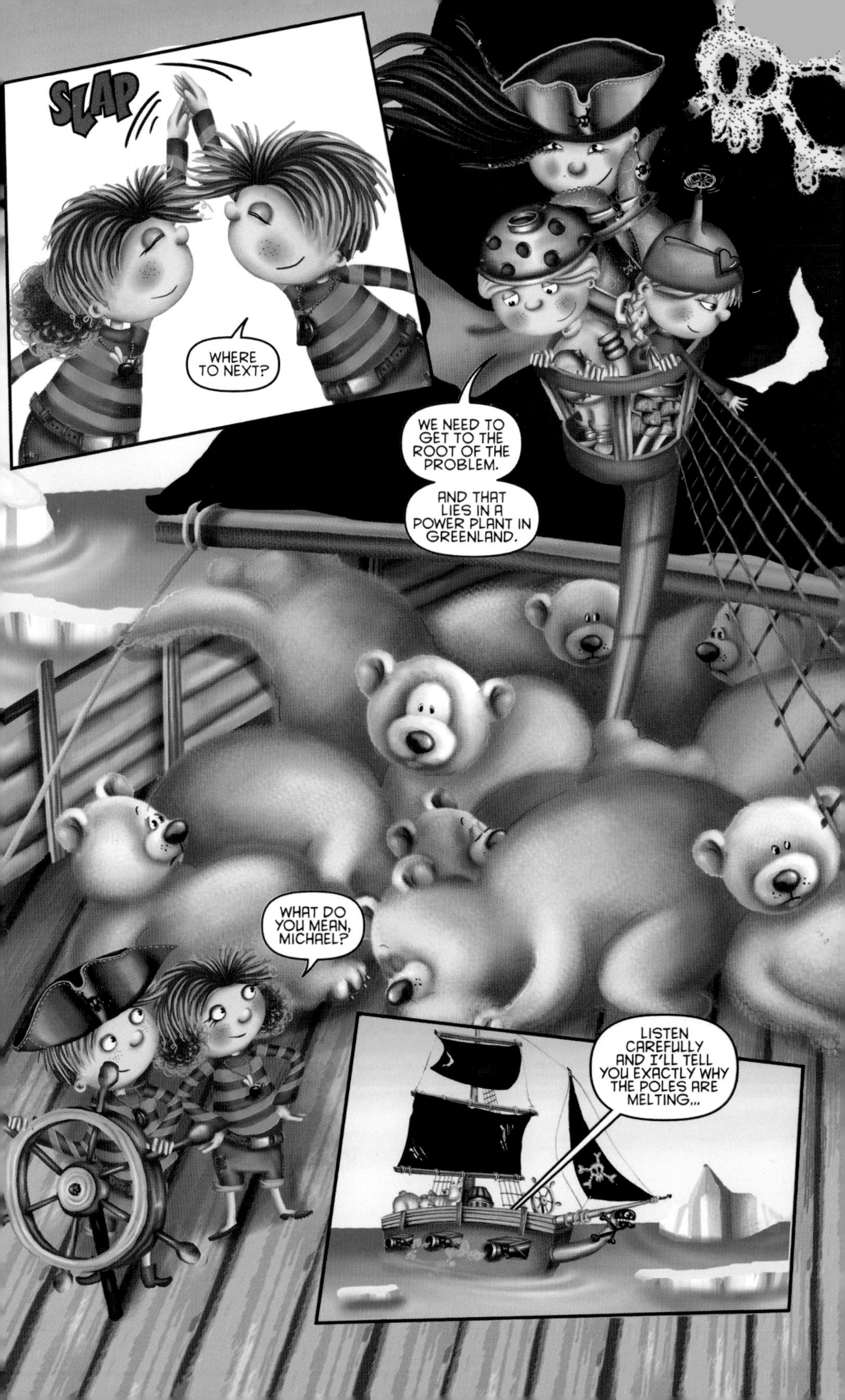
SLAP
WHERE TO NEXT?
WE NEED TO GET TO THE ROOT OF THE PROBLEM.
AND THAT LIES IN A POWER PLANT IN GREENLAND.
WHAT DO YOU MEAN, MICHAEL?
LISTEN CAREFULLY AND I'LL TELL YOU EXACTLY WHY THE POLES ARE MELTING...

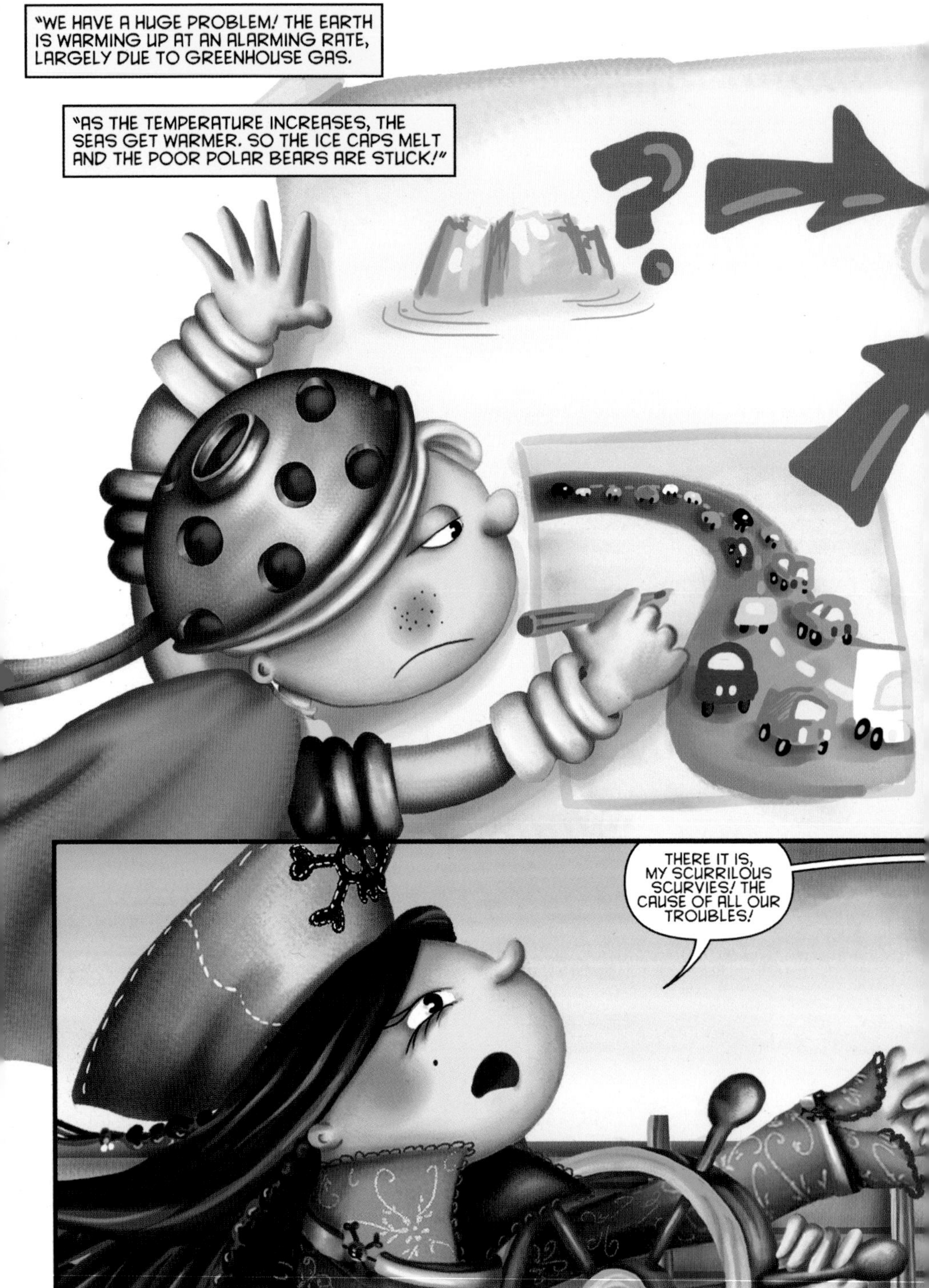
"WE HAVE A HUGE PROBLEM! THE EARTH IS WARMING UP AT AN ALARMING RATE, LARGELY DUE TO GREENHOUSE GAS.
"AS THE TEMPERATURE INCREASES, THE SEAS GET WARMER. SO THE ICE CAPS MELT AND THE POOR POLAR BEARS ARE STUCK!"
THERE IT IS, MY SCURRILOUS SCURVIES! THE CAUSE OF ALL OUR TROUBLES!

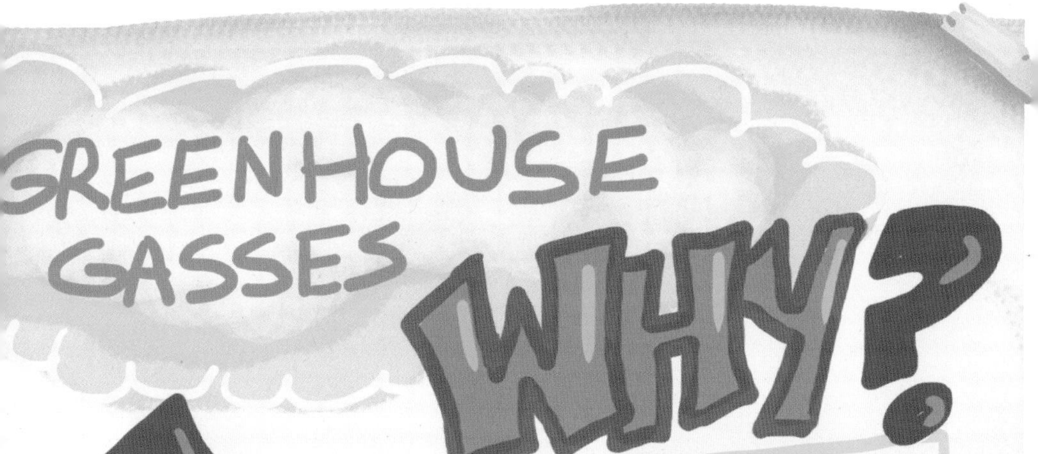
GREENHOUSE GASSES
WHY?
WHAT ELSE?
NEW ONE WHERE?

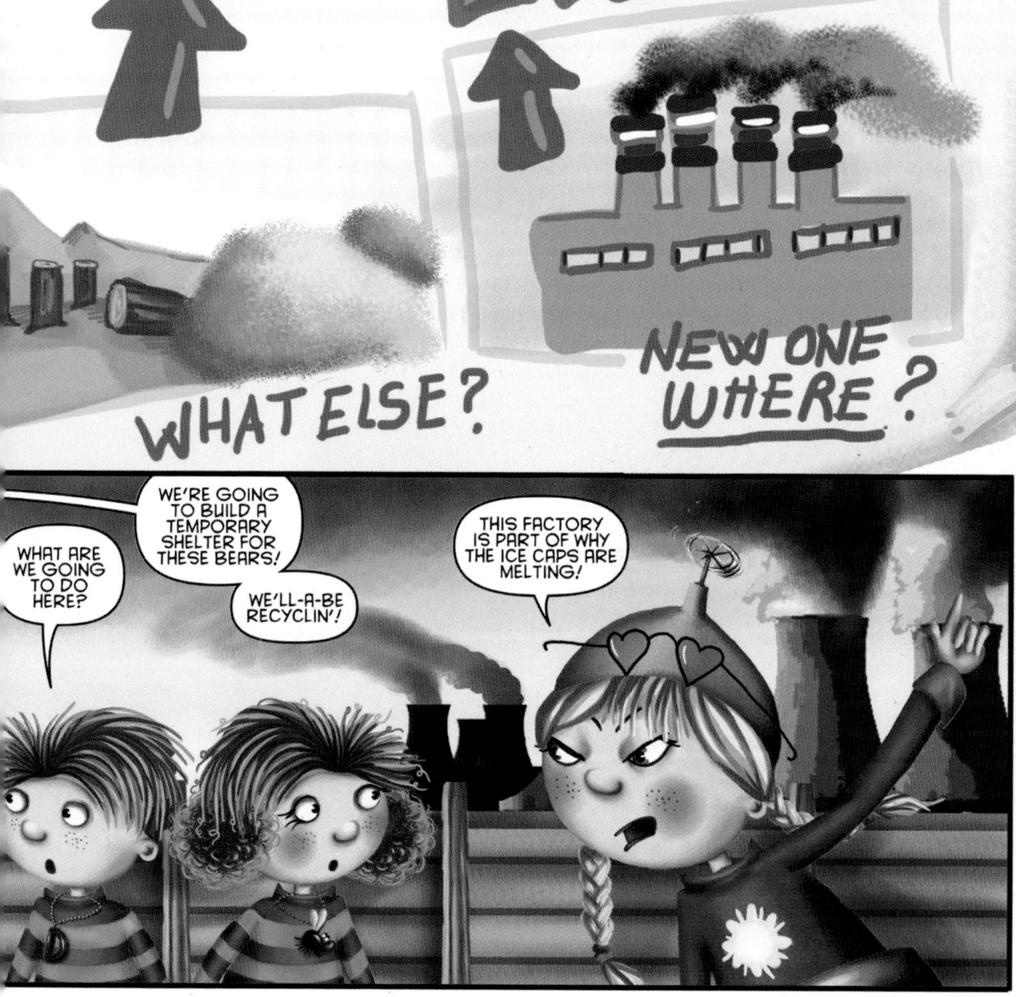
WHAT ARE WE GOING TO DO HERE?
WE'RE GOING TO BUILD A TEMPORARY SHELTER FOR THESE BEARS!
WE'LL-A-BE RECYCLIN'!
THIS FACTORY IS PART OF WHY THE ICE CAPS ARE MELTING!

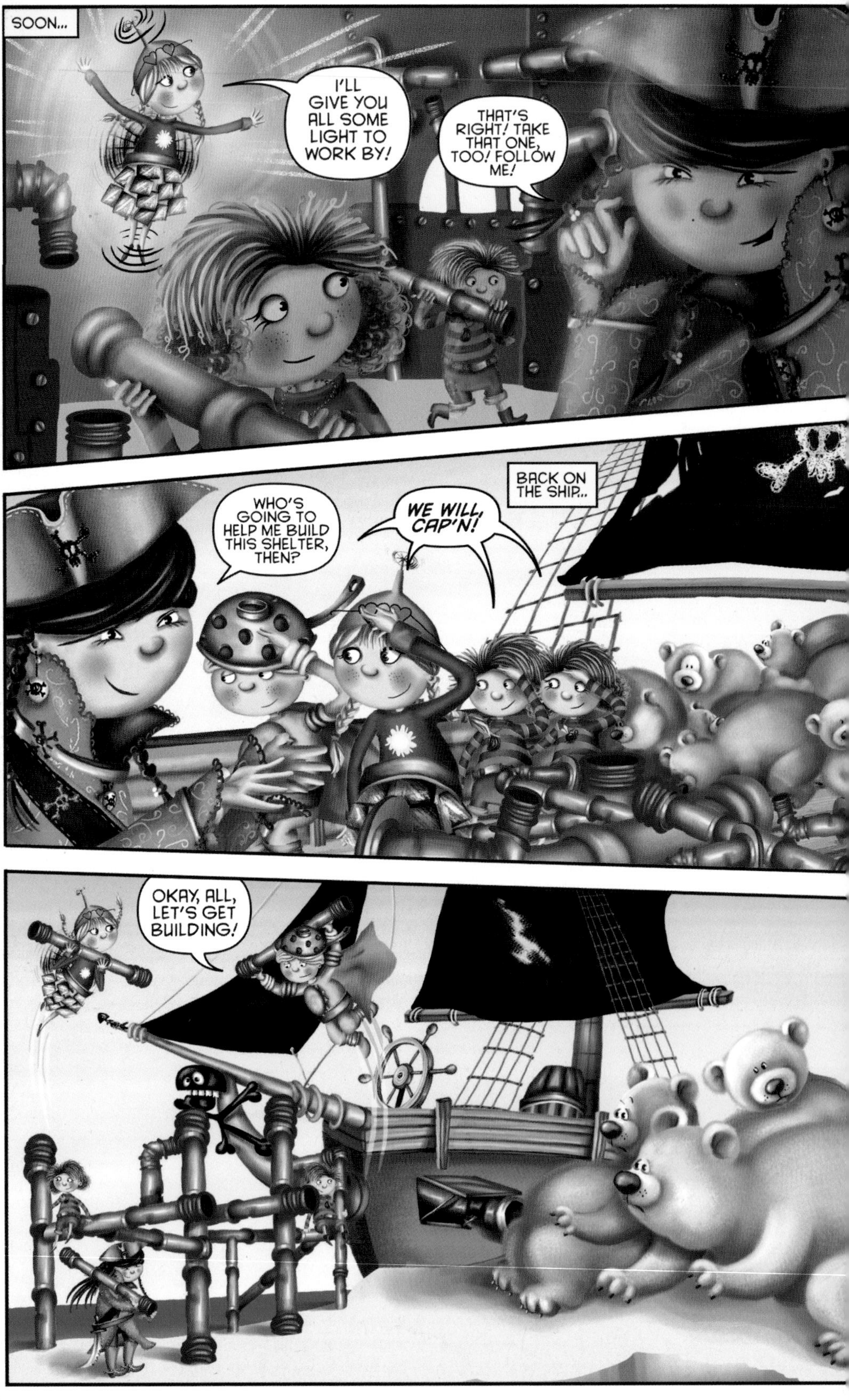
SOON...
I'LL GIVE YOU ALL SOME LIGHT TO WORK BY!
THAT'S RIGHT! TAKE THAT ONE, TOO! FOLLOW ME!
BACK ON THE SHIP...
WHO'S GOING TO HELP ME BUILD THIS SHELTER, THEN?
WE WILL, CAP'N!
OKAY, ALL, LET'S GET BUILDING!

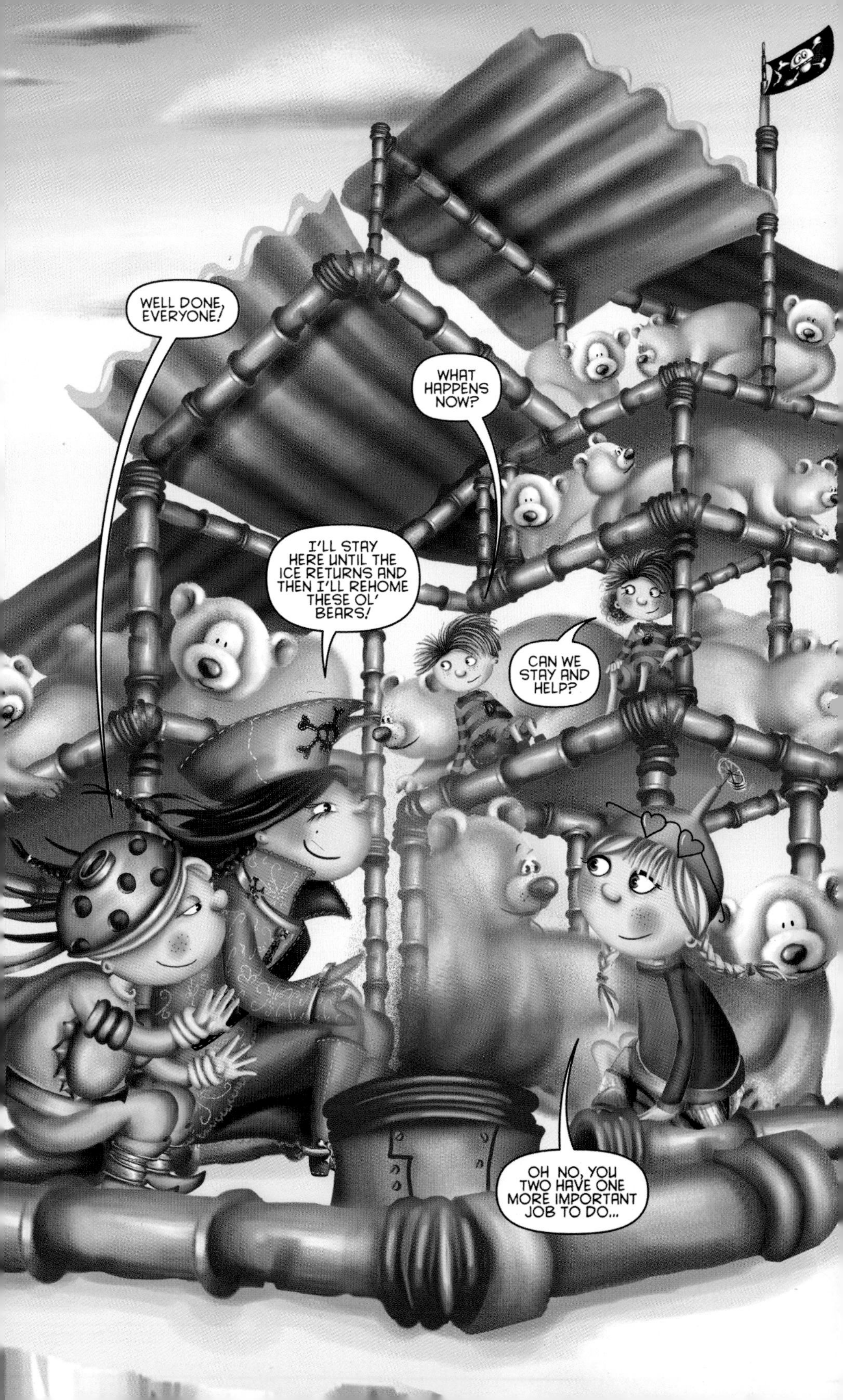
WELL DONE, EVERYONE!
WHAT HAPPENS NOW?
I'LL STAY HERE UNTIL THE ICE RETURNS AND THEN I'LL REHOME THESE OL' BEARS!
CAN WE STAY AND HELP?
OH NO, YOU TWO HAVE ONE MORE IMPORTANT JOB TO DO...

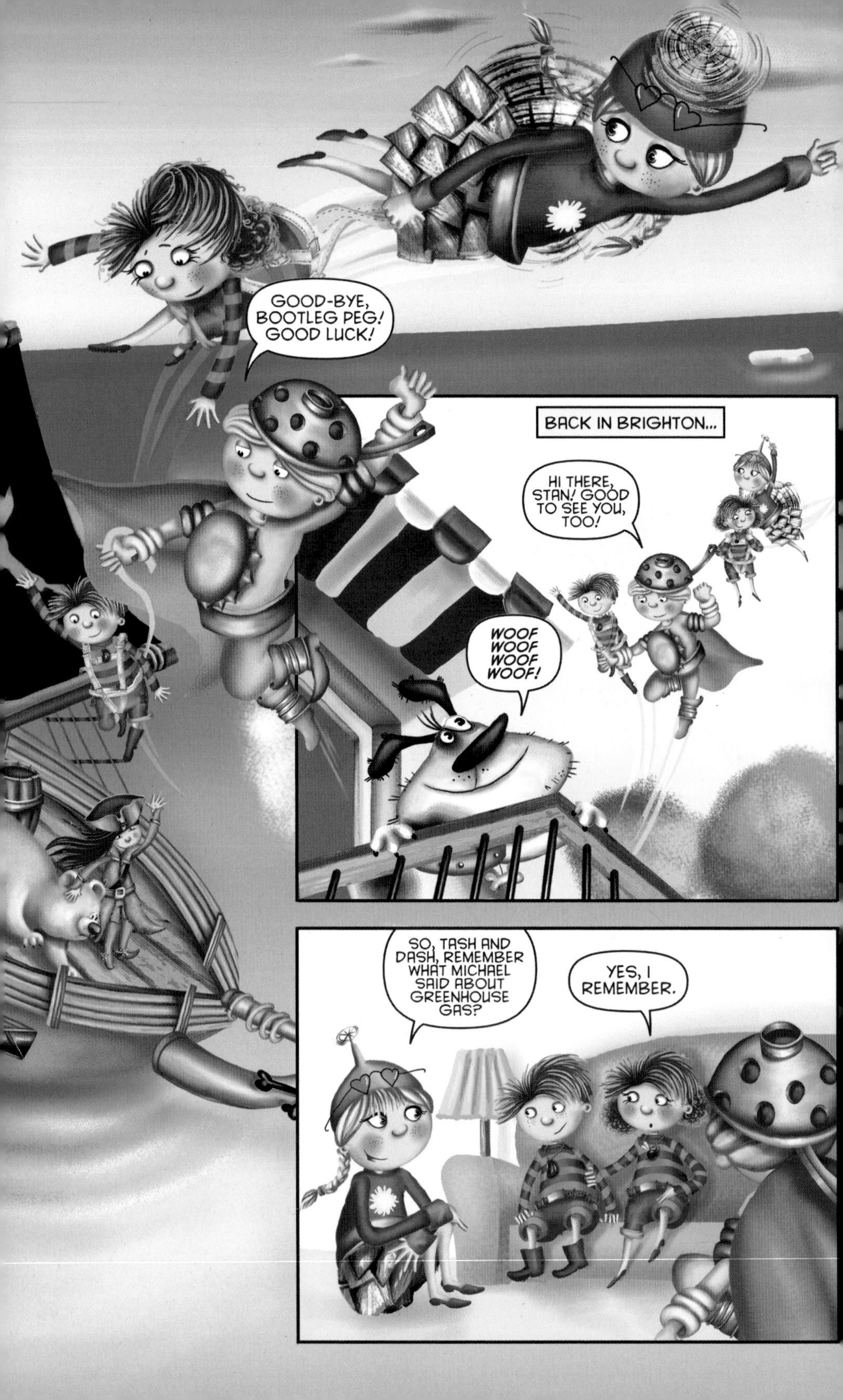
GOOD-BYE, BOOTLEG PEG! GOOD LUCK!
BACK IN BRIGHTON...
HI THERE, STAN! GOOD TO SEE YOU, TOO!
WOOF WOOF WOOF WOOF!
SO, TASH AND DASH, REMEMBER WHAT MICHAEL SAID ABOUT GREENHOUSE GAS?
YES, I REMEMBER.

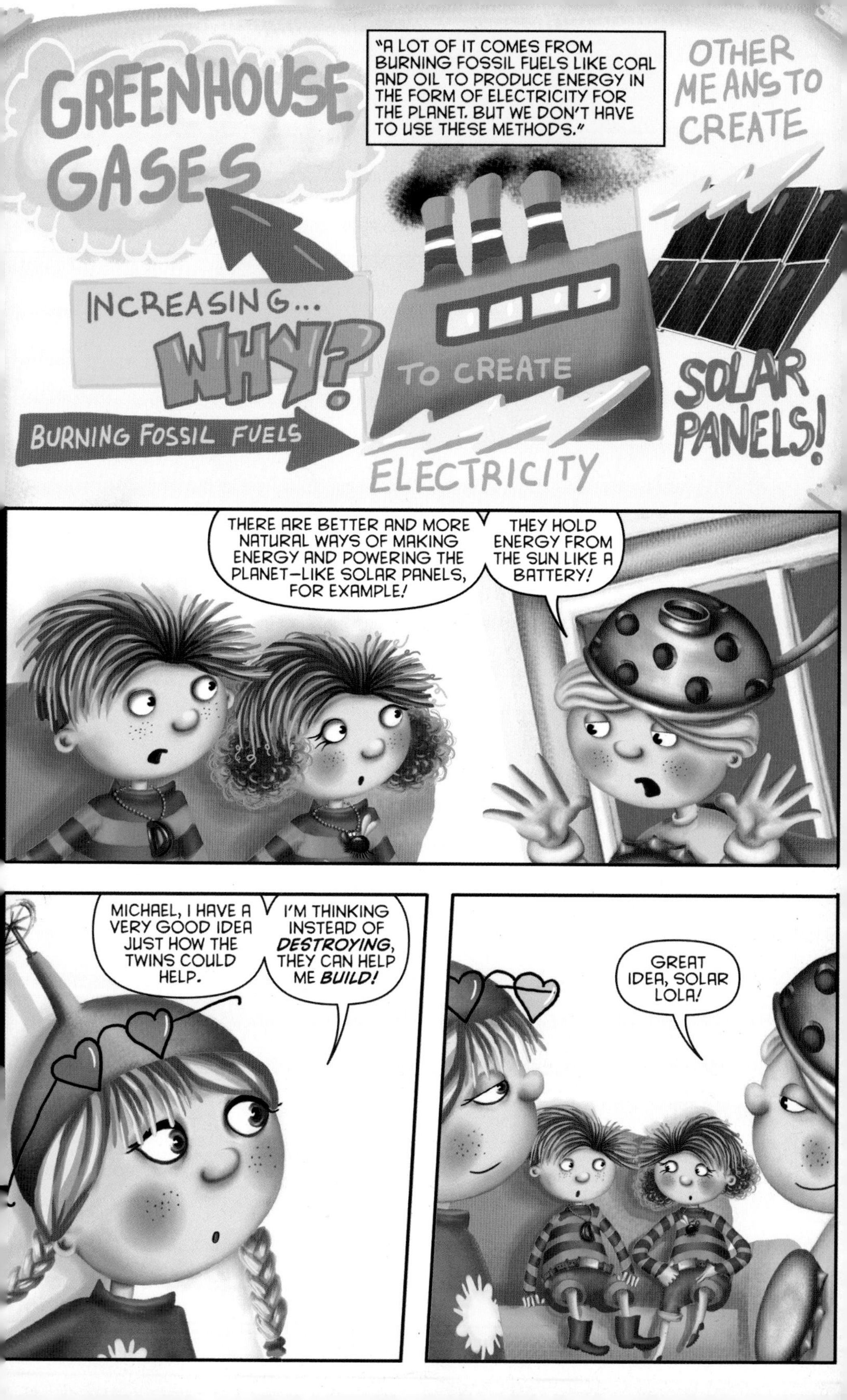
GREENHOUSE GASES
"A LOT OF IT COMES FROM BURNING FOSSIL FUELS LIKE COAL AND OIL TO PRODUCE ENERGY IN THE FORM OF ELECTRICITY FOR THE PLANET. BUT WE DON'T HAVE TO USE THESE METHODS."
OTHER MEANS TO CREATE
INCREASING...
WHY?
BURNING FOSSIL FUELS
TO CREATE
ELECTRICITY
SOLAR PANELS!
THERE ARE BETTER AND MORE NATURAL WAYS OF MAKING ENERGY AND POWERING THE PLANET—LIKE SOLAR PANELS, FOR EXAMPLE!
THEY HOLD ENERGY FROM THE SUN LIKE A BATTERY!
MICHAEL, I HAVE A VERY GOOD IDEA JUST HOW THE TWINS COULD HELP.
I'M THINKING INSTEAD OF *DESTROYING*, THEY CAN HELP ME *BUILD!*
GREAT IDEA, SOLAR LOLA!

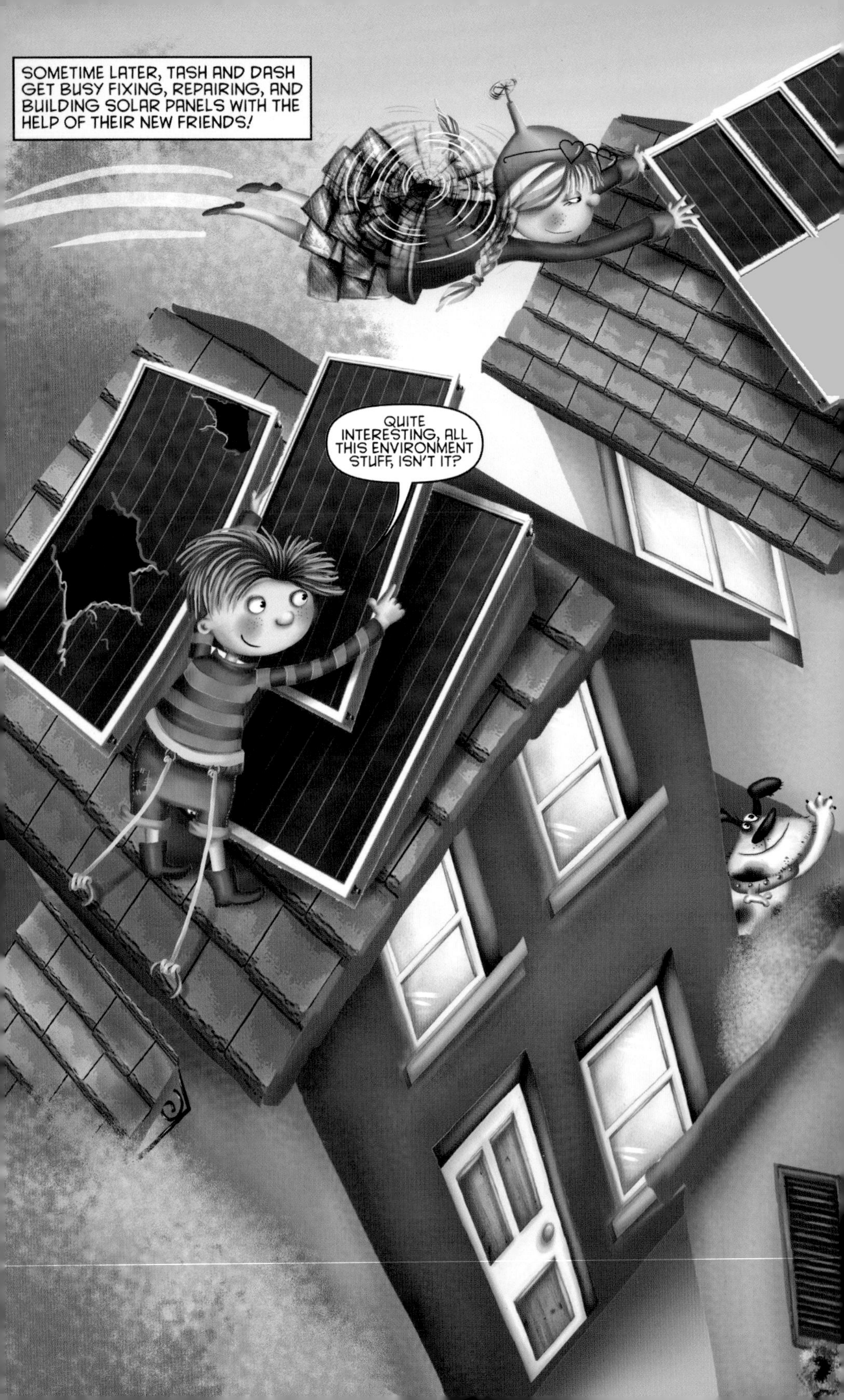
SOMETIME LATER, TASH AND DASH GET BUSY FIXING, REPAIRING, AND BUILDING SOLAR PANELS WITH THE HELP OF THEIR NEW FRIENDS!
QUITE INTERESTING, ALL THIS ENVIRONMENT STUFF, ISN'T IT?

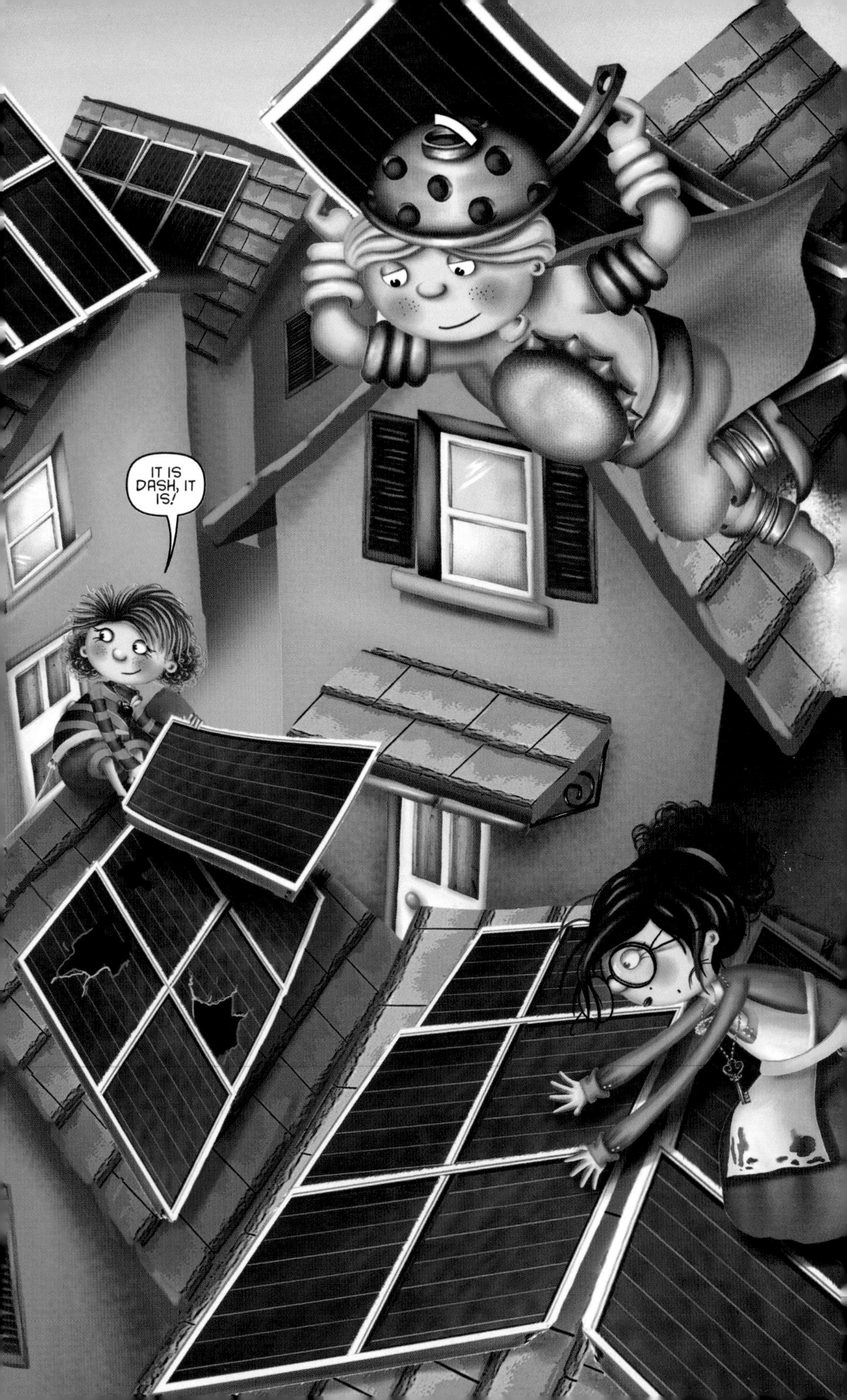
IT IS DASH, IT IS!

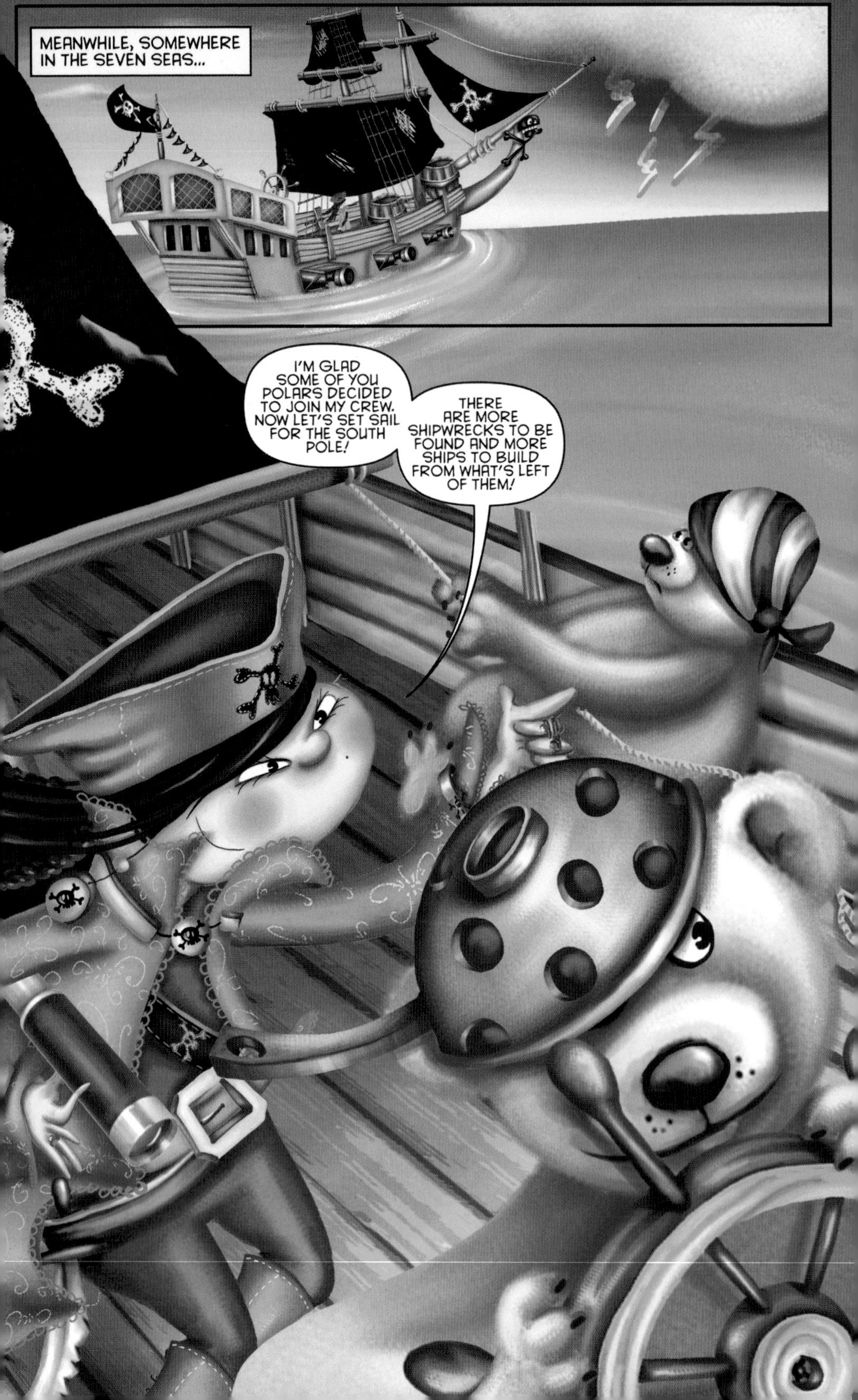
MEANWHILE, SOMEWHERE IN THE SEVEN SEAS...
I'M GLAD SOME OF YOU POLARS DECIDED TO JOIN MY CREW. NOW LET'S SET SAIL FOR THE SOUTH POLE!
THERE ARE MORE SHIPWRECKS TO BE FOUND AND MORE SHIPS TO BUILD FROM WHAT'S LEFT OF THEM!

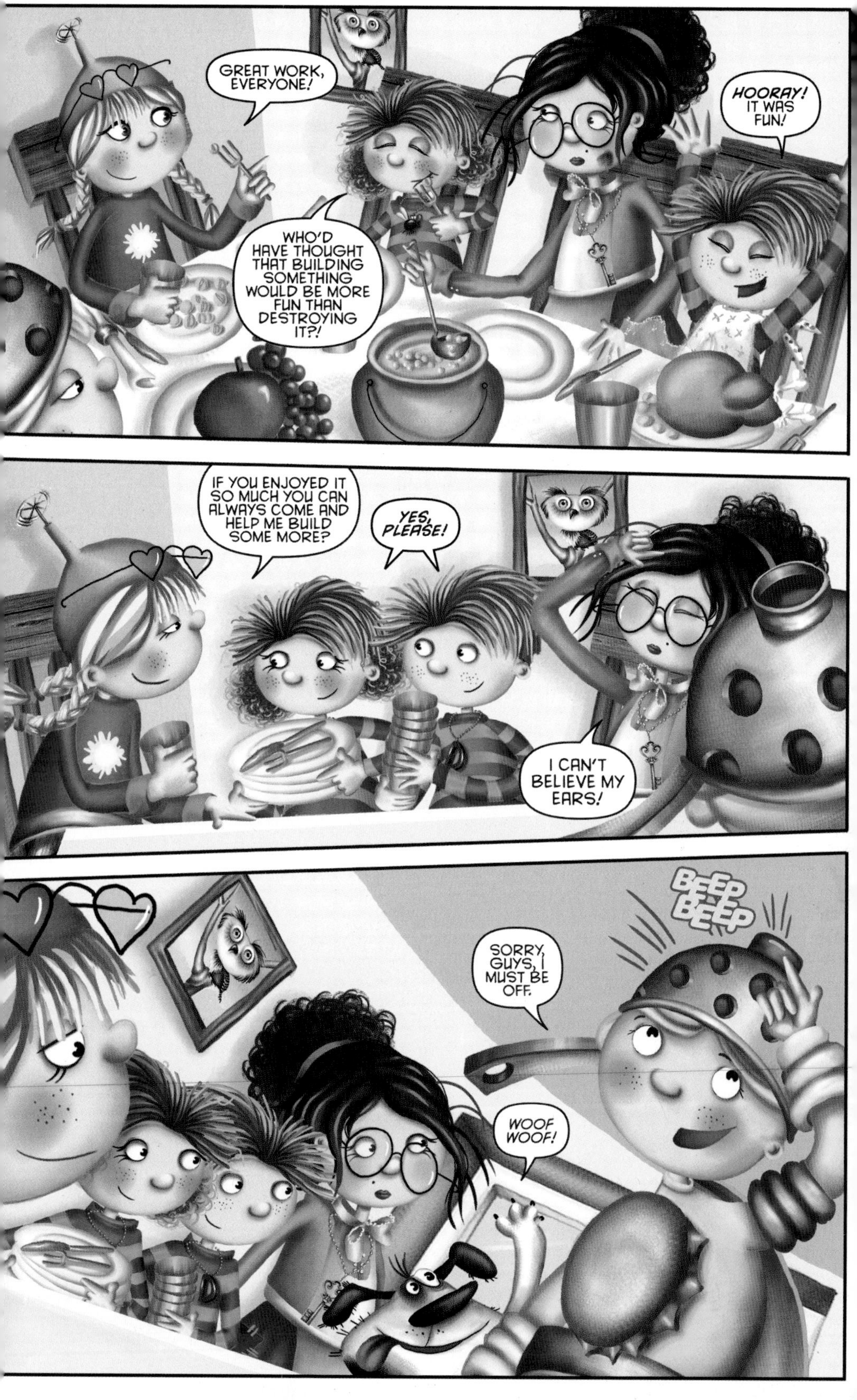
GREAT WORK, EVERYONE!
HOORAY! IT WAS FUN!
WHO'D HAVE THOUGHT THAT BUILDING SOMETHING WOULD BE MORE FUN THAN DESTROYING IT?!
IF YOU ENJOYED IT SO MUCH YOU CAN ALWAYS COME AND HELP ME BUILD SOME MORE?
YES, PLEASE!
I CAN'T BELIEVE MY EARS!
BEEP BEEP
SORRY, GUYS, I MUST BE OFF.
WOOF WOOF!

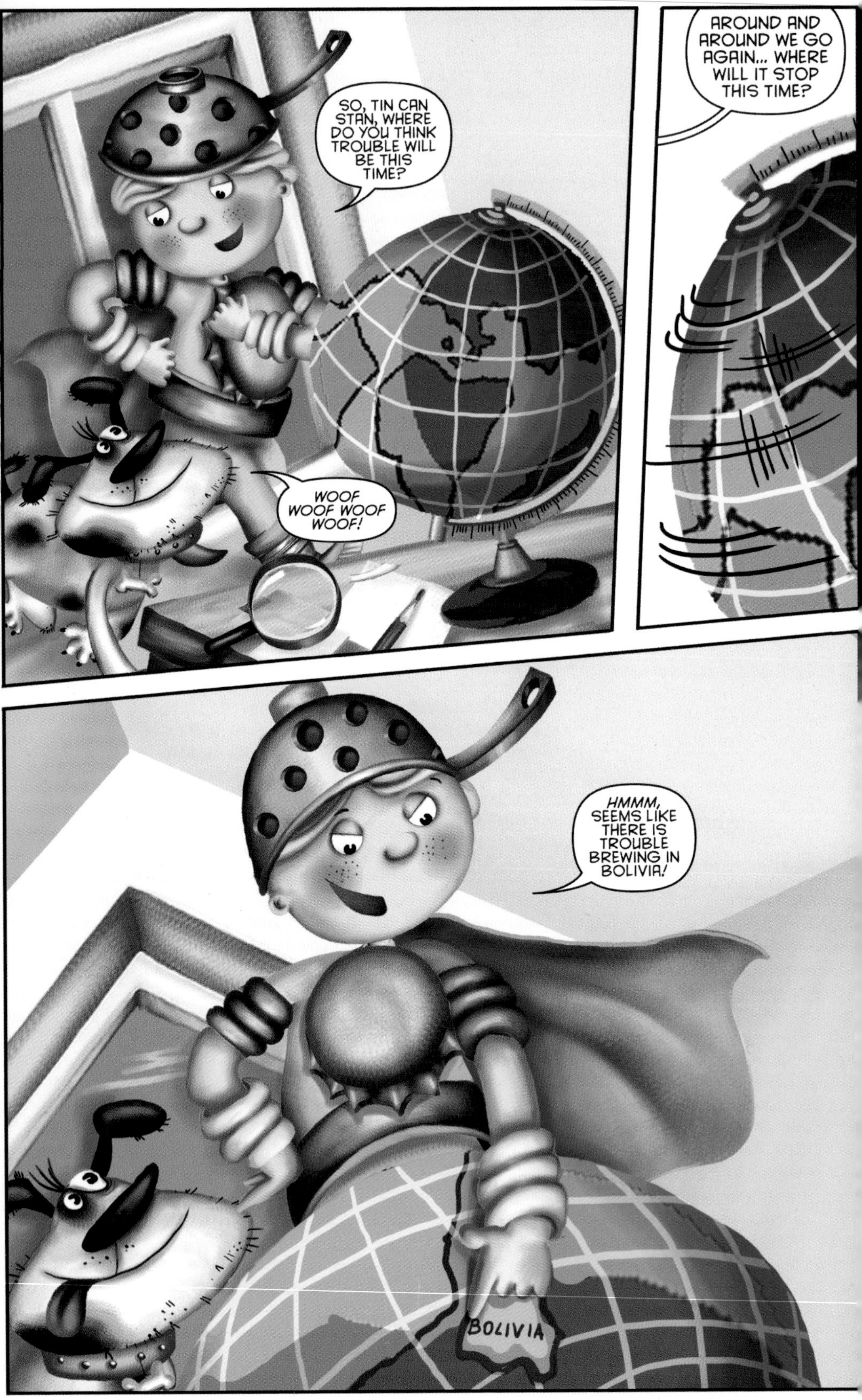
SO, TIN CAN STAN, WHERE DO YOU THINK TROUBLE WILL BE THIS TIME?
WOOF WOOF WOOF WOOF!
AROUND AND AROUND WE GO AGAIN... WHERE WILL IT STOP THIS TIME?
HMMM, SEEMS LIKE THERE IS TROUBLE BREWING IN BOLIVIA!
BOLIVIA

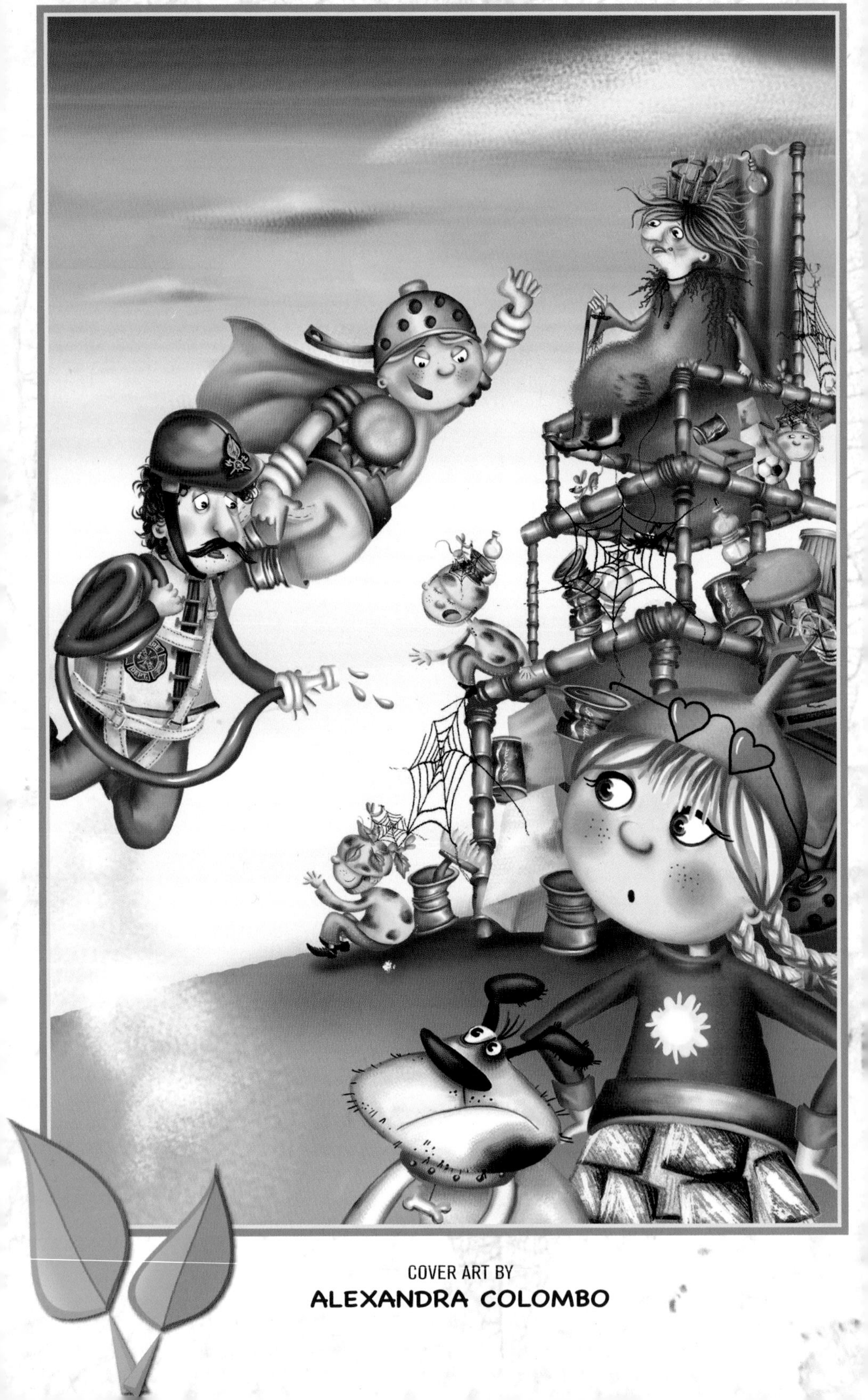

COVER ART BY
ALEXANDRA COLOMBO

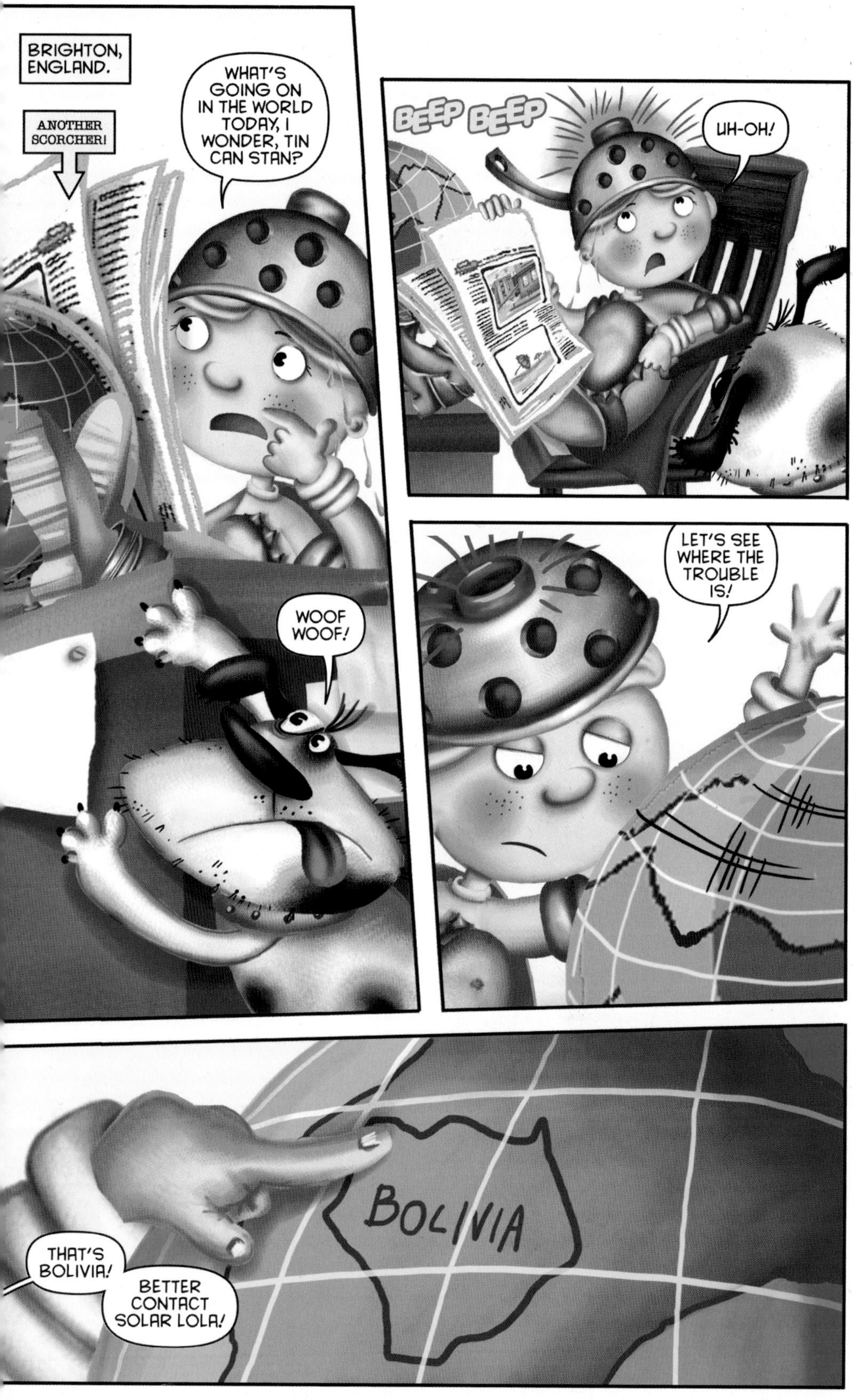

BRIGHTON, ENGLAND.
ANOTHER SCORCHER!
WHAT'S GOING ON IN THE WORLD TODAY, I WONDER, TIN CAN STAN?
BEEP BEEP
UH-OH!
WOOF WOOF!
LET'S SEE WHERE THE TROUBLE IS!
BOLIVIA
THAT'S BOLIVIA!
BETTER CONTACT SOLAR LOLA!

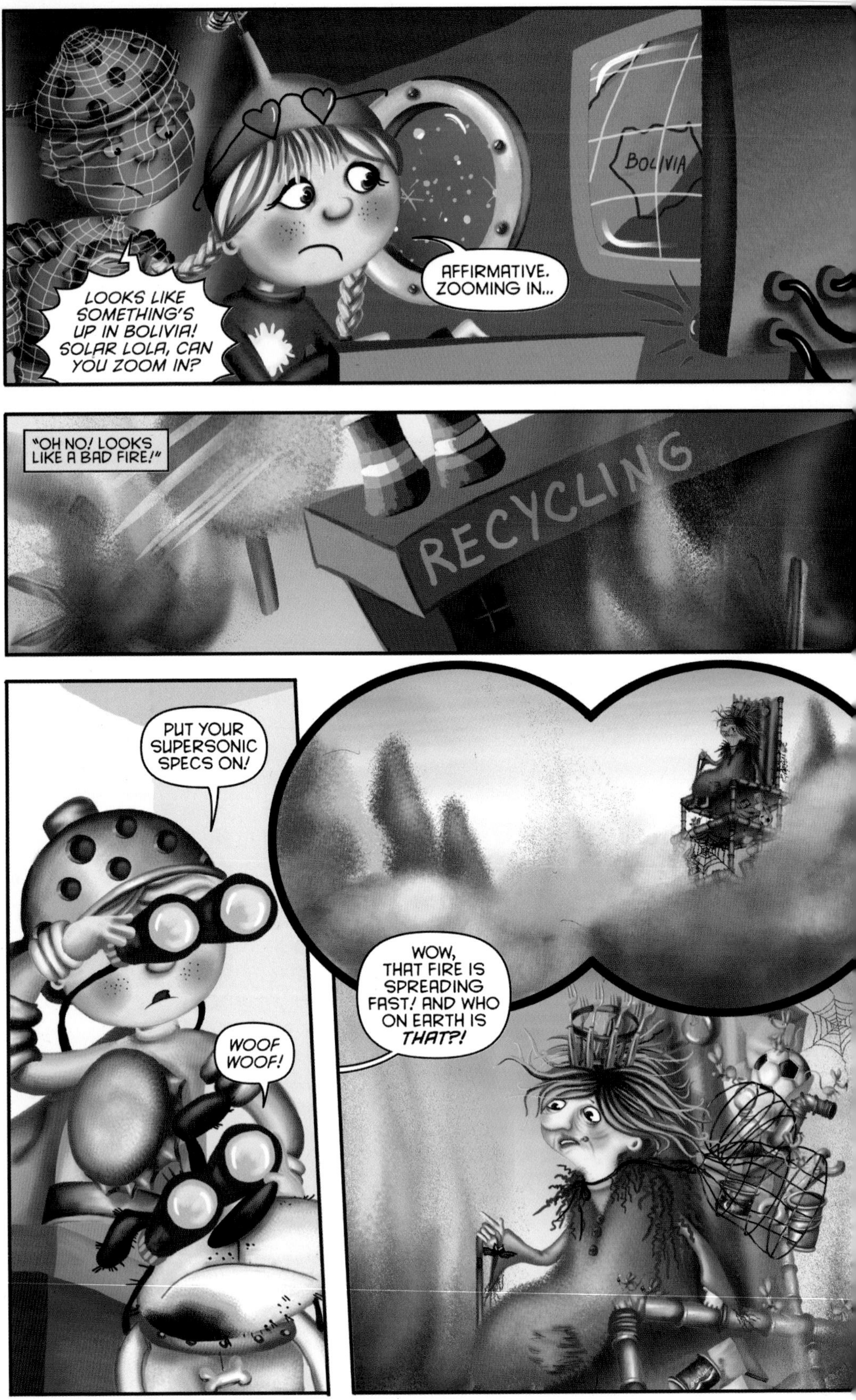
LOOKS LIKE SOMETHING'S UP IN BOLIVIA! SOLAR LOLA, CAN YOU ZOOM IN?
AFFIRMATIVE. ZOOMING IN...
BOLIVIA
"OH NO! LOOKS LIKE A BAD FIRE!"
RECYCLING
PUT YOUR SUPERSONIC SPECS ON!
WOOF WOOF!
WOW, THAT FIRE IS SPREADING FAST! AND WHO ON EARTH IS *THAT?!*

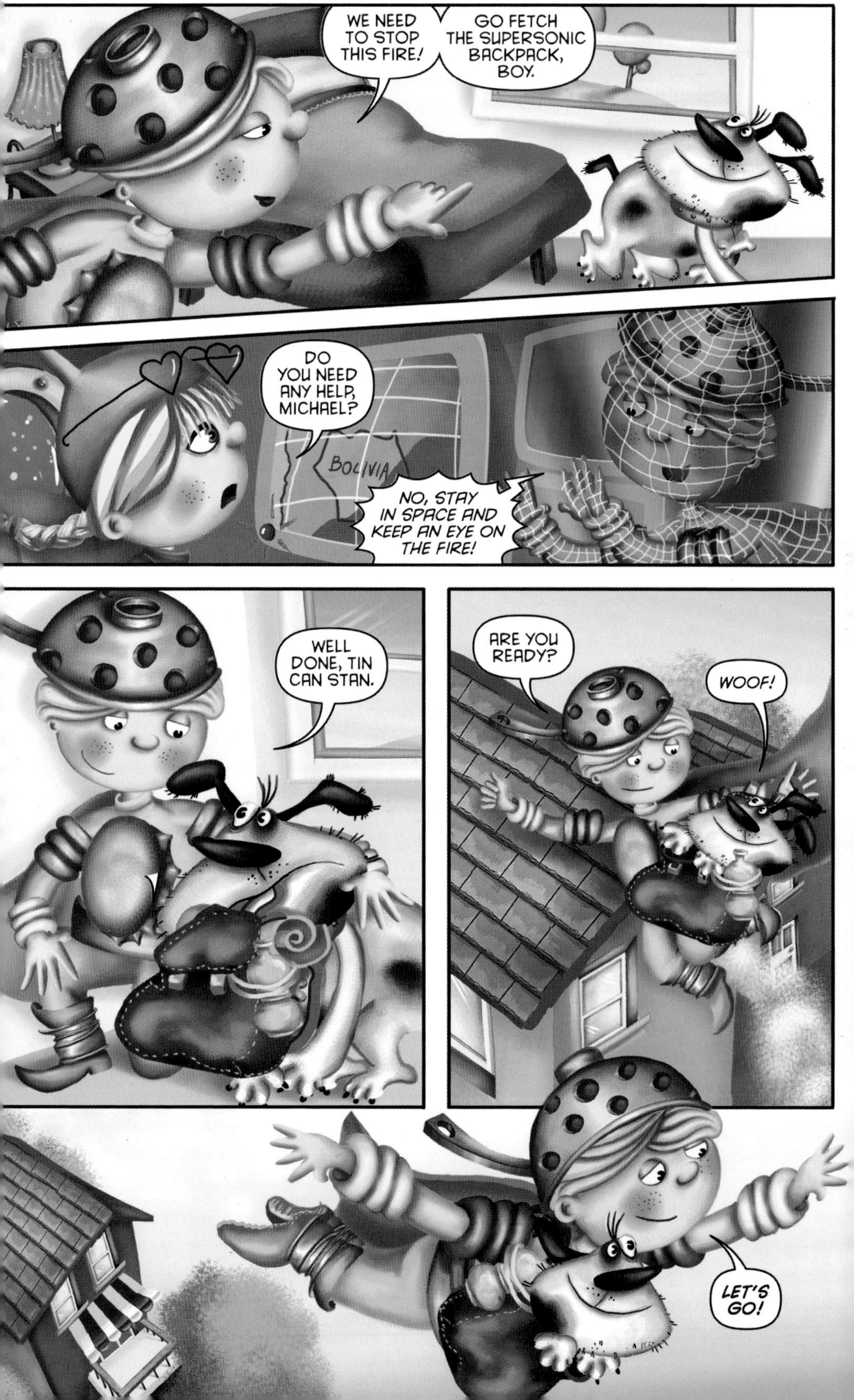
WE NEED TO STOP THIS FIRE!
GO FETCH THE SUPERSONIC BACKPACK, BOY.
DO YOU NEED ANY HELP, MICHAEL?
BOLIVIA
NO, STAY IN SPACE AND KEEP AN EYE ON THE FIRE!
WELL DONE, TIN CAN STAN.
ARE YOU READY?
WOOF!
LET'S GO!

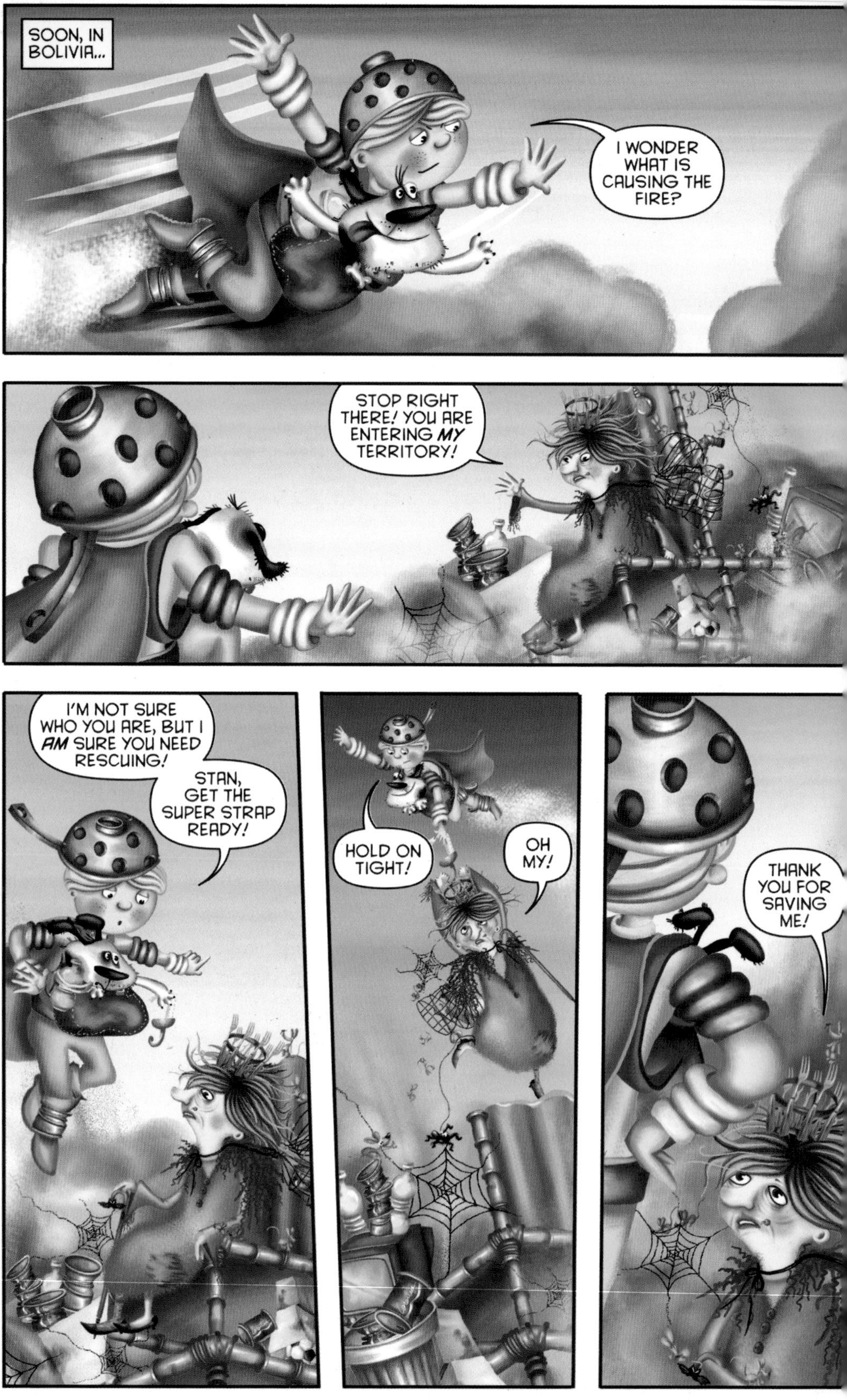
SOON, IN BOLIVIA...
I WONDER WHAT IS CAUSING THE FIRE?
STOP RIGHT THERE! YOU ARE ENTERING MY TERRITORY!
I'M NOT SURE WHO YOU ARE, BUT I AM SURE YOU NEED RESCUING!
STAN, GET THE SUPER STRAP READY!
HOLD ON TIGHT!
OH MY!
THANK YOU FOR SAVING ME!

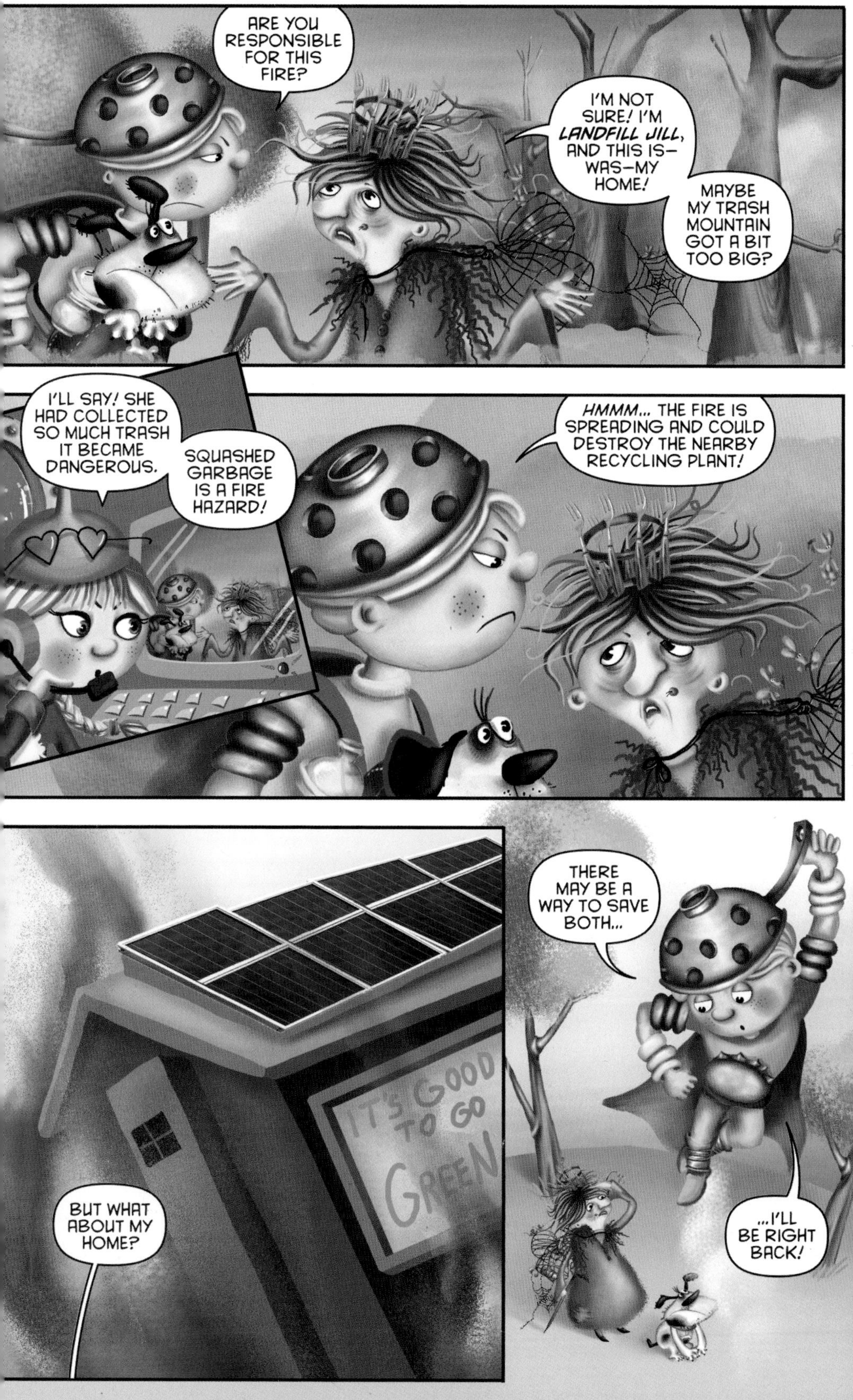
ARE YOU RESPONSIBLE FOR THIS FIRE?
I'M NOT SURE! I'M *LANDFILL JILL*, AND THIS IS—WAS—MY HOME!
MAYBE MY TRASH MOUNTAIN GOT A BIT TOO BIG?
I'LL SAY! SHE HAD COLLECTED SO MUCH TRASH IT BECAME DANGEROUS.
SQUASHED GARBAGE IS A FIRE HAZARD!
HMMM... THE FIRE IS SPREADING AND COULD DESTROY THE NEARBY RECYCLING PLANT!
IT'S GOOD TO GO GREEN
BUT WHAT ABOUT MY HOME?
THERE MAY BE A WAY TO SAVE BOTH...
...I'LL BE RIGHT BACK!

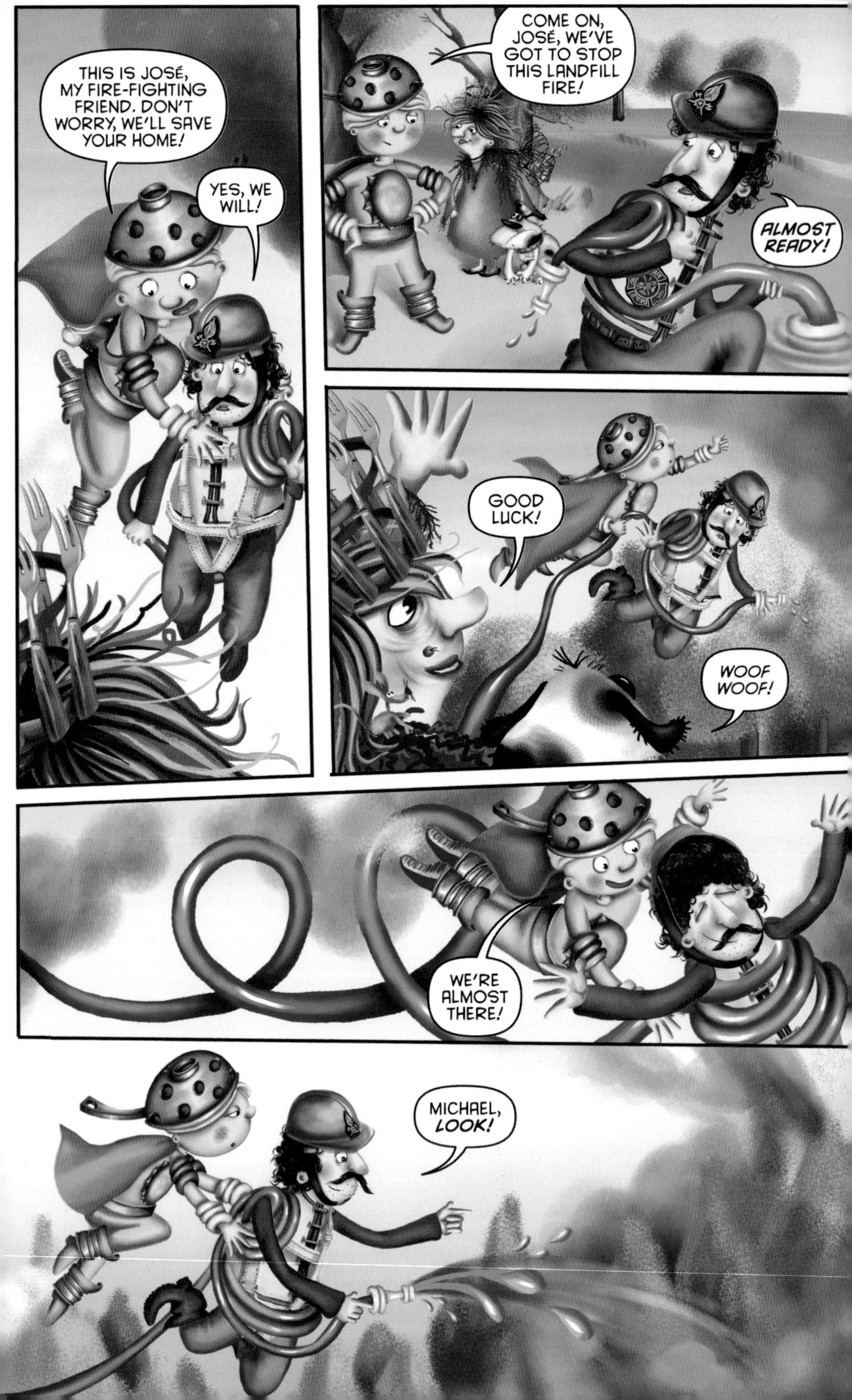
THIS IS JOSÉ, MY FIRE-FIGHTING FRIEND. DON'T WORRY, WE'LL SAVE YOUR HOME!
YES, WE WILL!
COME ON, JOSÉ, WE'VE GOT TO STOP THIS LANDFILL FIRE!
ALMOST READY!
GOOD LUCK!
WOOF WOOF!
WE'RE ALMOST THERE!
MICHAEL, LOOK!

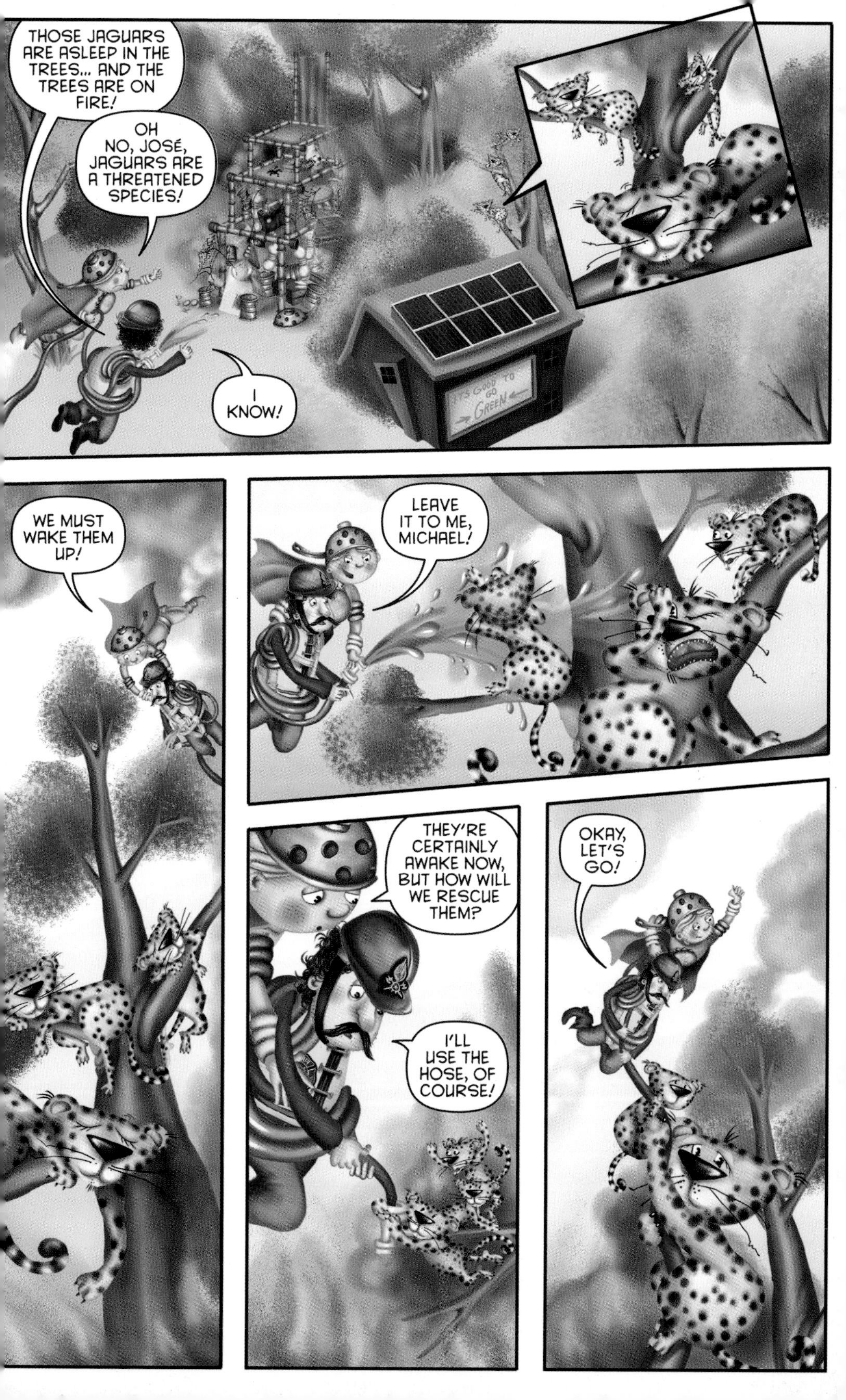
THOSE JAGUARS ARE ASLEEP IN THE TREES... AND THE TREES ARE ON FIRE!
OH NO, JOSÉ, JAGUARS ARE A THREATENED SPECIES!
I KNOW!
IT'S GOOD TO GO → GREEN ←
WE MUST WAKE THEM UP!
LEAVE IT TO ME, MICHAEL!
THEY'RE CERTAINLY AWAKE NOW, BUT HOW WILL WE RESCUE THEM?
I'LL USE THE HOSE, OF COURSE!
OKAY, LET'S GO!

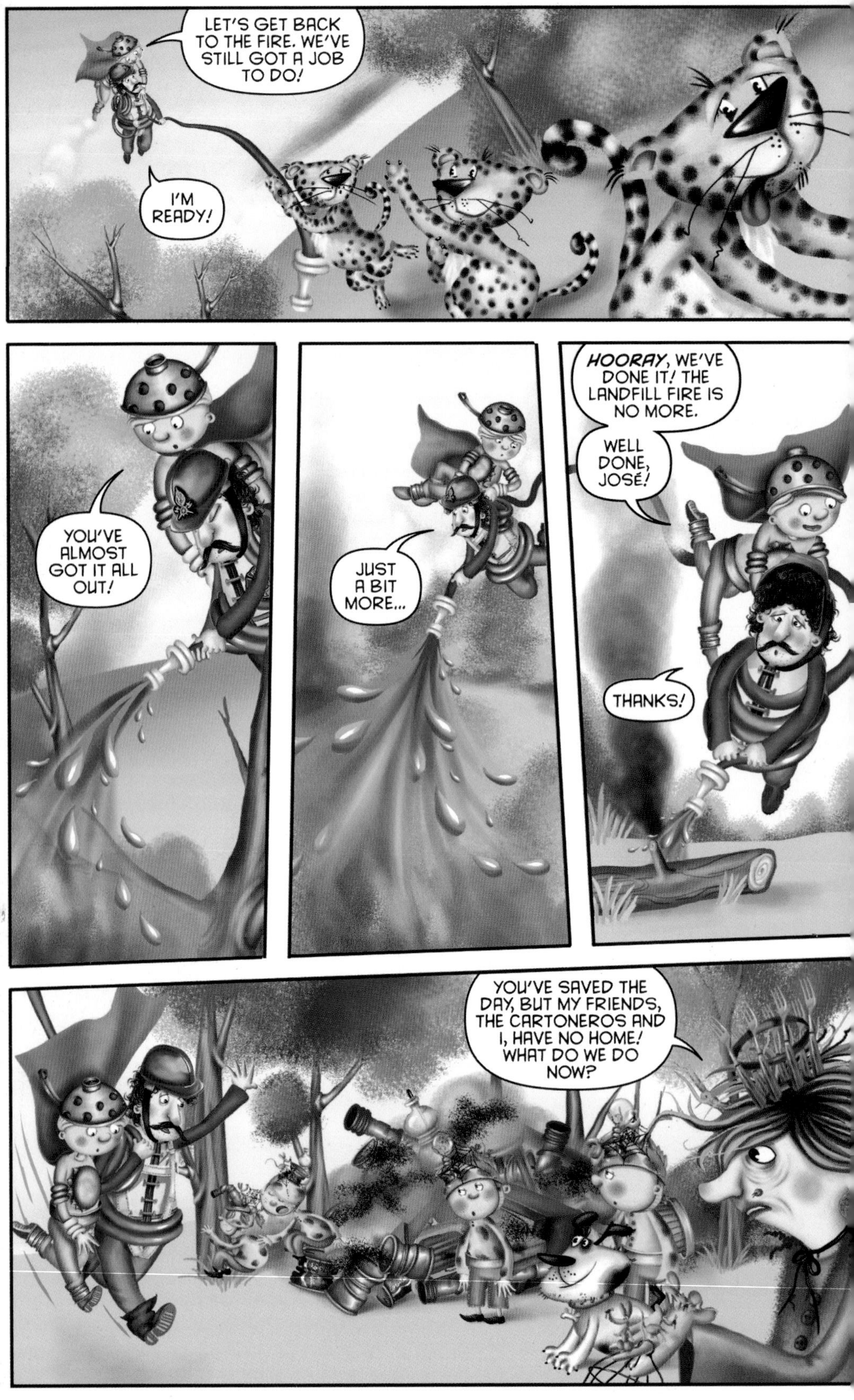
LET'S GET BACK TO THE FIRE. WE'VE STILL GOT A JOB TO DO!
I'M READY!
YOU'VE ALMOST GOT IT ALL OUT!
JUST A BIT MORE...
HOORAY, WE'VE DONE IT! THE LANDFILL FIRE IS NO MORE.
WELL DONE, JOSÉ!
THANKS!
YOU'VE SAVED THE DAY, BUT MY FRIENDS, THE CARTONEROS AND I, HAVE NO HOME! WHAT DO WE DO NOW?

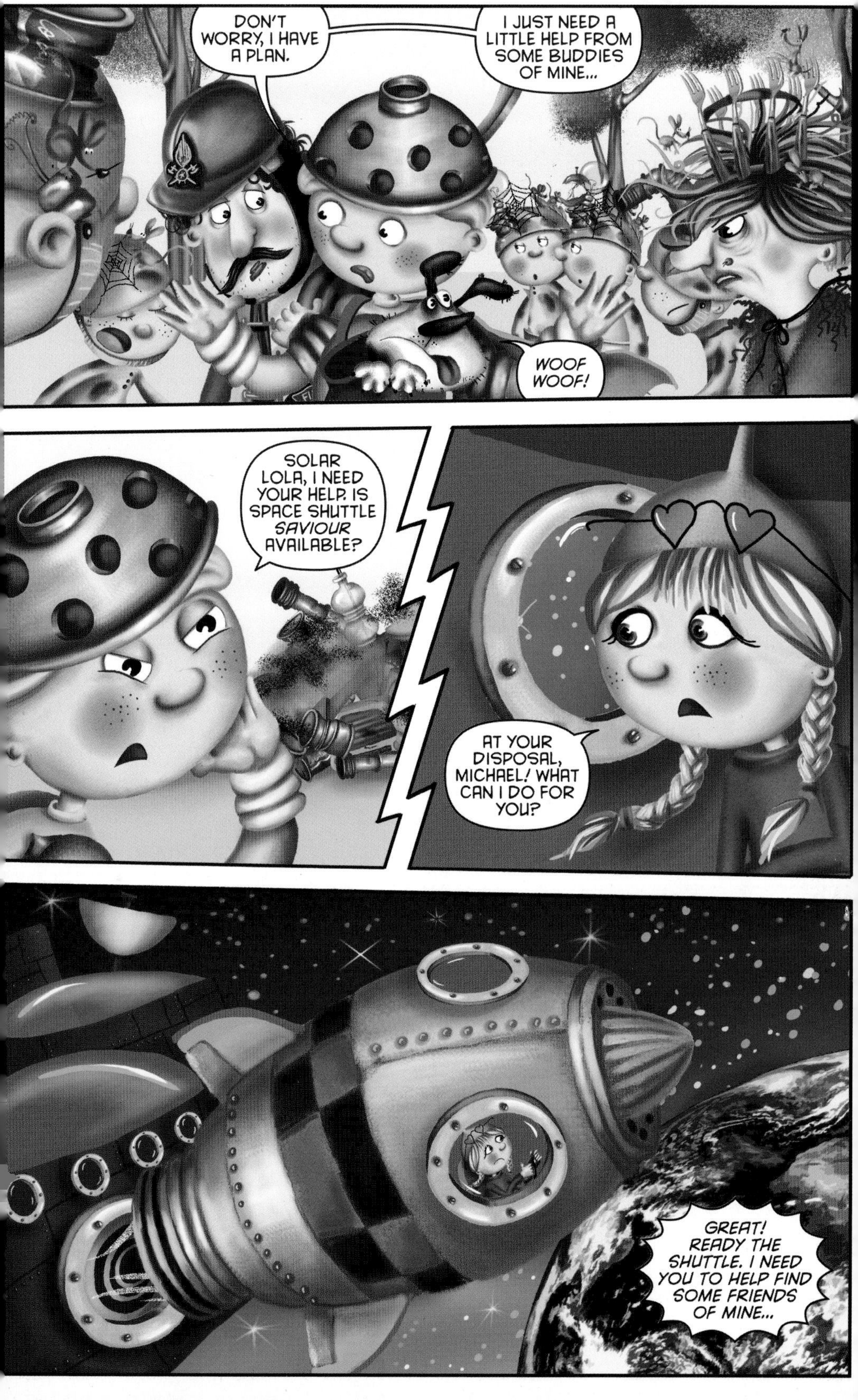
DON'T WORRY, I HAVE A PLAN.
I JUST NEED A LITTLE HELP FROM SOME BUDDIES OF MINE...
WOOF WOOF!
SOLAR LOLA, I NEED YOUR HELP. IS SPACE SHUTTLE *SAVIOUR* AVAILABLE?
AT YOUR DISPOSAL, MICHAEL! WHAT CAN I DO FOR YOU?
GREAT! READY THE SHUTTLE. I NEED YOU TO HELP FIND SOME FRIENDS OF MINE...

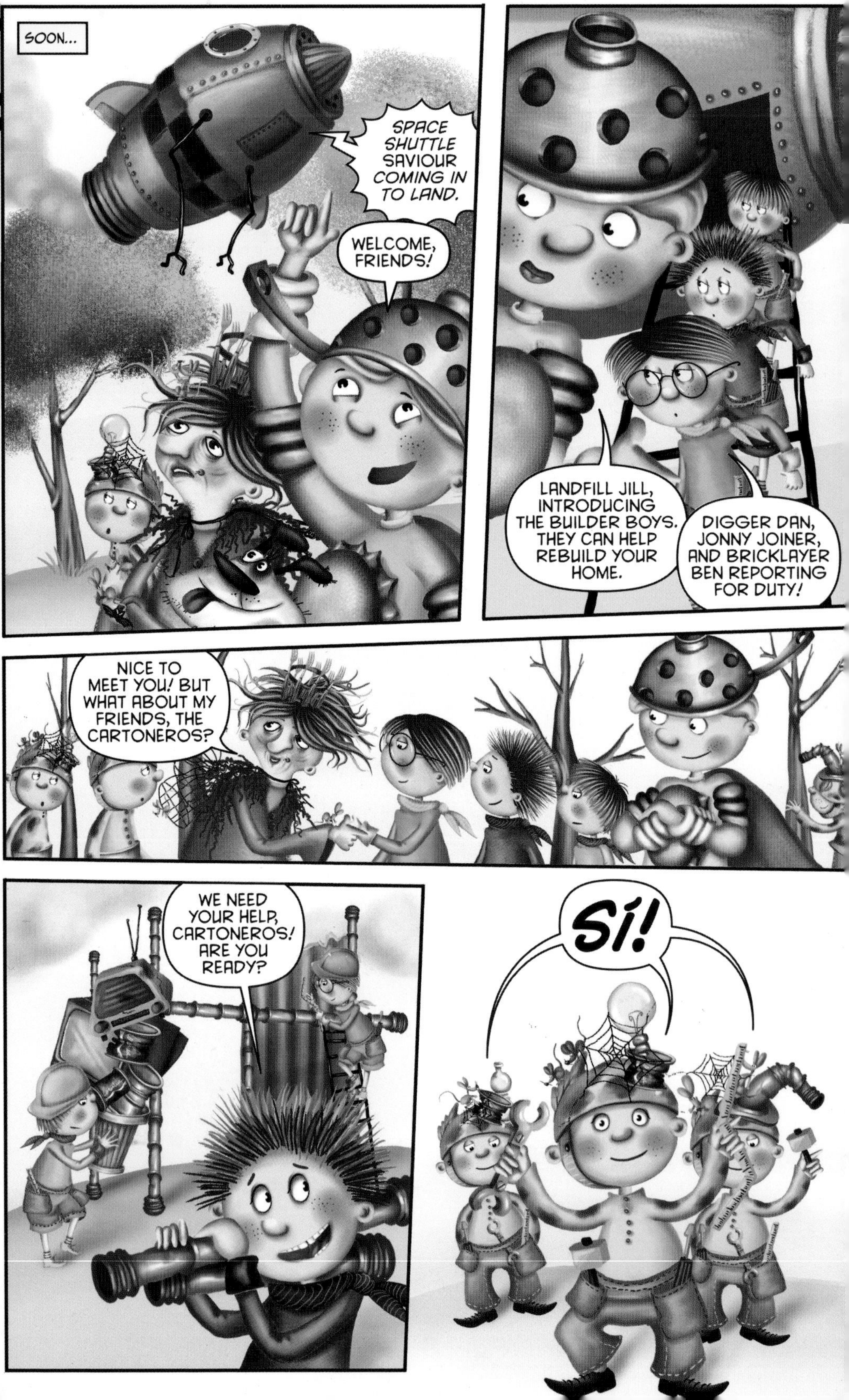
SOON...
SPACE SHUTTLE SAVIOUR COMING IN TO LAND.
WELCOME, FRIENDS!
LANDFILL JILL, INTRODUCING THE BUILDER BOYS. THEY CAN HELP REBUILD YOUR HOME.
DIGGER DAN, JONNY JOINER, AND BRICKLAYER BEN REPORTING FOR DUTY!
NICE TO MEET YOU! BUT WHAT ABOUT MY FRIENDS, THE CARTONEROS?
WE NEED YOUR HELP, CARTONEROS! ARE YOU READY?
SÍ!

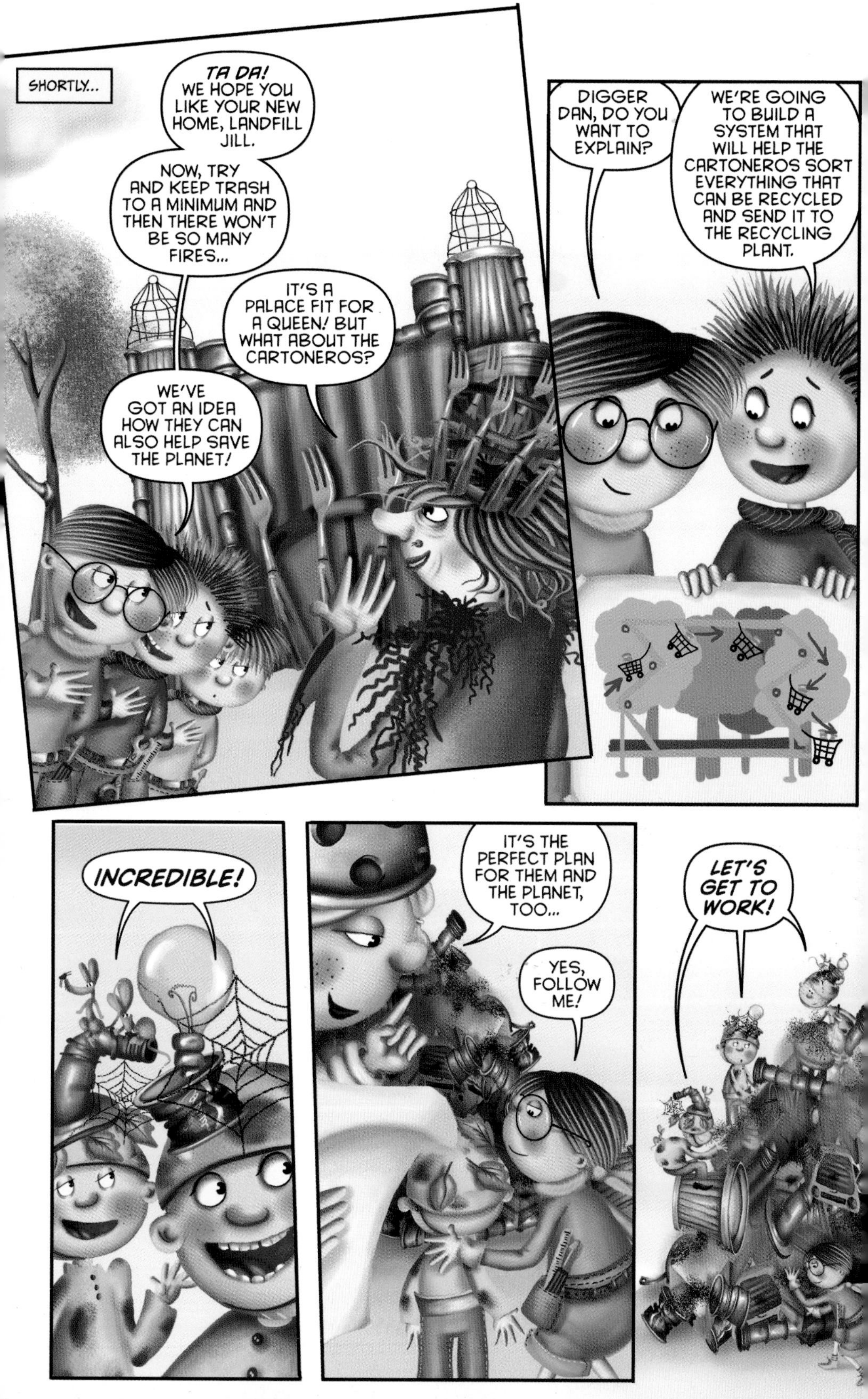
SHORTLY...
TA DA! WE HOPE YOU LIKE YOUR NEW HOME, LANDFILL JILL.
NOW, TRY AND KEEP TRASH TO A MINIMUM AND THEN THERE WON'T BE SO MANY FIRES...
IT'S A PALACE FIT FOR A QUEEN! BUT WHAT ABOUT THE CARTONEROS?
WE'VE GOT AN IDEA HOW THEY CAN ALSO HELP SAVE THE PLANET!
DIGGER DAN, DO YOU WANT TO EXPLAIN?
WE'RE GOING TO BUILD A SYSTEM THAT WILL HELP THE CARTONEROS SORT EVERYTHING THAT CAN BE RECYCLED AND SEND IT TO THE RECYCLING PLANT.
INCREDIBLE!
IT'S THE PERFECT PLAN FOR THEM AND THE PLANET, TOO...
YES, FOLLOW ME!
LET'S GET TO WORK!

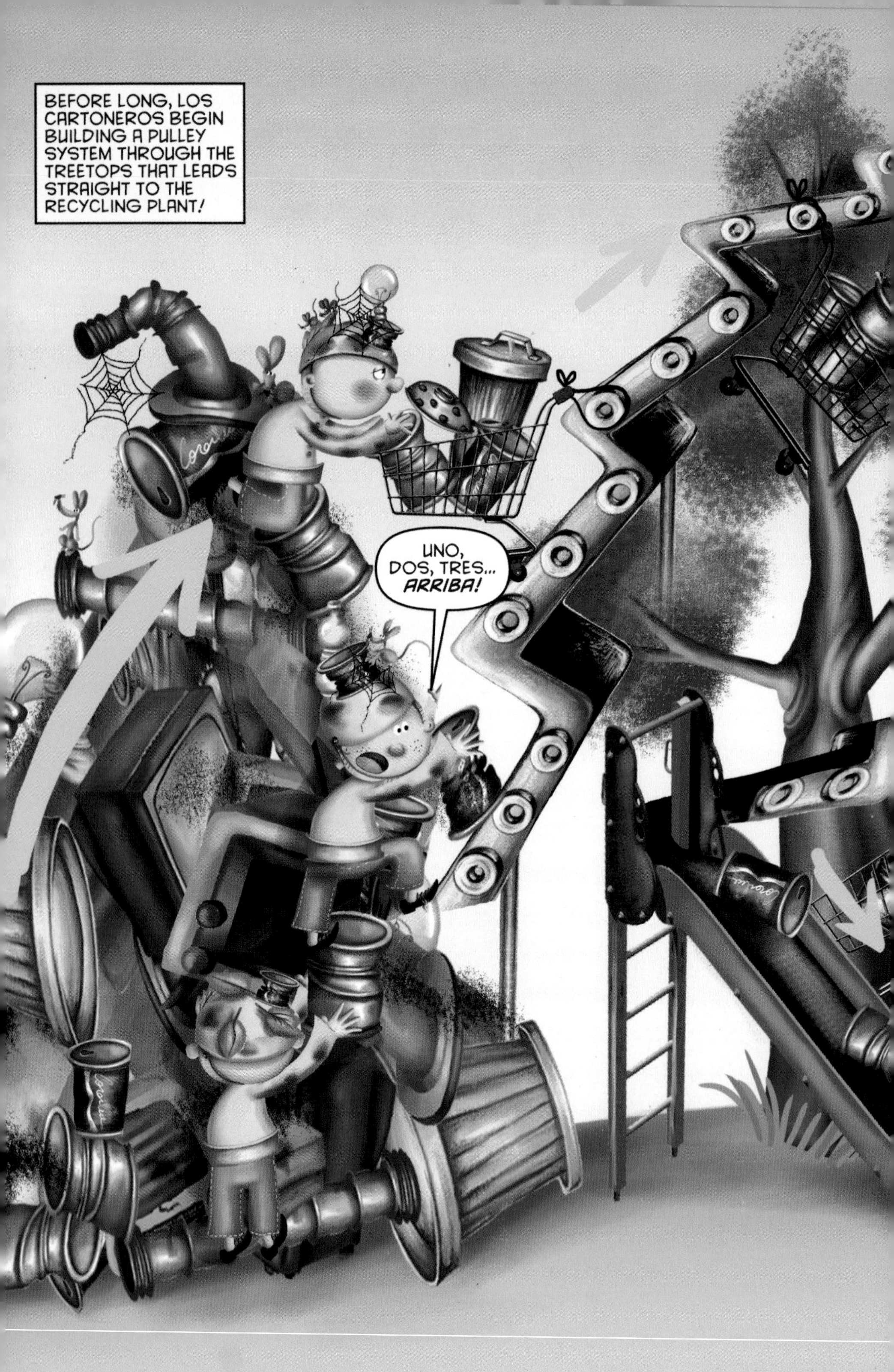
BEFORE LONG, LOS CARTONEROS BEGIN BUILDING A PULLEY SYSTEM THROUGH THE TREETOPS THAT LEADS STRAIGHT TO THE RECYCLING PLANT!
UNO, DOS, TRES... ARRIBA!

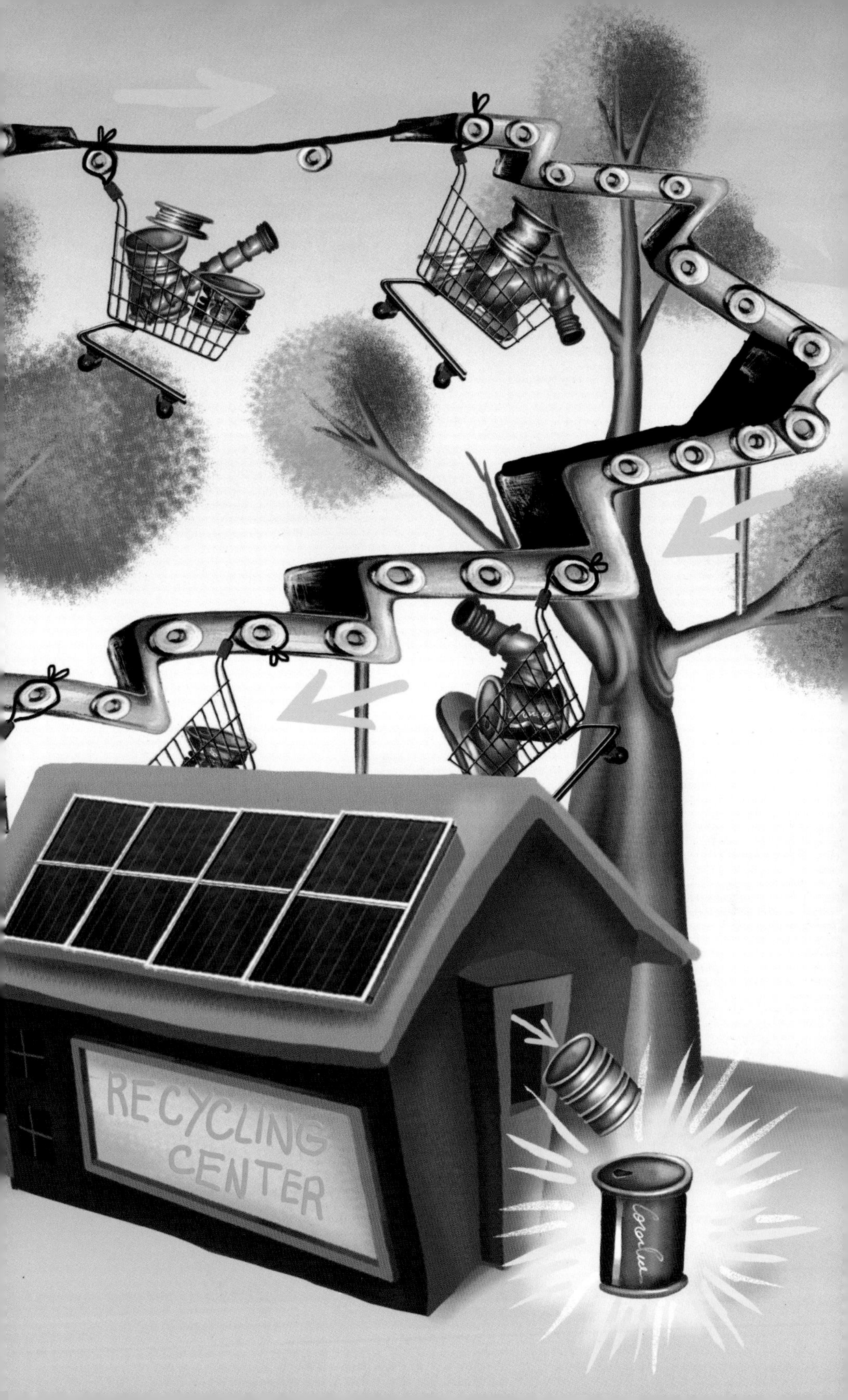
RECYCLING CENTER

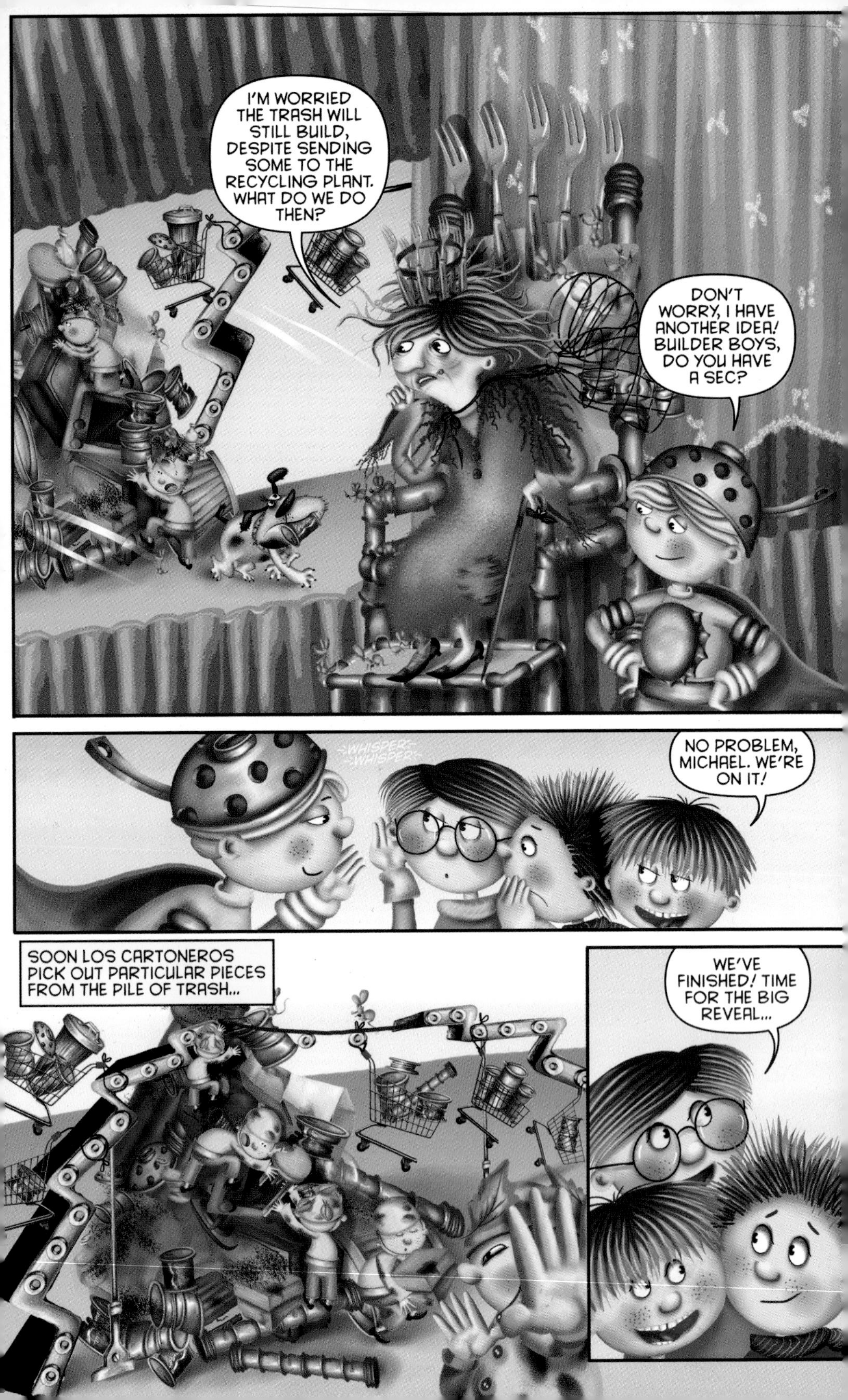
I'M WORRIED THE TRASH WILL STILL BUILD, DESPITE SENDING SOME TO THE RECYCLING PLANT. WHAT DO WE DO THEN?
DON'T WORRY, I HAVE ANOTHER IDEA! BUILDER BOYS, DO YOU HAVE A SEC?
WHISPER WHISPER
NO PROBLEM, MICHAEL. WE'RE ON IT!
SOON LOS CARTONEROS PICK OUT PARTICULAR PIECES FROM THE PILE OF TRASH...
WE'VE FINISHED! TIME FOR THE BIG REVEAL...

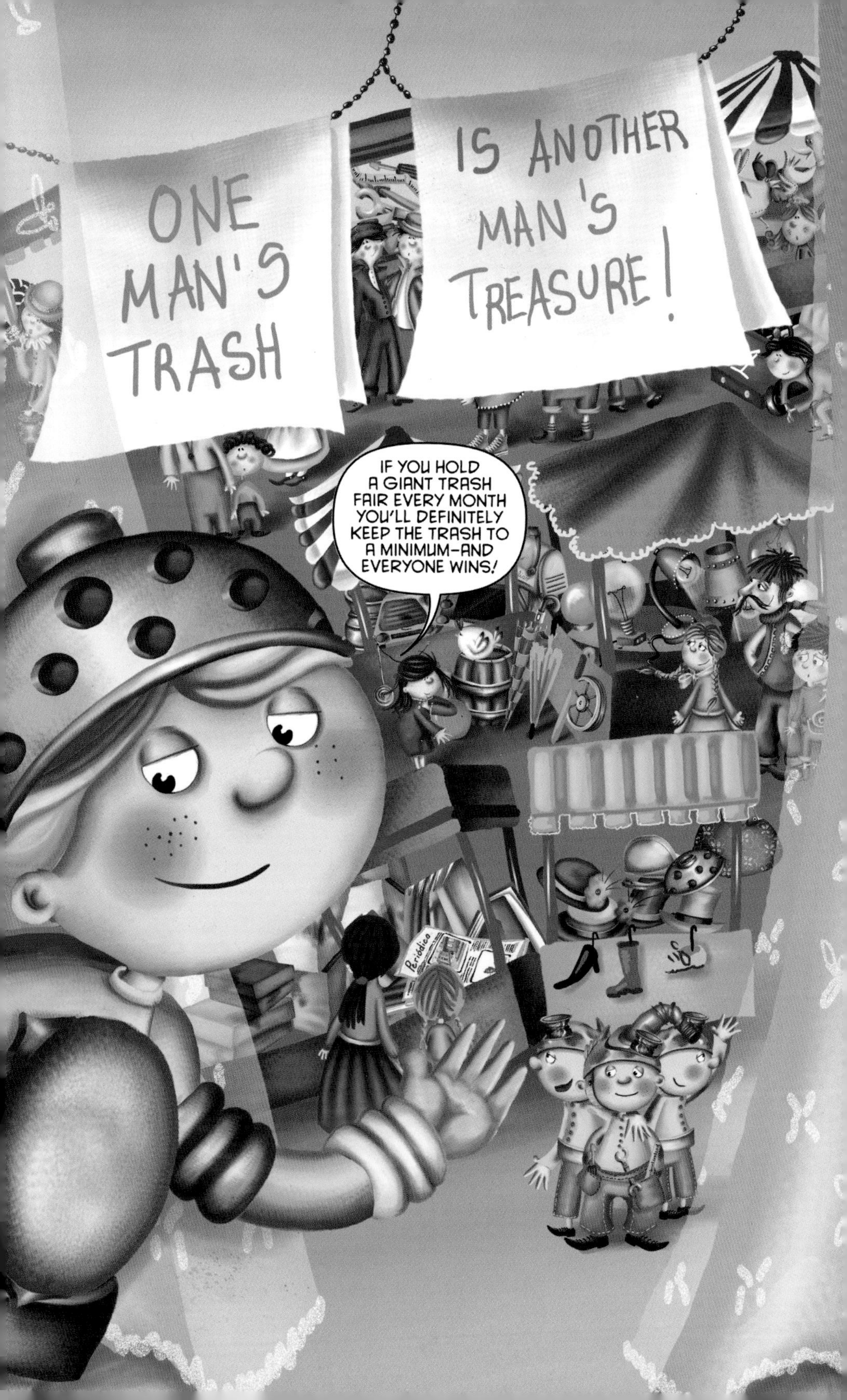
ONE MAN'S TRASH
IS ANOTHER MAN'S TREASURE!
IF YOU HOLD A GIANT TRASH FAIR EVERY MONTH YOU'LL DEFINITELY KEEP THE TRASH TO A MINIMUM—AND EVERYONE WINS!

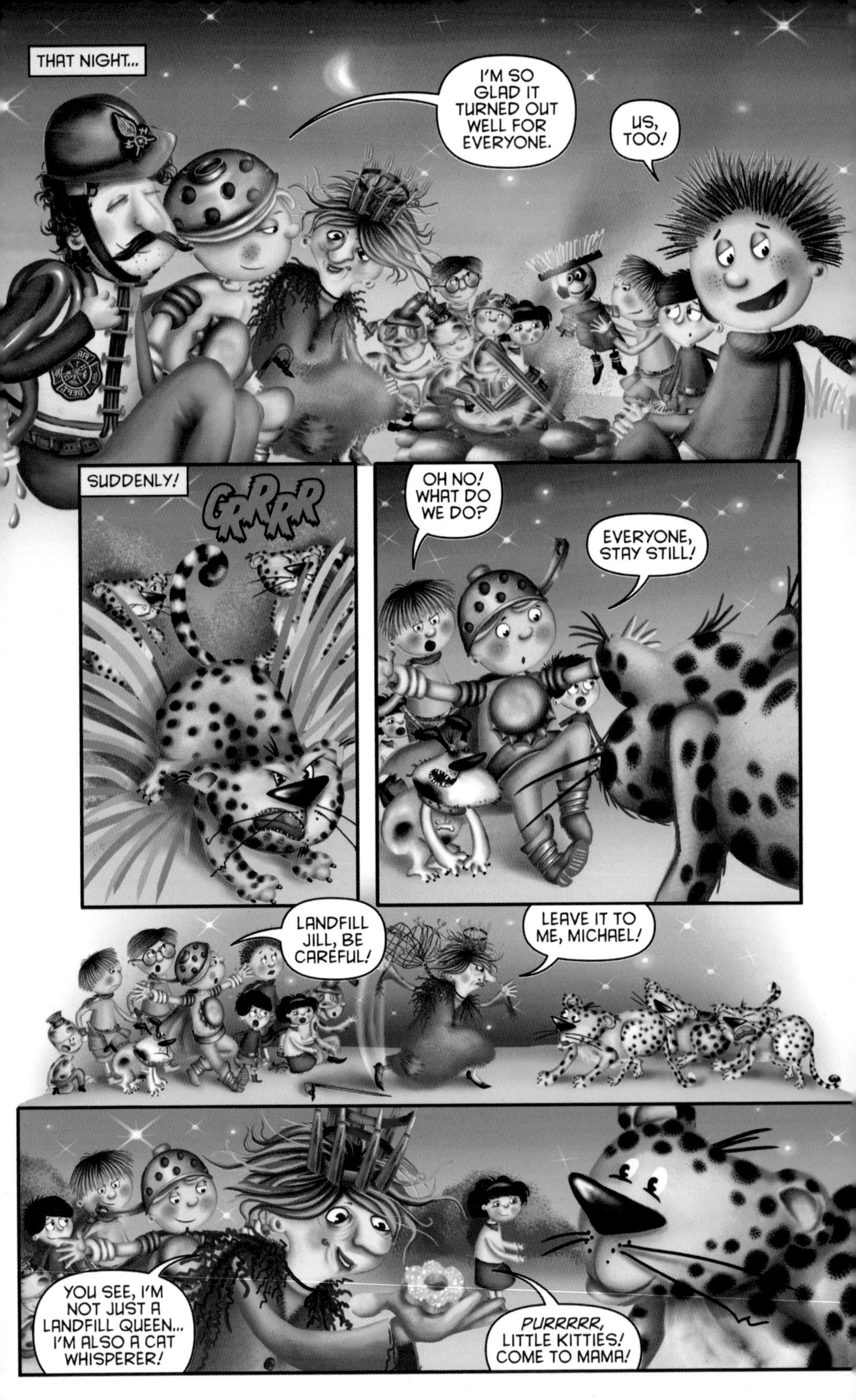
THAT NIGHT...
I'M SO GLAD IT TURNED OUT WELL FOR EVERYONE.
US, TOO!
SUDDENLY!
GRRRR
OH NO! WHAT DO WE DO?
EVERYONE, STAY STILL!
LANDFILL JILL, BE CAREFUL!
LEAVE IT TO ME, MICHAEL!
YOU SEE, I'M NOT JUST A LANDFILL QUEEN... I'M ALSO A CAT WHISPERER!
PURRRRR, LITTLE KITTIES! COME TO MAMA!

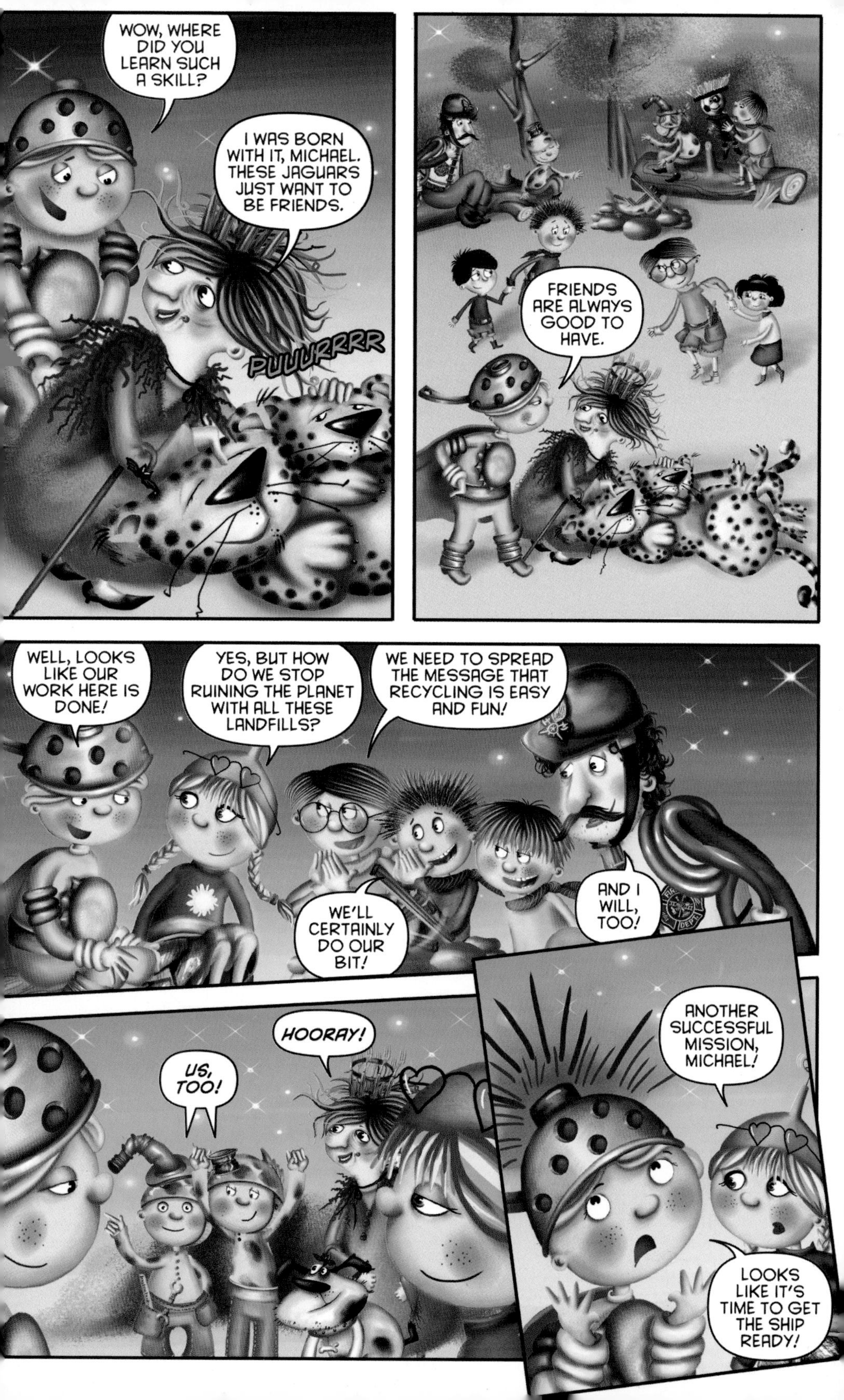
WOW, WHERE DID YOU LEARN SUCH A SKILL?
I WAS BORN WITH IT, MICHAEL. THESE JAGUARS JUST WANT TO BE FRIENDS.
PUUURRRR
FRIENDS ARE ALWAYS GOOD TO HAVE.
WELL, LOOKS LIKE OUR WORK HERE IS DONE!
YES, BUT HOW DO WE STOP RUINING THE PLANET WITH ALL THESE LANDFILLS?
WE NEED TO SPREAD THE MESSAGE THAT RECYCLING IS EASY AND FUN!
WE'LL CERTAINLY DO OUR BIT!
AND I WILL, TOO!
HOORAY!
US, TOO!
ANOTHER SUCCESSFUL MISSION, MICHAEL!
LOOKS LIKE IT'S TIME TO GET THE SHIP READY!

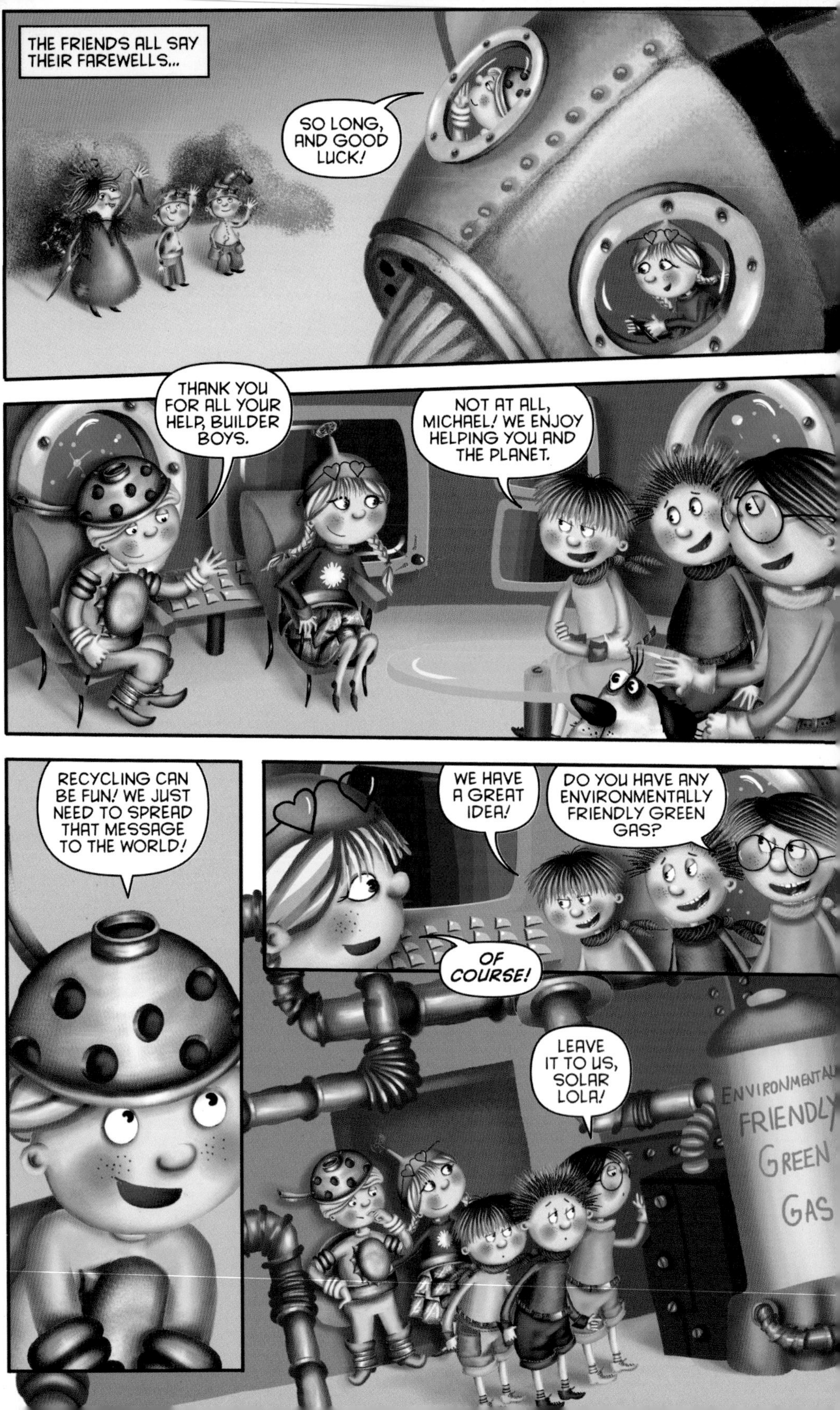
THE FRIENDS ALL SAY THEIR FAREWELLS...
SO LONG, AND GOOD LUCK!
THANK YOU FOR ALL YOUR HELP, BUILDER BOYS.
NOT AT ALL, MICHAEL! WE ENJOY HELPING YOU AND THE PLANET.
RECYCLING CAN BE FUN! WE JUST NEED TO SPREAD THAT MESSAGE TO THE WORLD!
WE HAVE A GREAT IDEA!
DO YOU HAVE ANY ENVIRONMENTALLY FRIENDLY GREEN GAS?
OF COURSE!
LEAVE IT TO US, SOLAR LOLA!
ENVIRONMENTAL FRIENDLY GREEN GAS

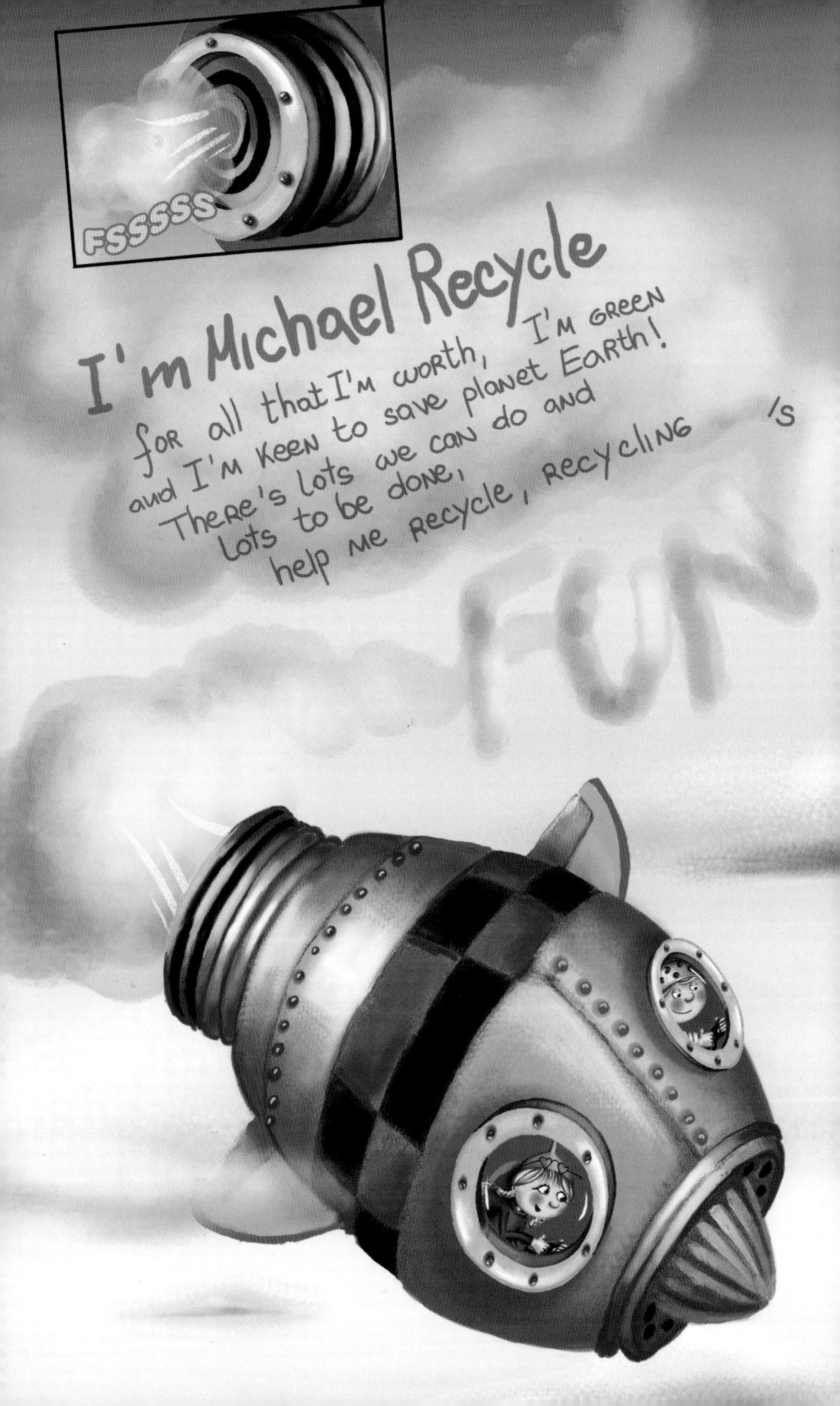
FSSSSS
I'm Michael Recycle
for all that I'm worth, I'm green
and I'm keen to save planet Earth!
There's lots we can do and
lots to be done,
help me recycle, recycling is
FUN

LOOK UP THERE!

RECYCLING IS FUN

BACK IN BRIGHTON...

AND IN ENVIRONMENTAL NEWS...

SO, TIN CAN STAN, WHERE DO YOU THINK WE'RE NEEDED NEXT?

WOOF WOOF WOOF WOOF WOOF!

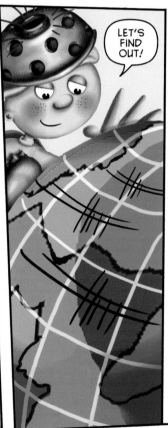

LET'S FIND OUT!

IT SEEMS LIKE THERE'S SOMETHING UP IN MEXICO! ARE YOU READY FOR ANOTHER ADVENTURE?

MEXICO

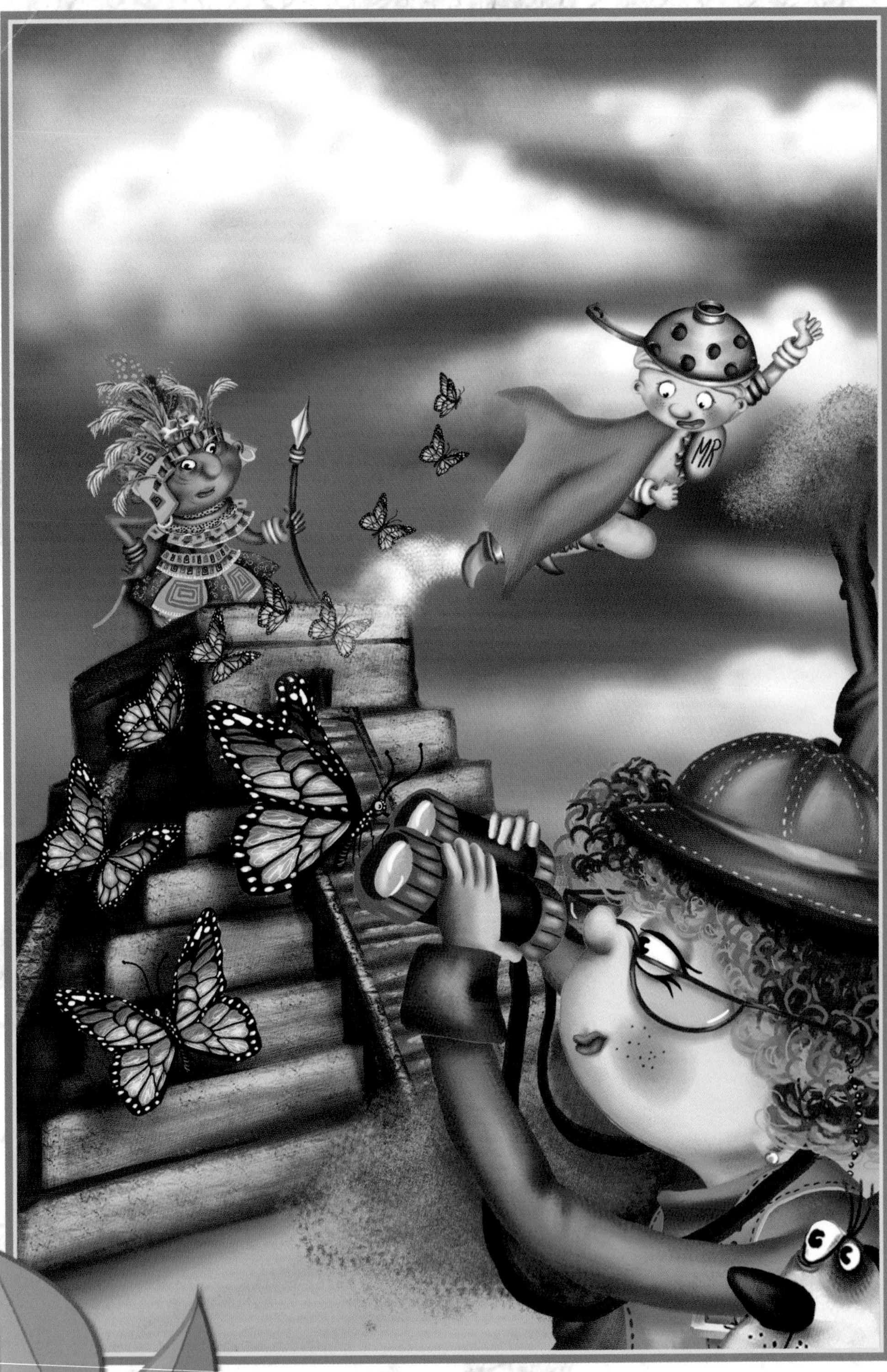
MR

COVER ART BY
ALEXANDRA COLOMBO

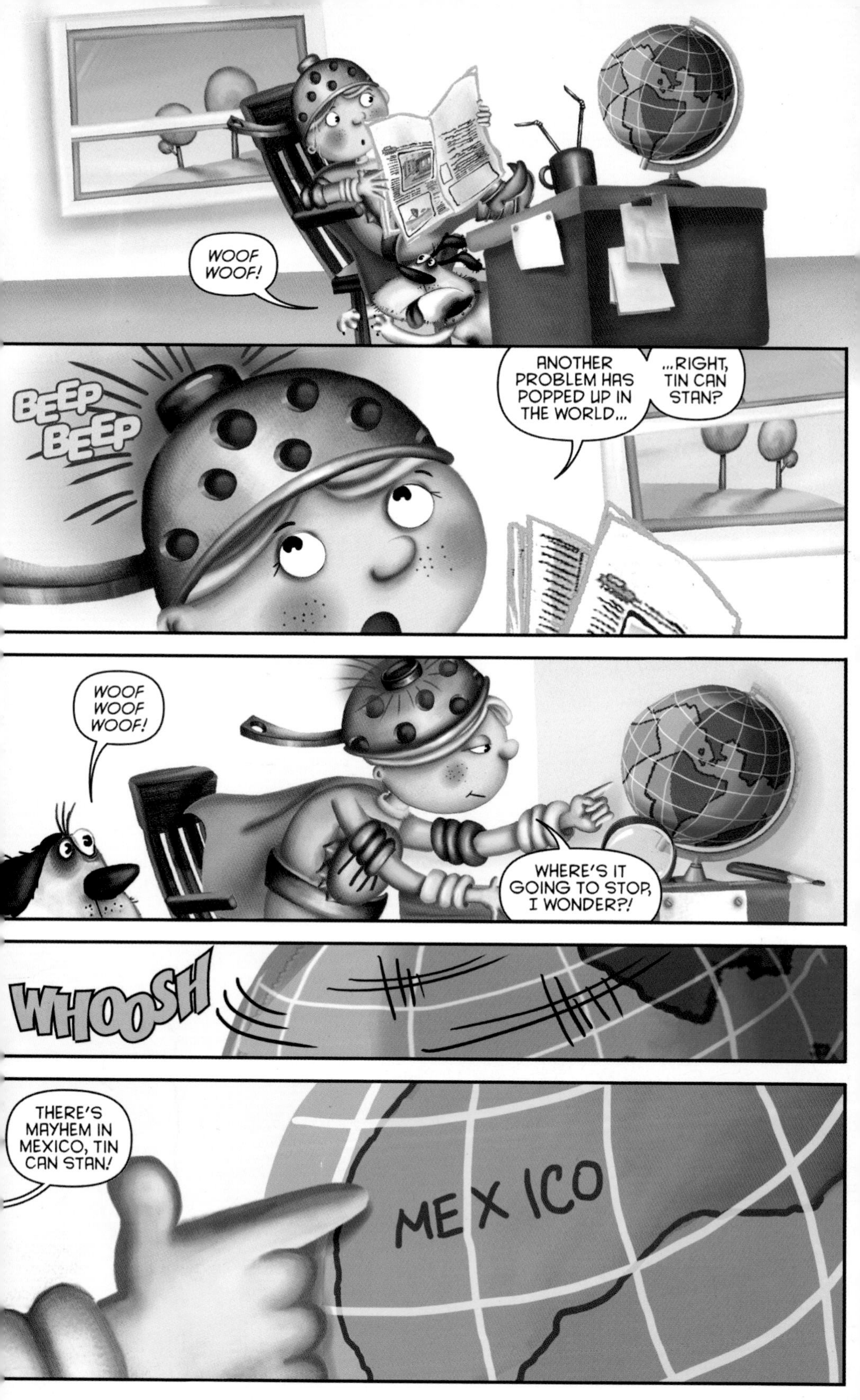
WOOF WOOF!
BEEP BEEP
ANOTHER PROBLEM HAS POPPED UP IN THE WORLD...
...RIGHT, TIN CAN STAN?
WOOF WOOF WOOF!
WHERE'S IT GOING TO STOP, I WONDER?!
WHOOSH
THERE'S MAYHEM IN MEXICO, TIN CAN STAN!
MEXICO

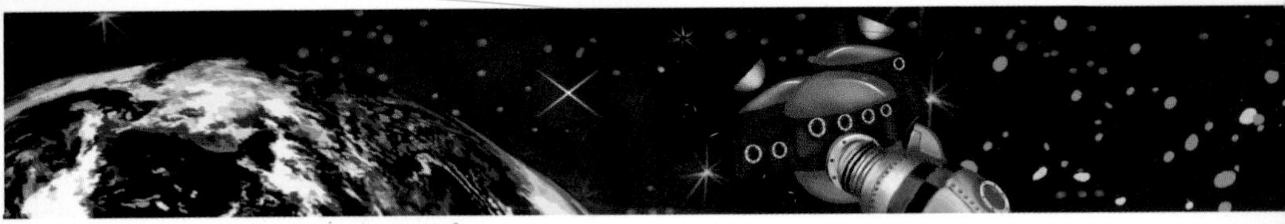

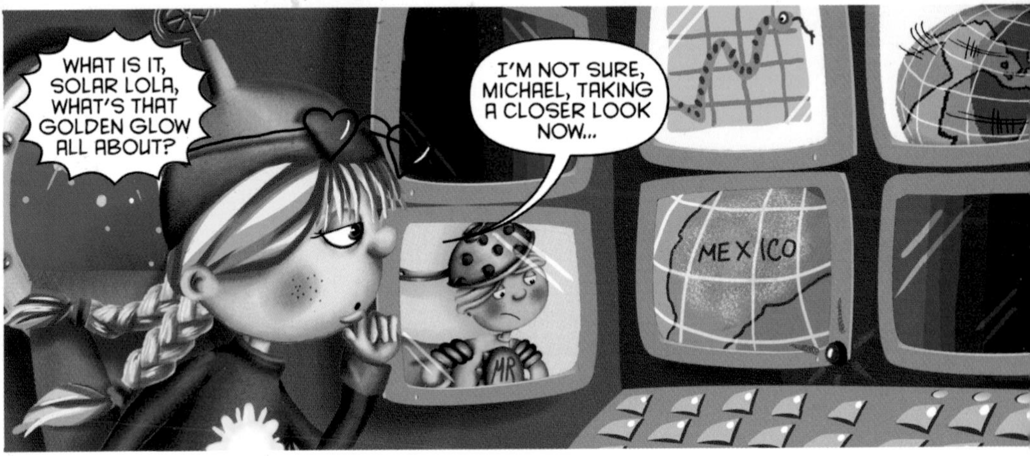

WHAT IS IT, SOLAR LOLA, WHAT'S THAT GOLDEN GLOW ALL ABOUT?
I'M NOT SURE, MICHAEL, TAKING A CLOSER LOOK NOW...
MR
MEXICO

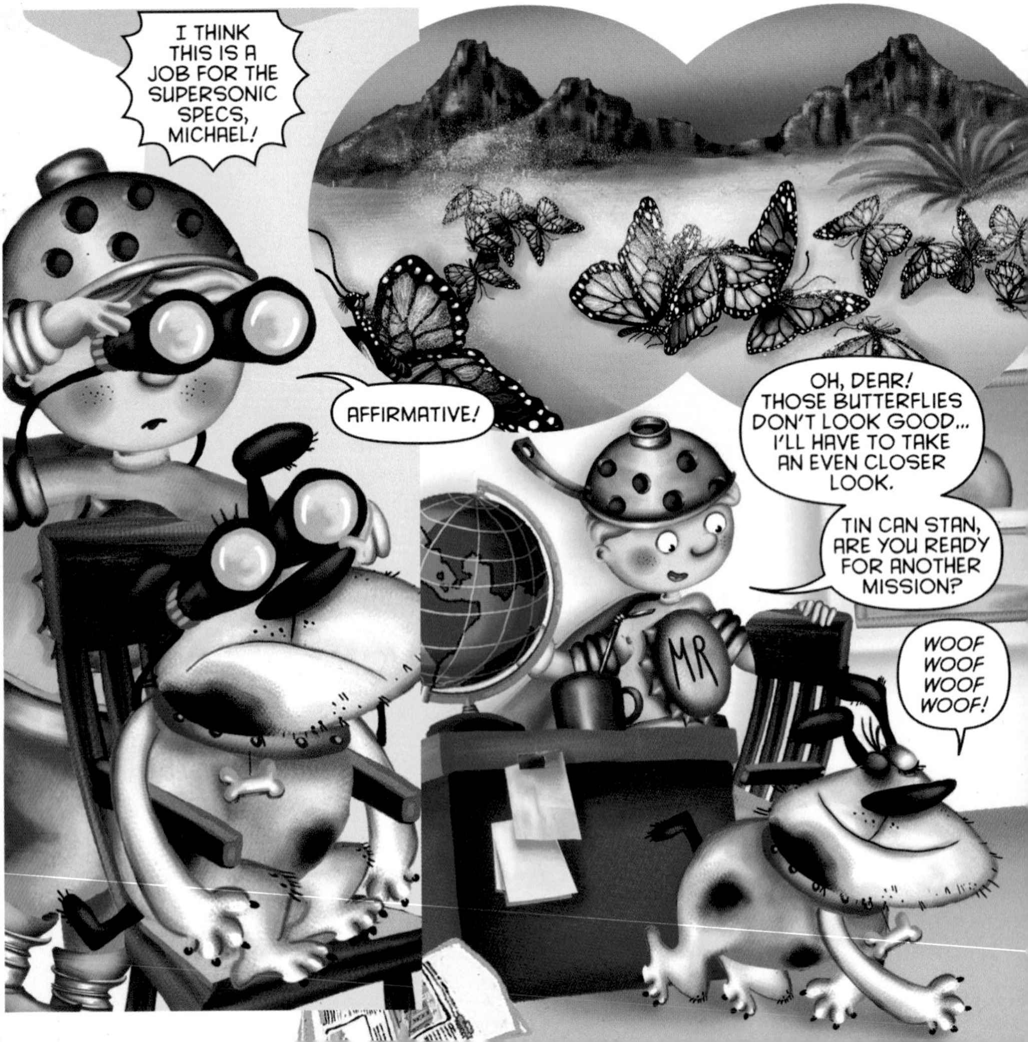

I THINK THIS IS A JOB FOR THE SUPERSONIC SPECS, MICHAEL!
AFFIRMATIVE!
OH, DEAR! THOSE BUTTERFLIES DON'T LOOK GOOD... I'LL HAVE TO TAKE AN EVEN CLOSER LOOK.
TIN CAN STAN, ARE YOU READY FOR ANOTHER MISSION?
WOOF WOOF WOOF WOOF!
MR

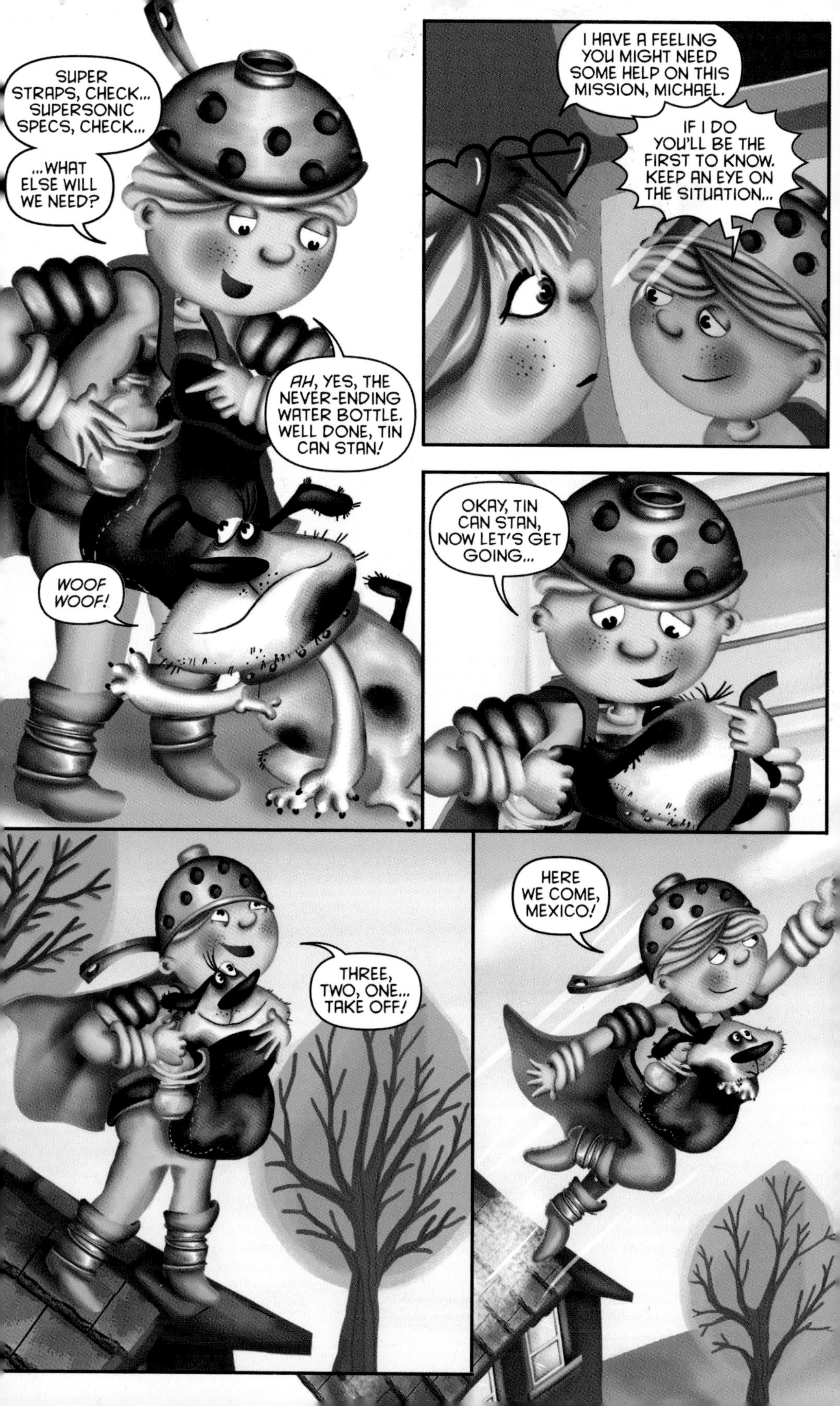
SUPER STRAPS, CHECK... SUPERSONIC SPECS, CHECK...
...WHAT ELSE WILL WE NEED?
AH, YES, THE NEVER-ENDING WATER BOTTLE. WELL DONE, TIN CAN STAN!
WOOF WOOF!
I HAVE A FEELING YOU MIGHT NEED SOME HELP ON THIS MISSION, MICHAEL.
IF I DO YOU'LL BE THE FIRST TO KNOW. KEEP AN EYE ON THE SITUATION...
OKAY, TIN CAN STAN, NOW LET'S GET GOING...
THREE, TWO, ONE... TAKE OFF!
HERE WE COME, MEXICO!

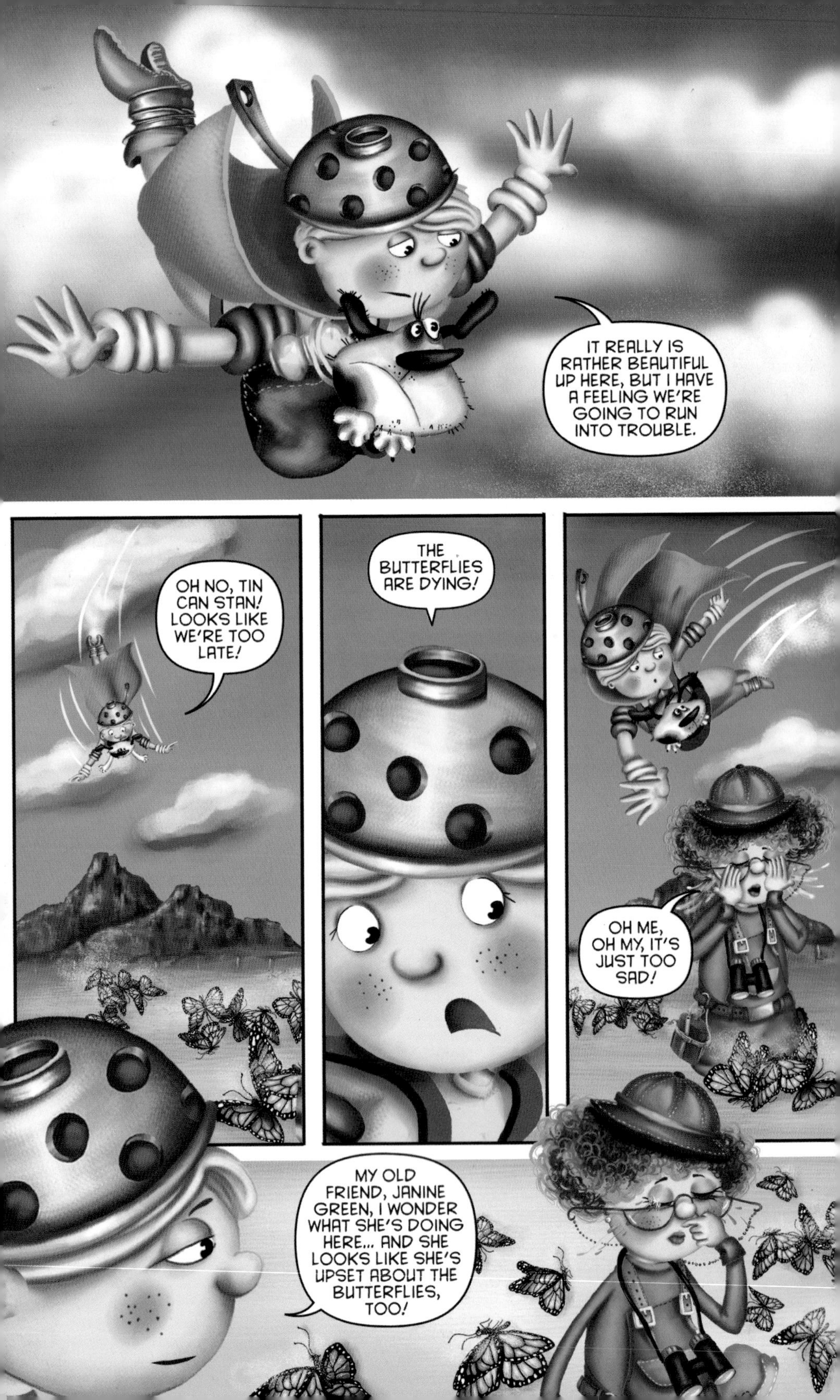
IT REALLY IS RATHER BEAUTIFUL UP HERE, BUT I HAVE A FEELING WE'RE GOING TO RUN INTO TROUBLE.
OH NO, TIN CAN STAN! LOOKS LIKE WE'RE TOO LATE!
THE BUTTERFLIES ARE DYING!
OH ME, OH MY, IT'S JUST TOO SAD!
MY OLD FRIEND, JANINE GREEN, I WONDER WHAT SHE'S DOING HERE... AND SHE LOOKS LIKE SHE'S UPSET ABOUT THE BUTTERFLIES, TOO!

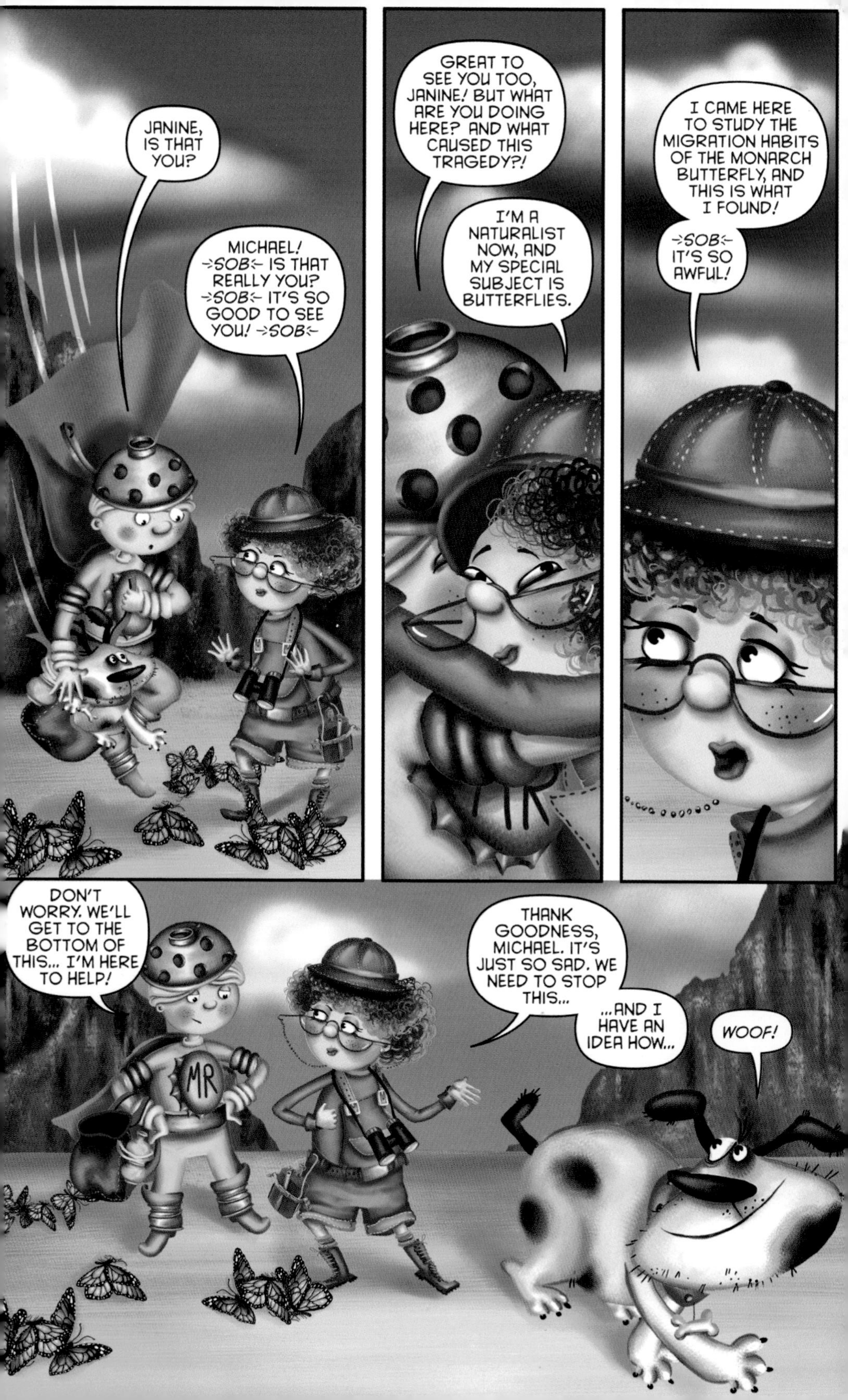
JANINE, IS THAT YOU?
MICHAEL! -SOB- IS THAT REALLY YOU? -SOB- IT'S SO GOOD TO SEE YOU! -SOB-
GREAT TO SEE YOU TOO, JANINE! BUT WHAT ARE YOU DOING HERE? AND WHAT CAUSED THIS TRAGEDY?!
I'M A NATURALIST NOW, AND MY SPECIAL SUBJECT IS BUTTERFLIES.
I CAME HERE TO STUDY THE MIGRATION HABITS OF THE MONARCH BUTTERFLY, AND THIS IS WHAT I FOUND!
-SOB- IT'S SO AWFUL!
DON'T WORRY. WE'LL GET TO THE BOTTOM OF THIS... I'M HERE TO HELP!
MR
THANK GOODNESS, MICHAEL. IT'S JUST SO SAD. WE NEED TO STOP THIS...
...AND I HAVE AN IDEA HOW...
WOOF!

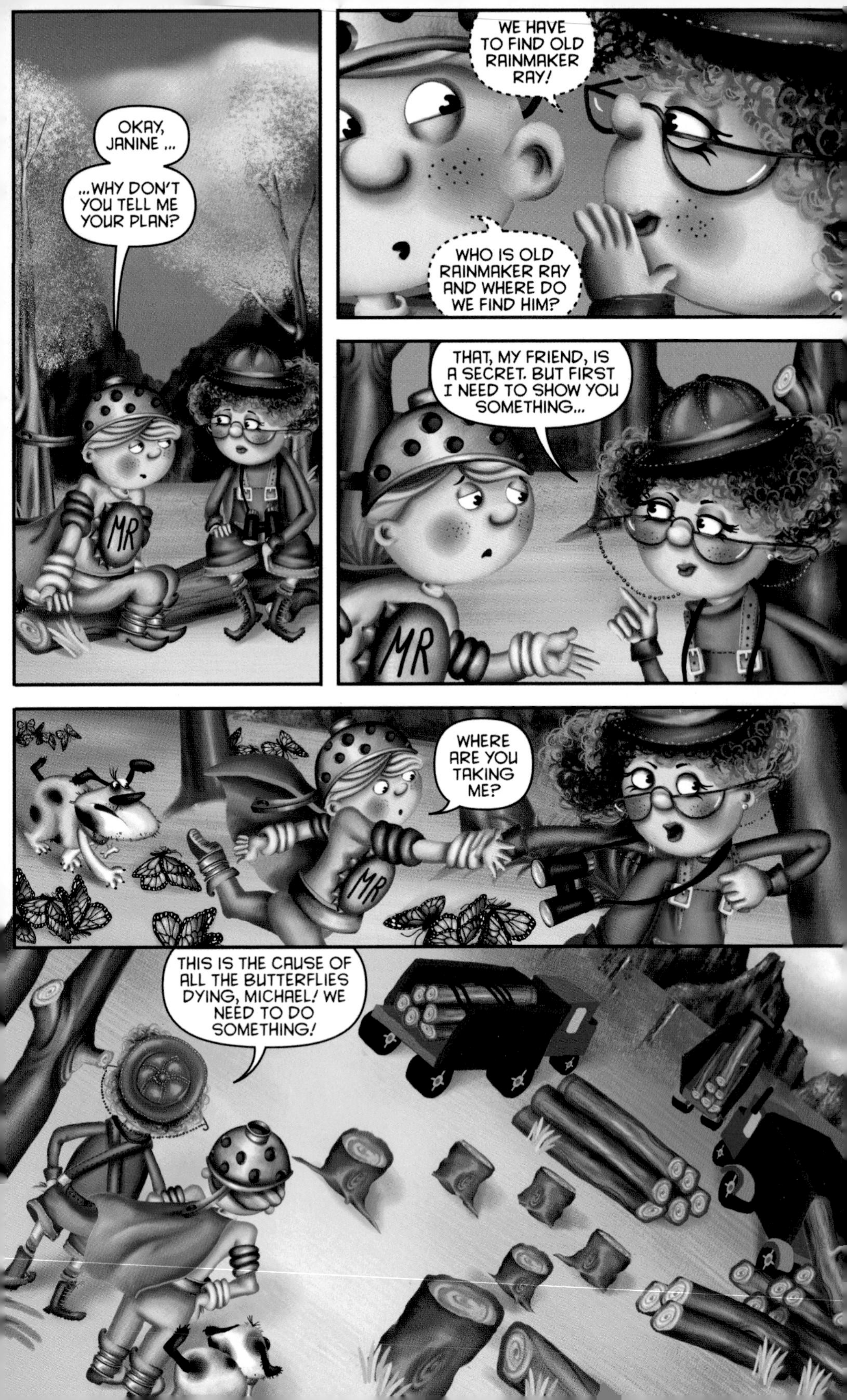
OKAY, JANINE ...
...WHY DON'T YOU TELL ME YOUR PLAN?
WE HAVE TO FIND OLD RAINMAKER RAY!
WHO IS OLD RAINMAKER RAY AND WHERE DO WE FIND HIM?
THAT, MY FRIEND, IS A SECRET. BUT FIRST I NEED TO SHOW YOU SOMETHING...
MR
WHERE ARE YOU TAKING ME?
THIS IS THE CAUSE OF ALL THE BUTTERFLIES DYING, MICHAEL! WE NEED TO DO SOMETHING!

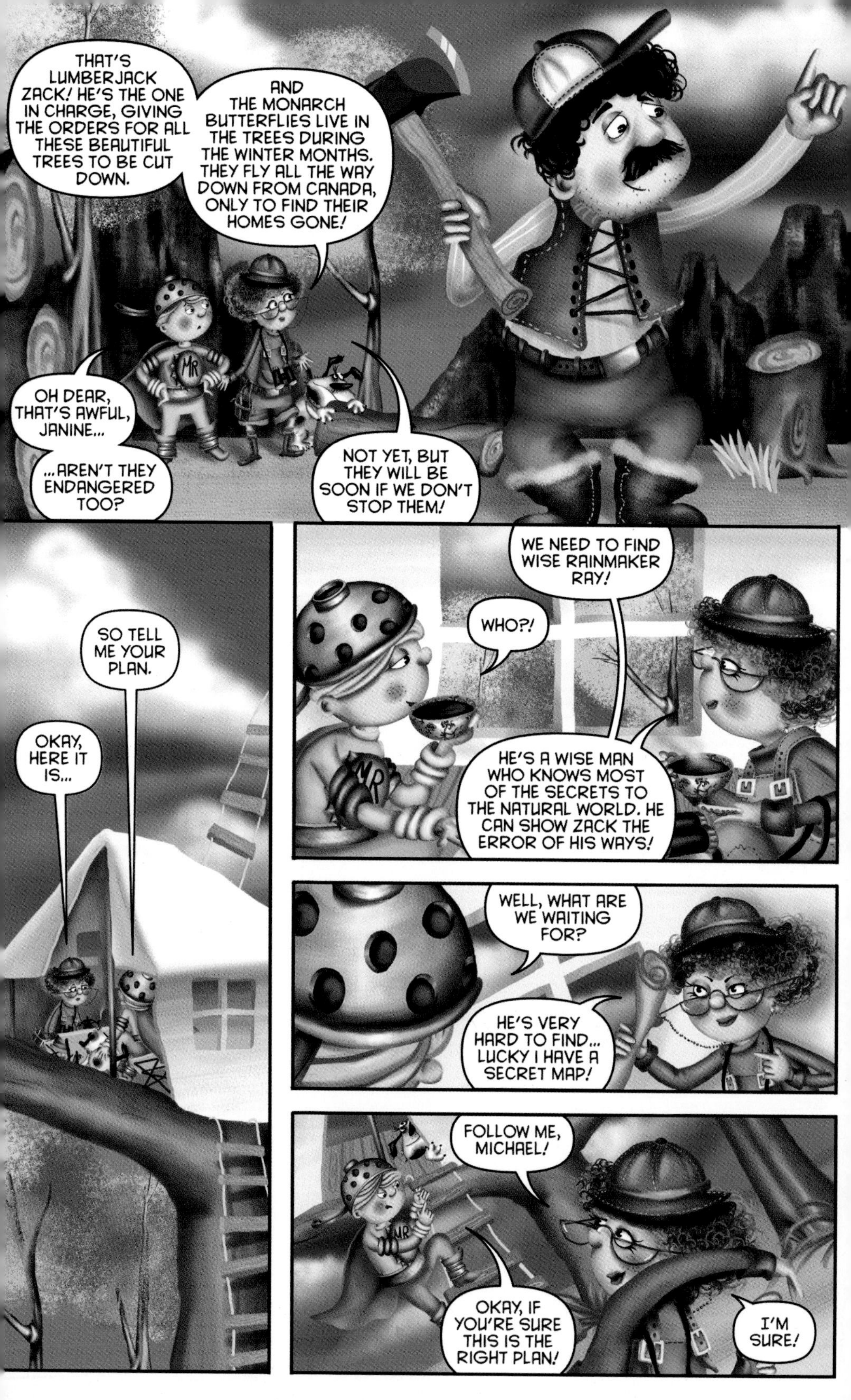
THAT'S LUMBERJACK ZACK! HE'S THE ONE IN CHARGE, GIVING THE ORDERS FOR ALL THESE BEAUTIFUL TREES TO BE CUT DOWN.
AND THE MONARCH BUTTERFLIES LIVE IN THE TREES DURING THE WINTER MONTHS. THEY FLY ALL THE WAY DOWN FROM CANADA, ONLY TO FIND THEIR HOMES GONE!
OH DEAR, THAT'S AWFUL, JANINE...
...AREN'T THEY ENDANGERED TOO?
NOT YET, BUT THEY WILL BE SOON IF WE DON'T STOP THEM!
SO TELL ME YOUR PLAN.
OKAY, HERE IT IS...
WE NEED TO FIND WISE RAINMAKER RAY!
WHO?!
HE'S A WISE MAN WHO KNOWS MOST OF THE SECRETS TO THE NATURAL WORLD. HE CAN SHOW ZACK THE ERROR OF HIS WAYS!
WELL, WHAT ARE WE WAITING FOR?
HE'S VERY HARD TO FIND... LUCKY I HAVE A SECRET MAP!
FOLLOW ME, MICHAEL!
OKAY, IF YOU'RE SURE THIS IS THE RIGHT PLAN!
I'M SURE!

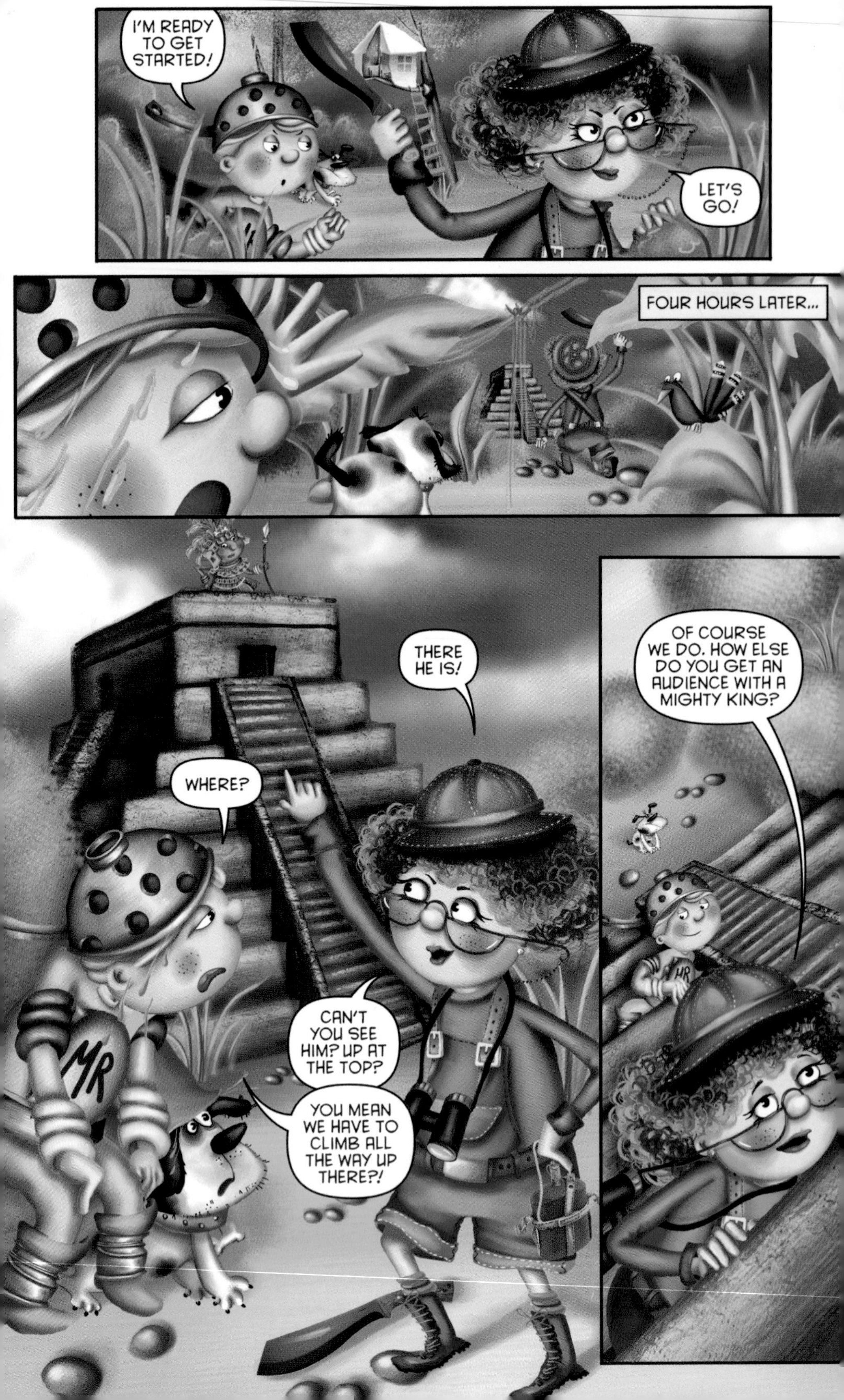
I'M READY TO GET STARTED!
LET'S GO!
FOUR HOURS LATER...
THERE HE IS!
WHERE?
CAN'T YOU SEE HIM? UP AT THE TOP?
YOU MEAN WE HAVE TO CLIMB ALL THE WAY UP THERE?!
OF COURSE WE DO. HOW ELSE DO YOU GET AN AUDIENCE WITH A MIGHTY KING?

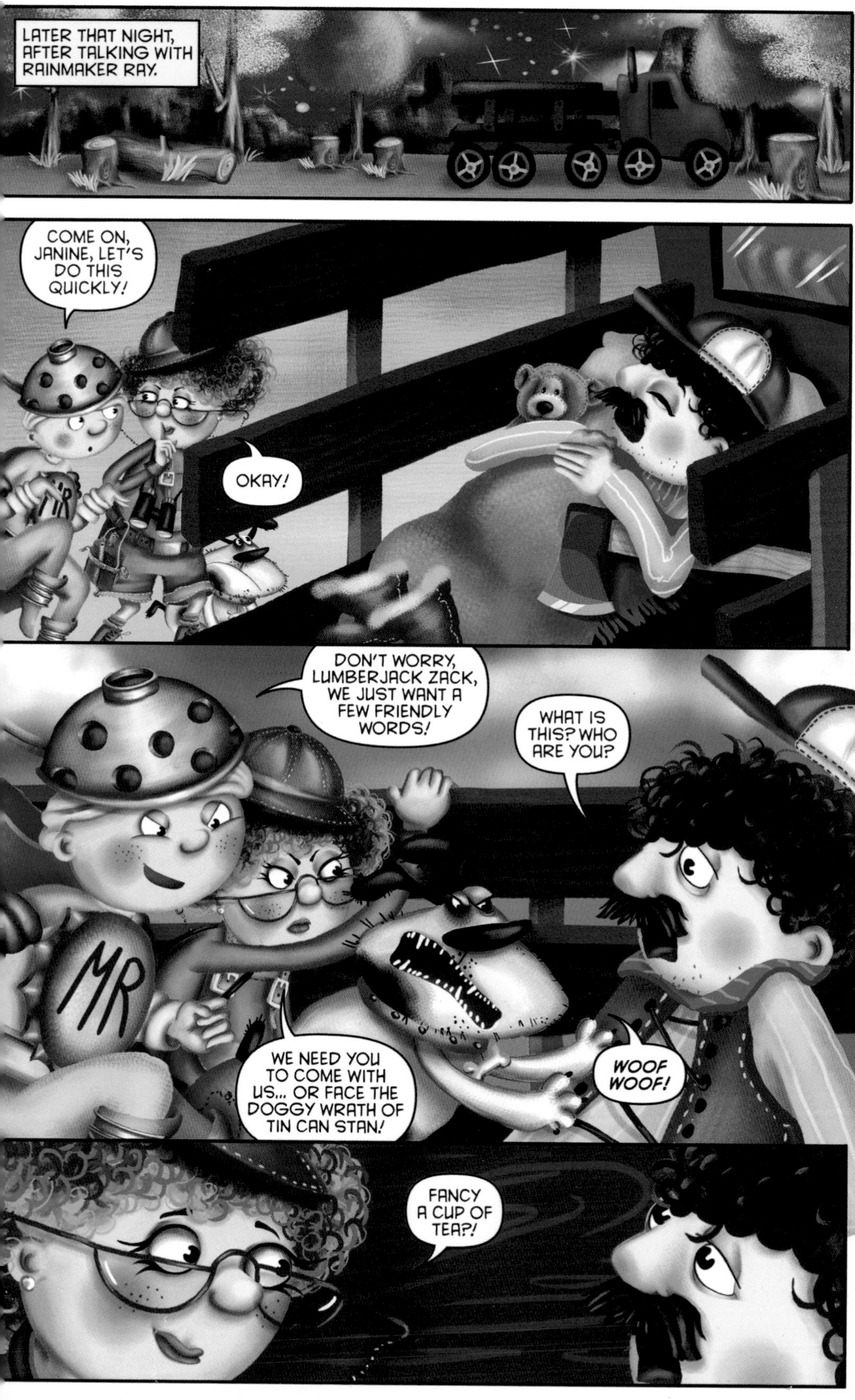
LATER THAT NIGHT, AFTER TALKING WITH RAINMAKER RAY.
COME ON, JANINE, LET'S DO THIS QUICKLY!
OKAY!
DON'T WORRY, LUMBERJACK ZACK, WE JUST WANT A FEW FRIENDLY WORDS!
WHAT IS THIS? WHO ARE YOU?
WE NEED YOU TO COME WITH US... OR FACE THE DOGGY WRATH OF TIN CAN STAN!
WOOF WOOF!
MR
FANCY A CUP OF TEA?!

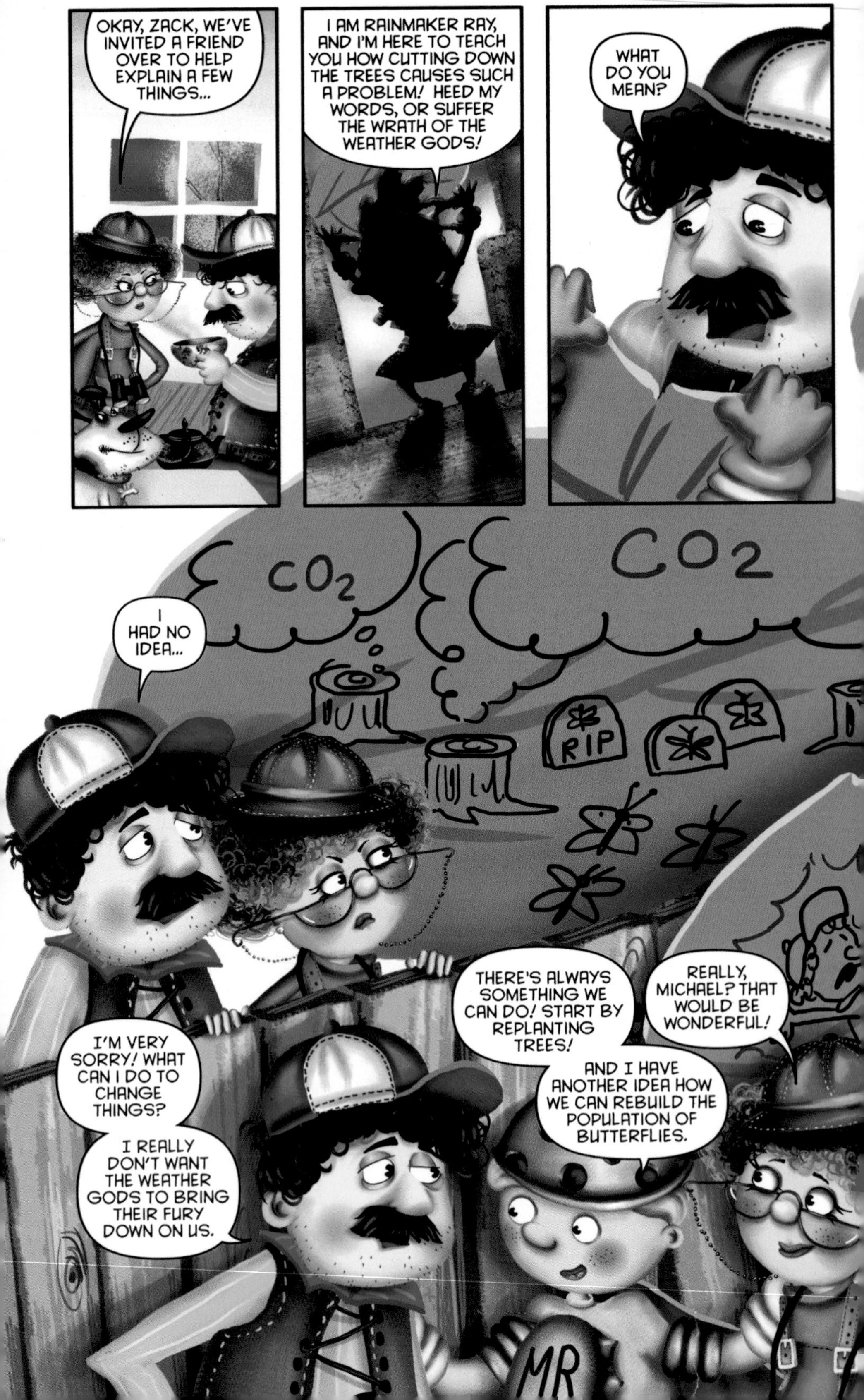
OKAY, ZACK, WE'VE INVITED A FRIEND OVER TO HELP EXPLAIN A FEW THINGS...
I AM RAINMAKER RAY, AND I'M HERE TO TEACH YOU HOW CUTTING DOWN THE TREES CAUSES SUCH A PROBLEM! HEED MY WORDS, OR SUFFER THE WRATH OF THE WEATHER GODS!
WHAT DO YOU MEAN?
I HAD NO IDEA...
CO2
CO2
RIP
I'M VERY SORRY! WHAT CAN I DO TO CHANGE THINGS?
I REALLY DON'T WANT THE WEATHER GODS TO BRING THEIR FURY DOWN ON US.
THERE'S ALWAYS SOMETHING WE CAN DO! START BY REPLANTING TREES!
AND I HAVE ANOTHER IDEA HOW WE CAN REBUILD THE POPULATION OF BUTTERFLIES.
REALLY, MICHAEL? THAT WOULD BE WONDERFUL!
MR

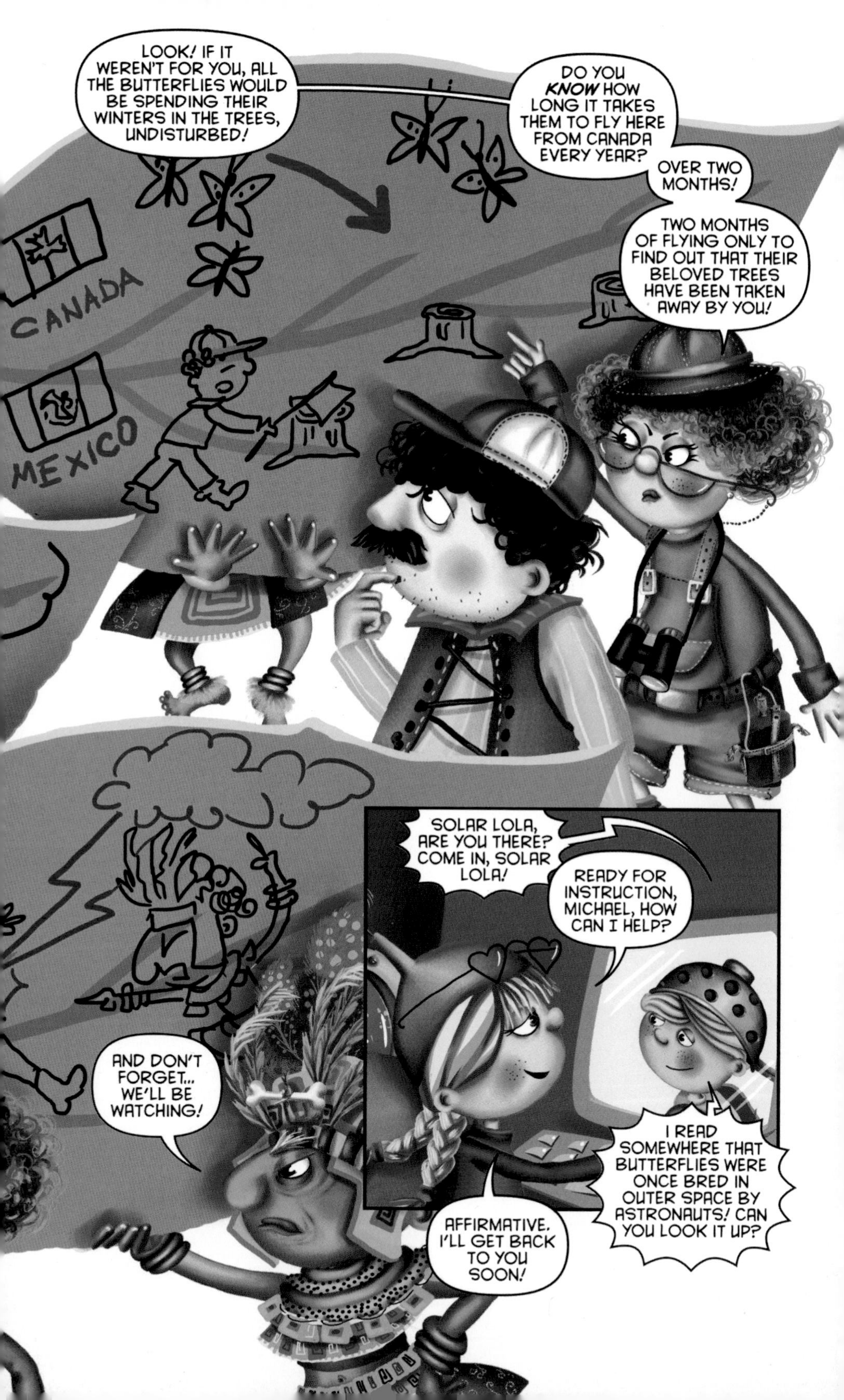
LOOK! IF IT WEREN'T FOR YOU, ALL THE BUTTERFLIES WOULD BE SPENDING THEIR WINTERS IN THE TREES, UNDISTURBED!
DO YOU KNOW HOW LONG IT TAKES THEM TO FLY HERE FROM CANADA EVERY YEAR?
OVER TWO MONTHS!
TWO MONTHS OF FLYING ONLY TO FIND OUT THAT THEIR BELOVED TREES HAVE BEEN TAKEN AWAY BY YOU!
CANADA
MEXICO
AND DON'T FORGET... WE'LL BE WATCHING!
SOLAR LOLA, ARE YOU THERE? COME IN, SOLAR LOLA!
READY FOR INSTRUCTION, MICHAEL, HOW CAN I HELP?
I READ SOMEWHERE THAT BUTTERFLIES WERE ONCE BRED IN OUTER SPACE BY ASTRONAUTS! CAN YOU LOOK IT UP?
AFFIRMATIVE. I'LL GET BACK TO YOU SOON!

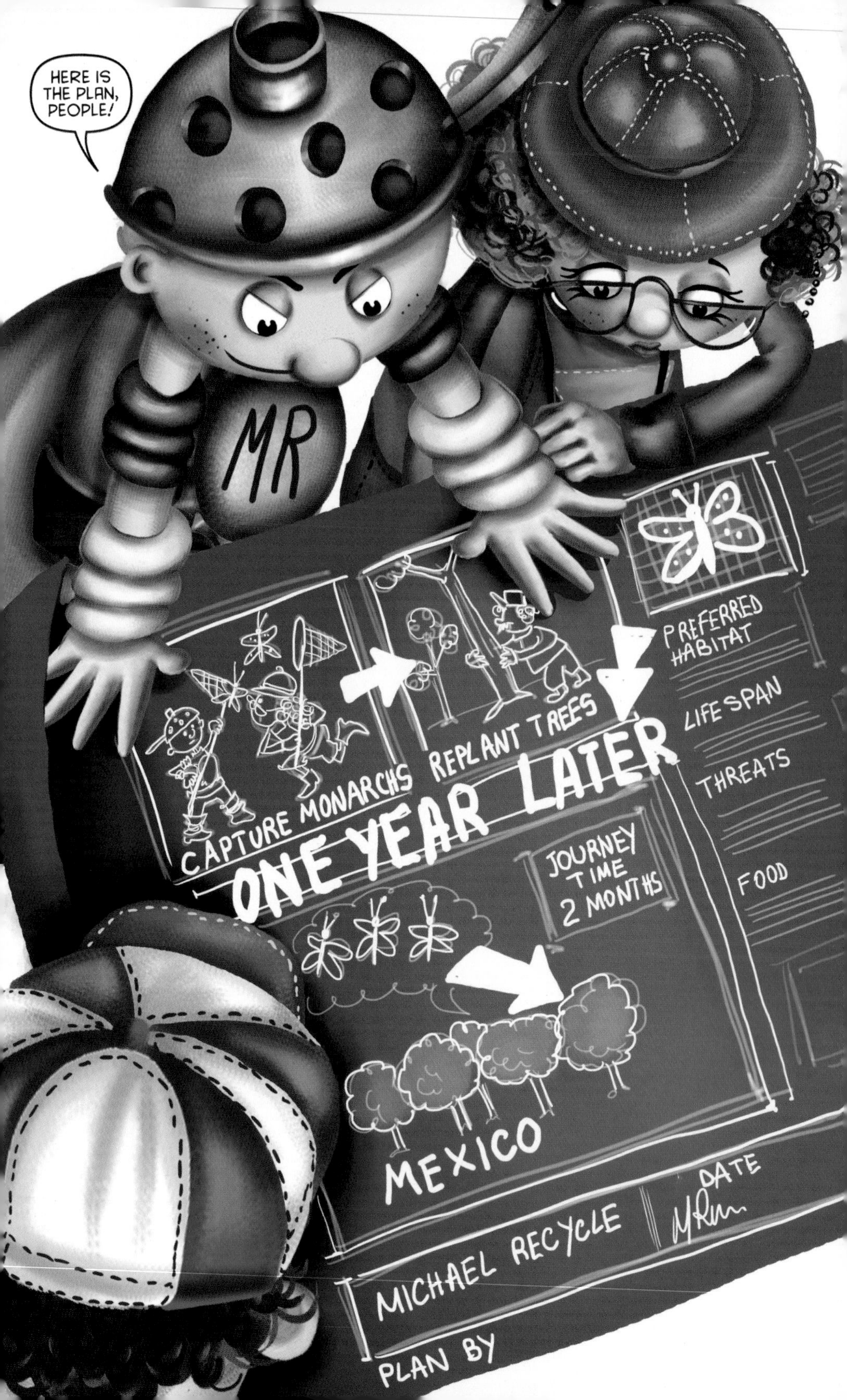
HERE IS THE PLAN, PEOPLE!
MR
CAPTURE MONARCHS
REPLANT TREES
PREFERRED HABITAT
LIFESPAN
THREATS
FOOD
ONE YEAR LATER
JOURNEY TIME 2 MONTHS
MEXICO
DATE
MICHAEL RECYCLE
PLAN BY

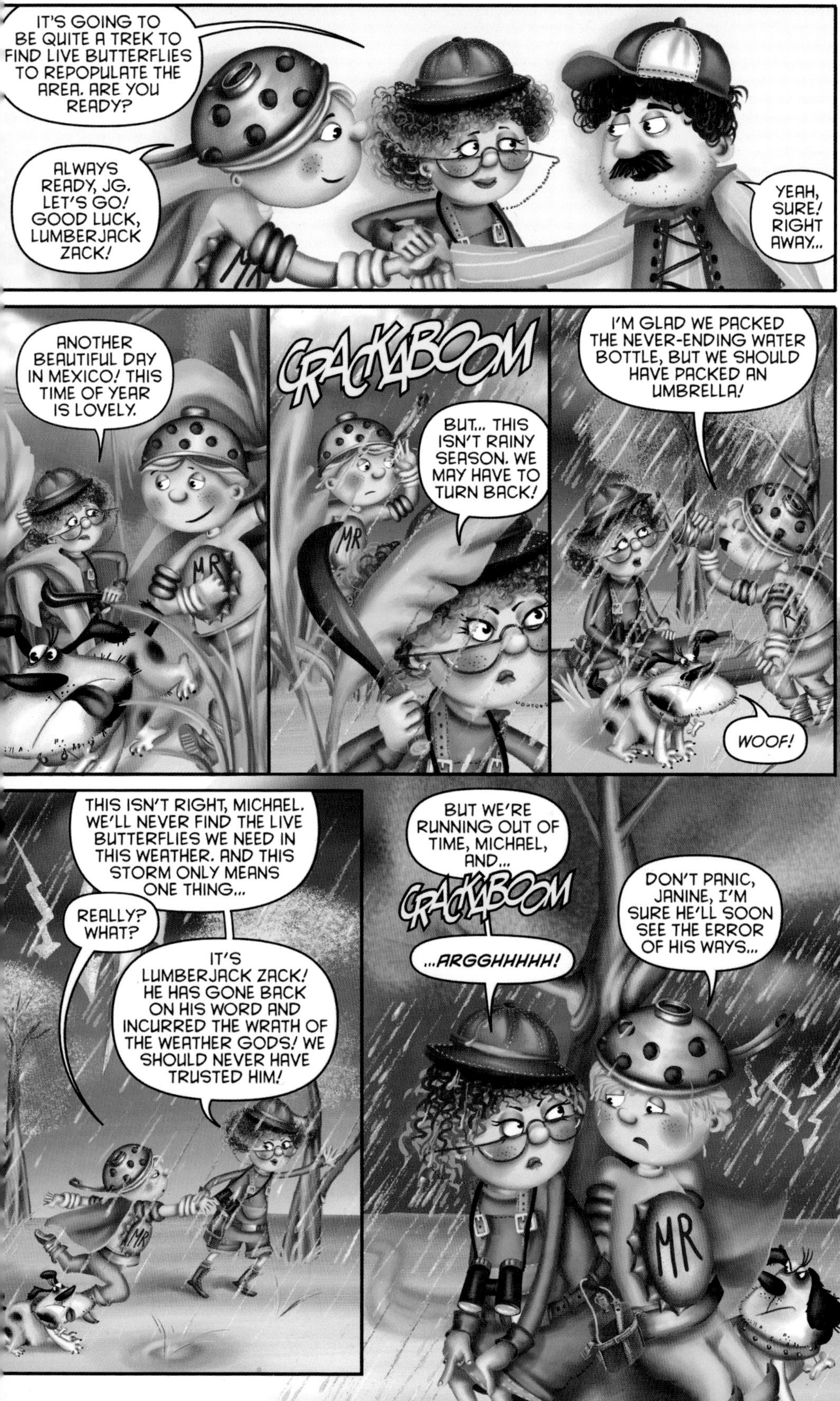
IT'S GOING TO BE QUITE A TREK TO FIND LIVE BUTTERFLIES TO REPOPULATE THE AREA. ARE YOU READY?
ALWAYS READY, JG. LET'S GO! GOOD LUCK, LUMBERJACK ZACK!
YEAH, SURE! RIGHT AWAY...
ANOTHER BEAUTIFUL DAY IN MEXICO! THIS TIME OF YEAR IS LOVELY.
CRACKABOOM
BUT... THIS ISN'T RAINY SEASON. WE MAY HAVE TO TURN BACK!
I'M GLAD WE PACKED THE NEVER-ENDING WATER BOTTLE, BUT WE SHOULD HAVE PACKED AN UMBRELLA!
WOOF!
THIS ISN'T RIGHT, MICHAEL. WE'LL NEVER FIND THE LIVE BUTTERFLIES WE NEED IN THIS WEATHER. AND THIS STORM ONLY MEANS ONE THING...
REALLY? WHAT?
IT'S LUMBERJACK ZACK! HE HAS GONE BACK ON HIS WORD AND INCURRED THE WRATH OF THE WEATHER GODS! WE SHOULD NEVER HAVE TRUSTED HIM!
BUT WE'RE RUNNING OUT OF TIME, MICHAEL, AND...
CRACKABOOM
...ARGGHHHHH!
DON'T PANIC, JANINE, I'M SURE HE'LL SOON SEE THE ERROR OF HIS WAYS...

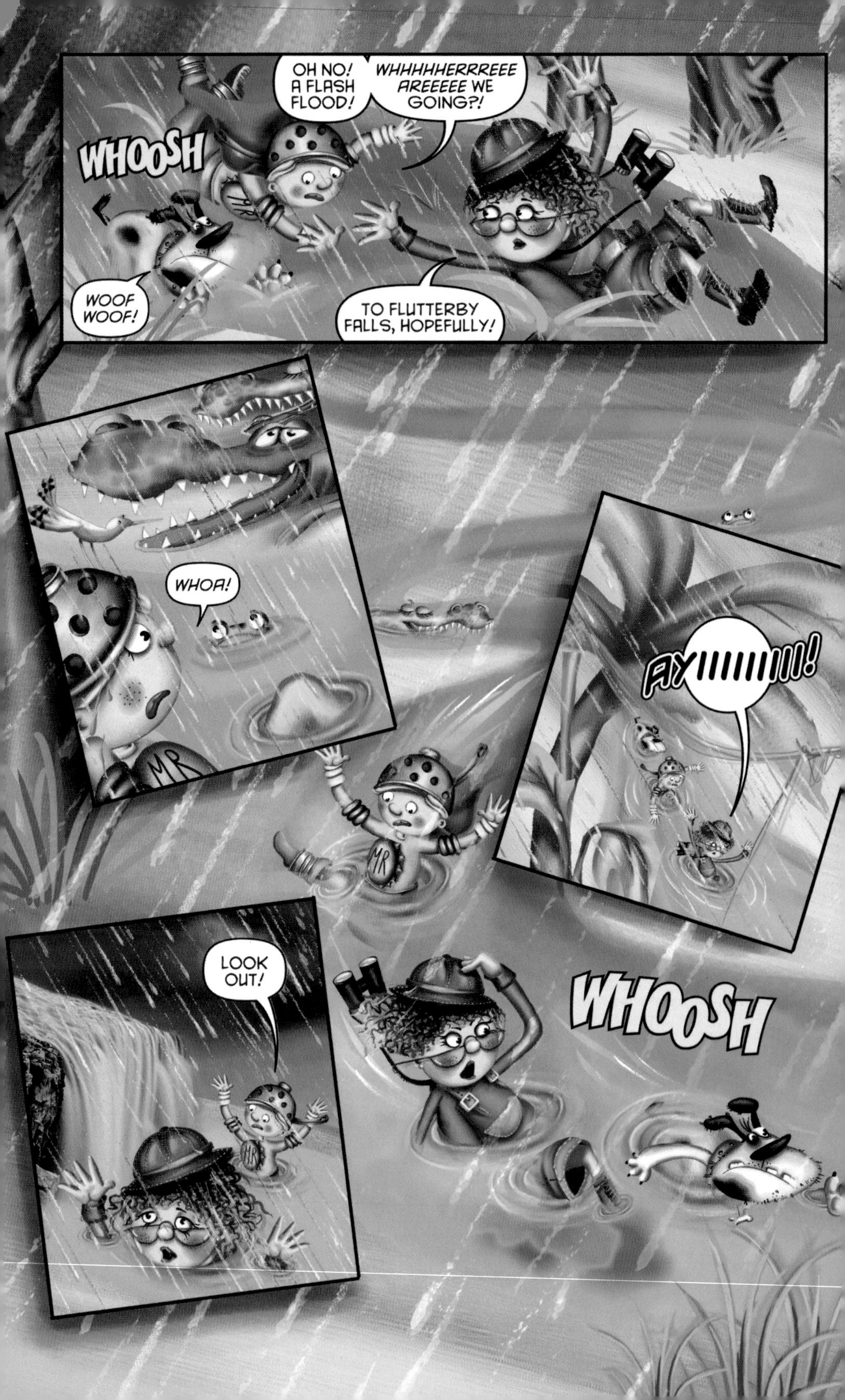
OH NO! A FLASH FLOOD!
WHHHHHERRREEE AREEEEE WE GOING?!
WHOOSH
WOOF WOOF!
TO FLUTTERBY FALLS, HOPEFULLY!
WHOA!
AYIIIIIIIII!
LOOK OUT!
WHOOSH

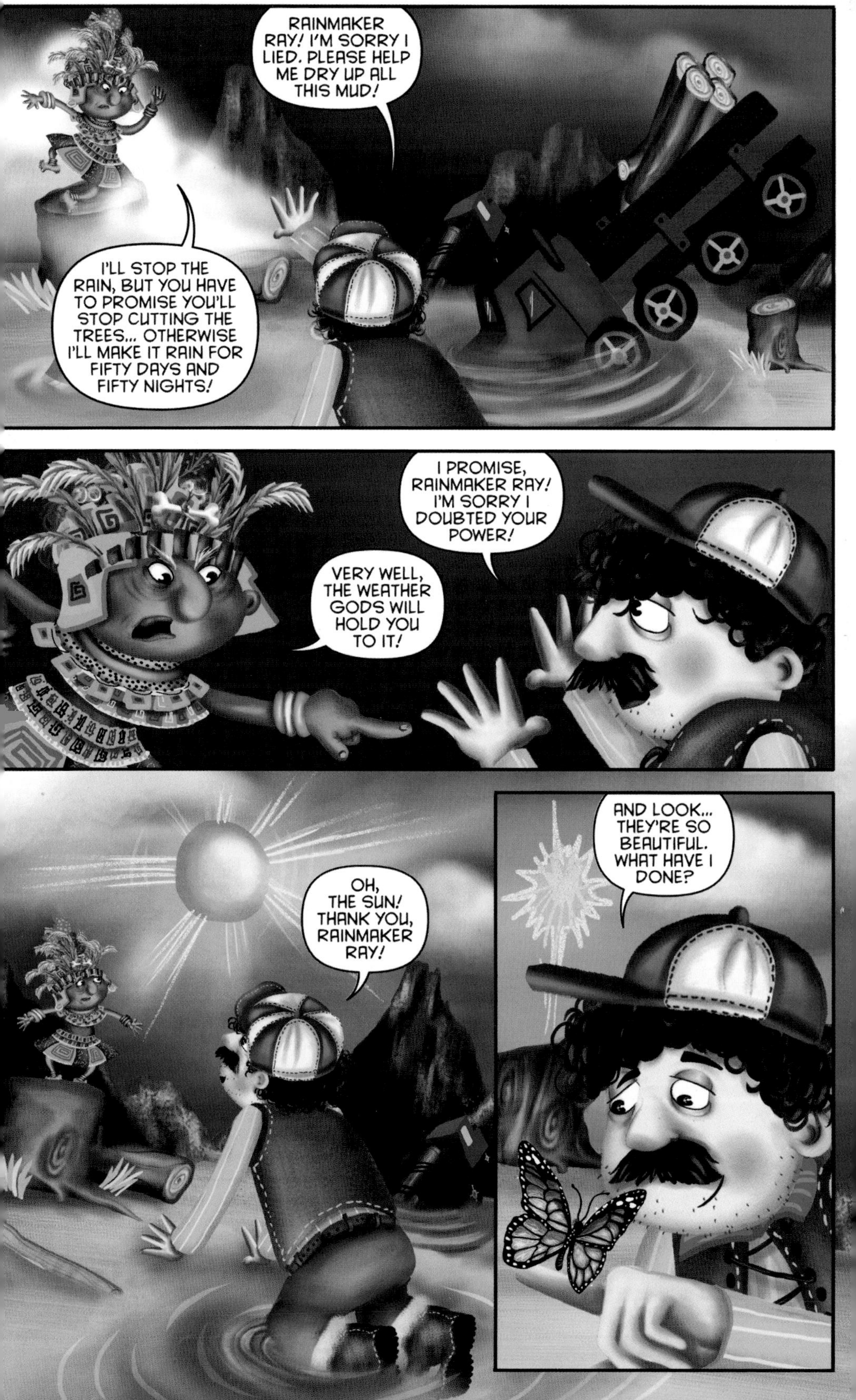
RAINMAKER RAY! I'M SORRY I LIED. PLEASE HELP ME DRY UP ALL THIS MUD!
I'LL STOP THE RAIN, BUT YOU HAVE TO PROMISE YOU'LL STOP CUTTING THE TREES... OTHERWISE I'LL MAKE IT RAIN FOR FIFTY DAYS AND FIFTY NIGHTS!
I PROMISE, RAINMAKER RAY! I'M SORRY I DOUBTED YOUR POWER!
VERY WELL, THE WEATHER GODS WILL HOLD YOU TO IT!
OH, THE SUN! THANK YOU, RAINMAKER RAY!
AND LOOK... THEY'RE SO BEAUTIFUL. WHAT HAVE I DONE?

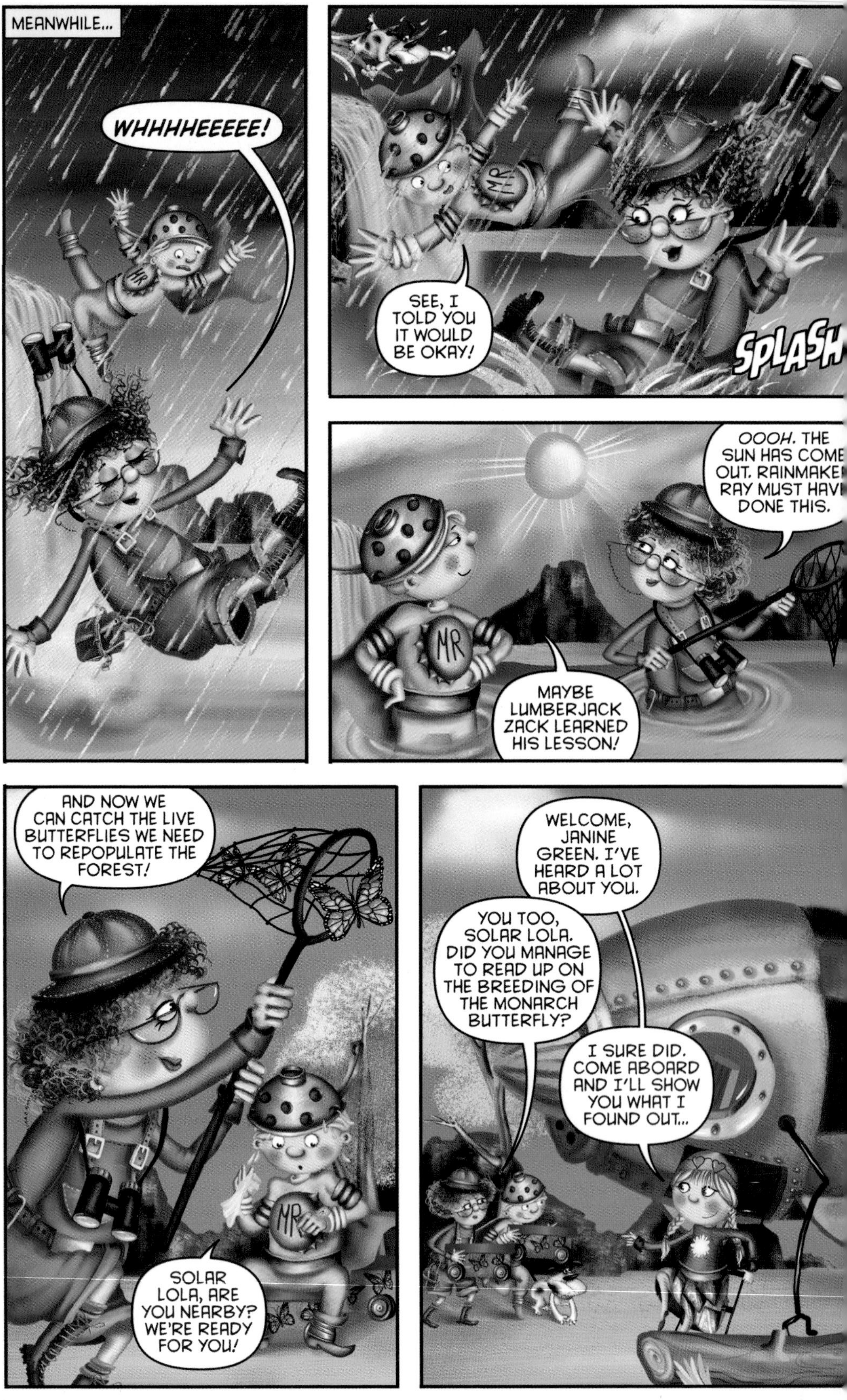
MEANWHILE...
WHHHHEEEEE!
SEE, I TOLD YOU IT WOULD BE OKAY!
SPLASH
OOOH. THE SUN HAS COME OUT. RAINMAKER RAY MUST HAVE DONE THIS.
MAYBE LUMBERJACK ZACK LEARNED HIS LESSON!
AND NOW WE CAN CATCH THE LIVE BUTTERFLIES WE NEED TO REPOPULATE THE FOREST!
SOLAR LOLA, ARE YOU NEARBY? WE'RE READY FOR YOU!
WELCOME, JANINE GREEN. I'VE HEARD A LOT ABOUT YOU.
YOU TOO, SOLAR LOLA. DID YOU MANAGE TO READ UP ON THE BREEDING OF THE MONARCH BUTTERFLY?
I SURE DID. COME ABOARD AND I'LL SHOW YOU WHAT I FOUND OUT...

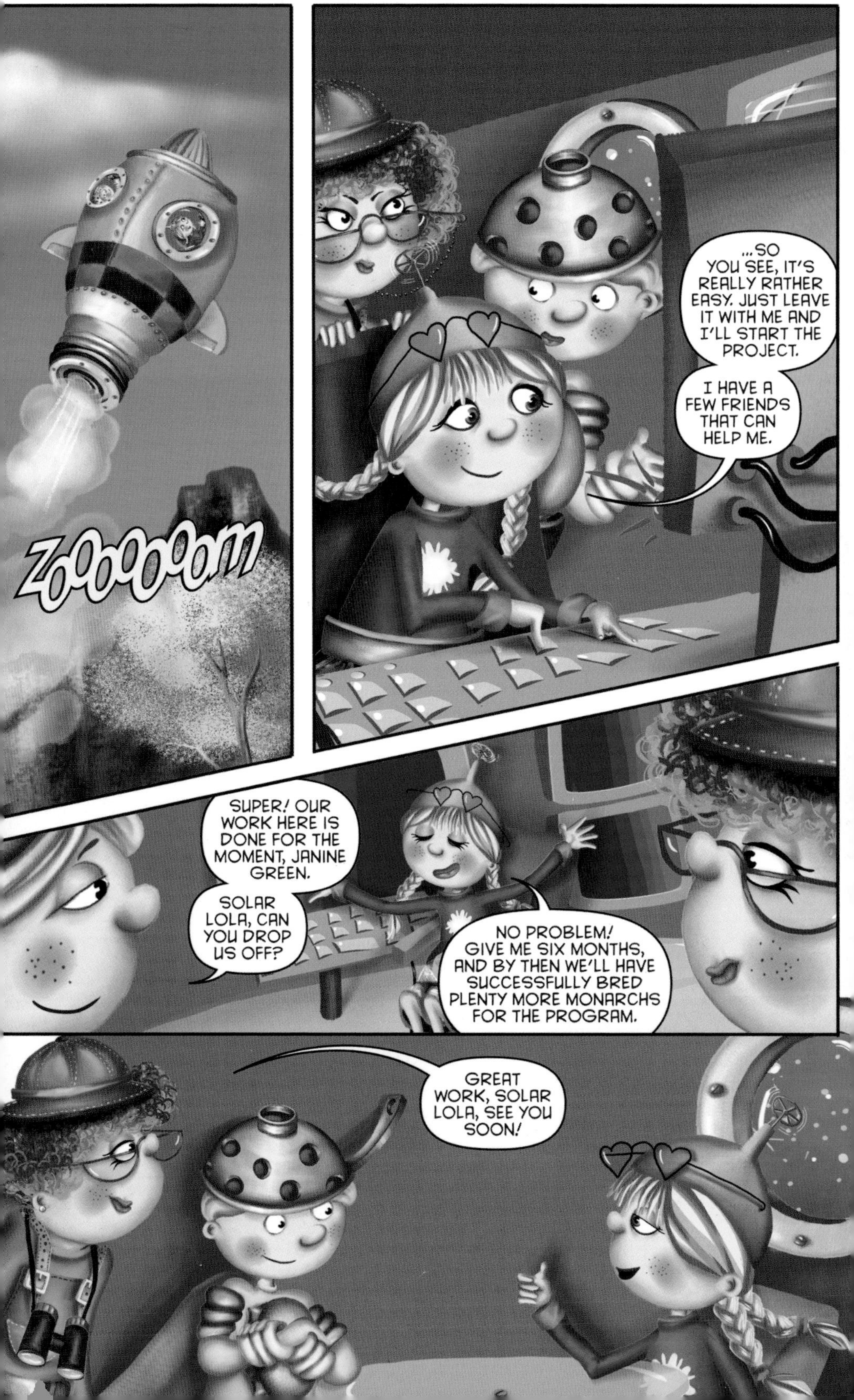
ZOOOOOOOM
...SO YOU SEE, IT'S REALLY RATHER EASY. JUST LEAVE IT WITH ME AND I'LL START THE PROJECT.
I HAVE A FEW FRIENDS THAT CAN HELP ME.
SUPER! OUR WORK HERE IS DONE FOR THE MOMENT, JANINE GREEN.
SOLAR LOLA, CAN YOU DROP US OFF?
NO PROBLEM! GIVE ME SIX MONTHS, AND BY THEN WE'LL HAVE SUCCESSFULLY BRED PLENTY MORE MONARCHS FOR THE PROGRAM.
GREAT WORK, SOLAR LOLA, SEE YOU SOON!

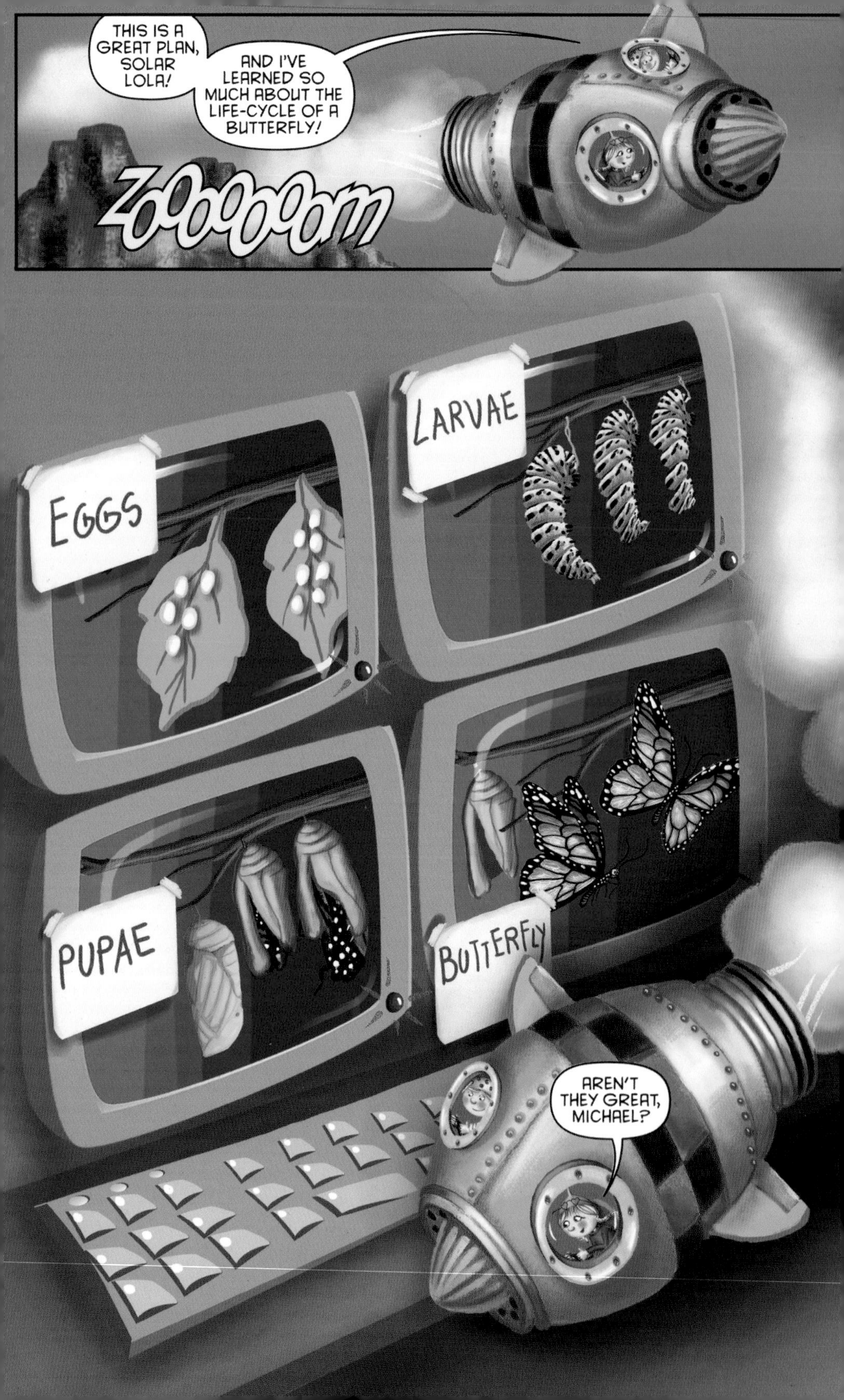
THIS IS A GREAT PLAN, SOLAR LOLA!
AND I'VE LEARNED SO MUCH ABOUT THE LIFE-CYCLE OF A BUTTERFLY!
ZOOOOOOOM
EGGS
LARVAE
PUPAE
BUTTERFLY
AREN'T THEY GREAT, MICHAEL?

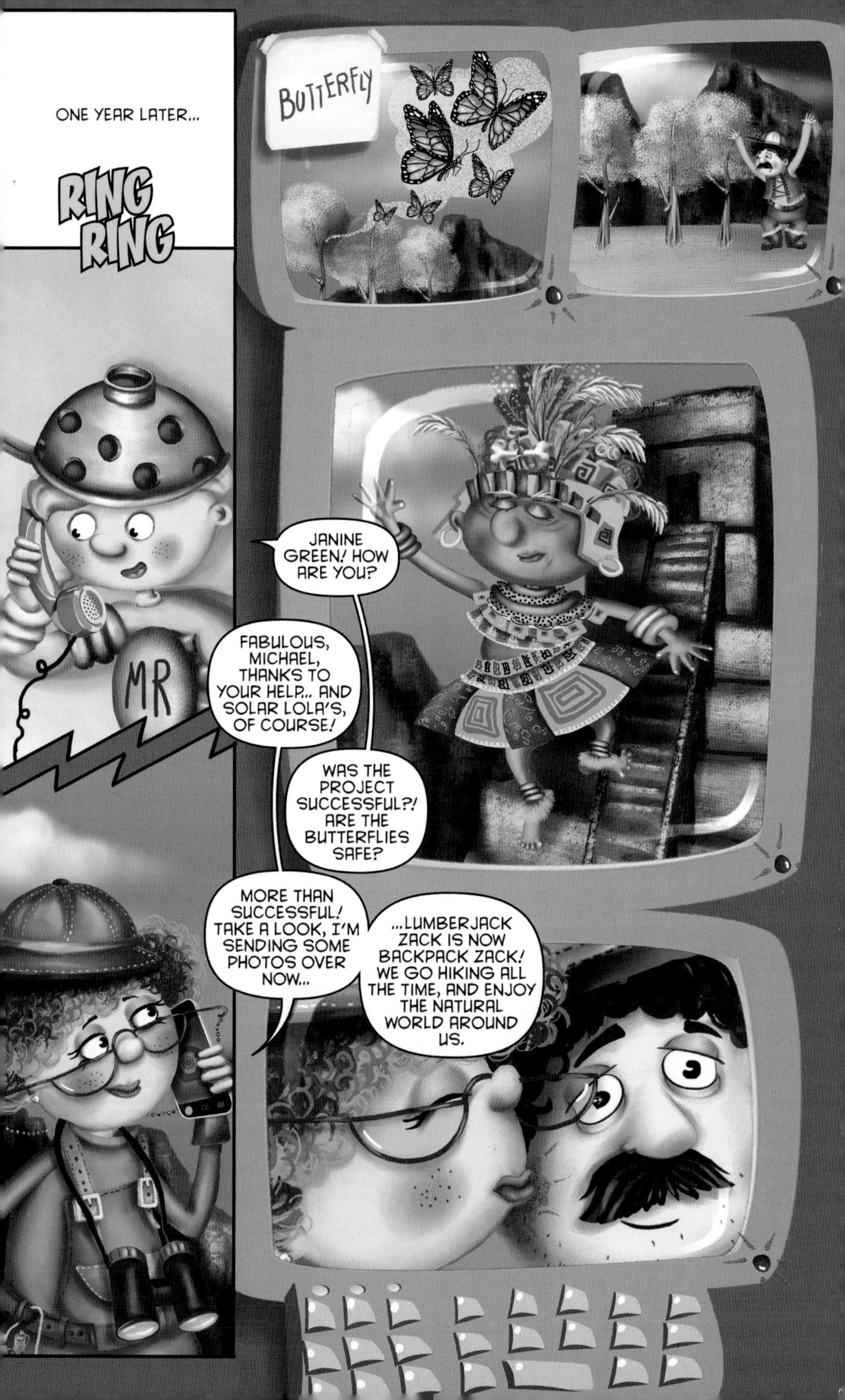
ONE YEAR LATER...
RING RING
BUTTERFLY
JANINE GREEN! HOW ARE YOU?
FABULOUS, MICHAEL, THANKS TO YOUR HELP... AND SOLAR LOLA'S, OF COURSE!
MR
WAS THE PROJECT SUCCESSFUL?! ARE THE BUTTERFLIES SAFE?
MORE THAN SUCCESSFUL! TAKE A LOOK, I'M SENDING SOME PHOTOS OVER NOW...
...LUMBERJACK ZACK IS NOW BACKPACK ZACK! WE GO HIKING ALL THE TIME, AND ENJOY THE NATURAL WORLD AROUND US.

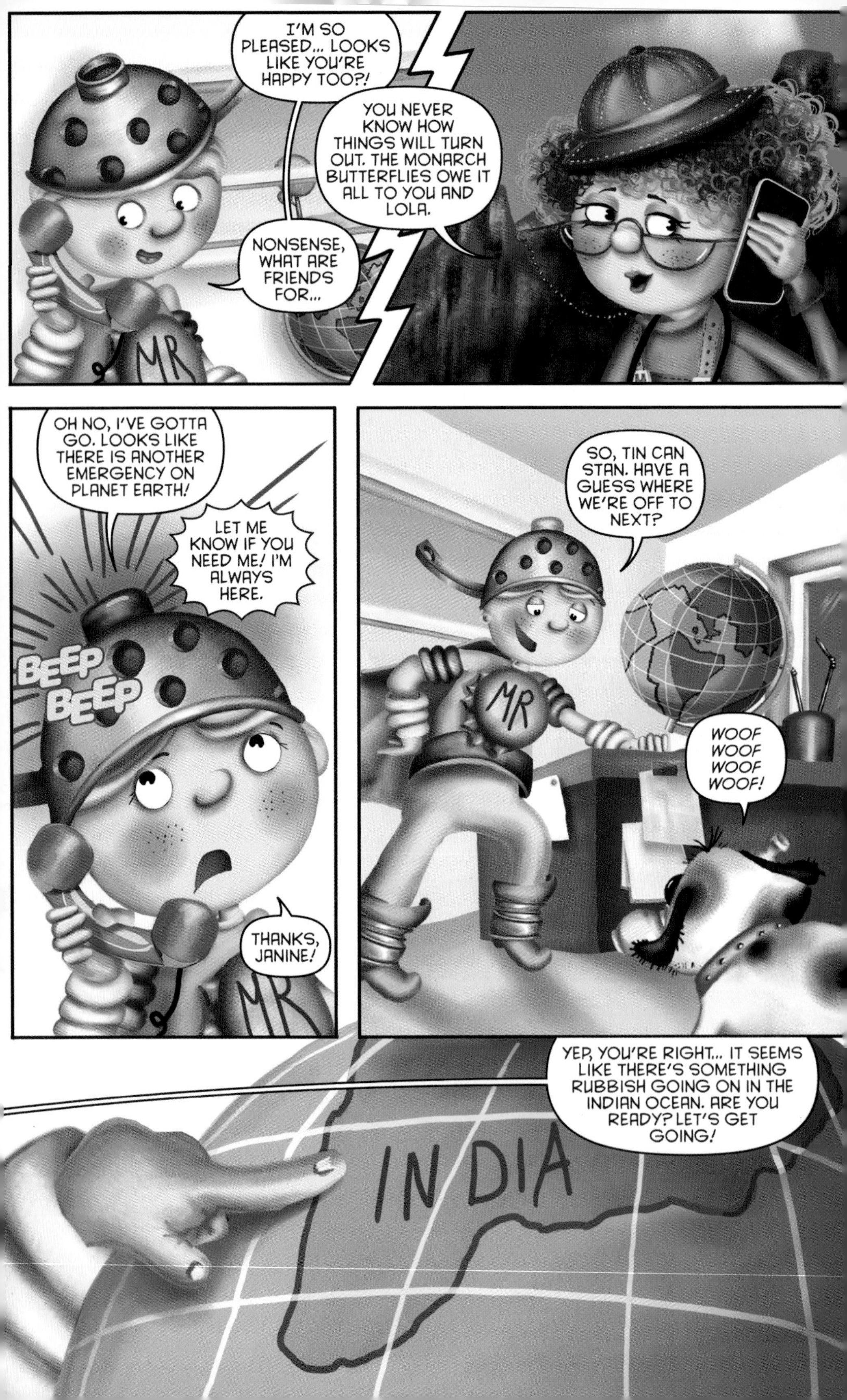
I'M SO PLEASED... LOOKS LIKE YOU'RE HAPPY TOO?!
YOU NEVER KNOW HOW THINGS WILL TURN OUT. THE MONARCH BUTTERFLIES OWE IT ALL TO YOU AND LOLA.
NONSENSE, WHAT ARE FRIENDS FOR...
MR
OH NO, I'VE GOTTA GO. LOOKS LIKE THERE IS ANOTHER EMERGENCY ON PLANET EARTH!
LET ME KNOW IF YOU NEED ME! I'M ALWAYS HERE.
BEEP BEEP
THANKS, JANINE!
MR
SO, TIN CAN STAN. HAVE A GUESS WHERE WE'RE OFF TO NEXT?
MR
WOOF WOOF WOOF WOOF!
YEP, YOU'RE RIGHT... IT SEEMS LIKE THERE'S SOMETHING RUBBISH GOING ON IN THE INDIAN OCEAN. ARE YOU READY? LET'S GET GOING!
INDIA

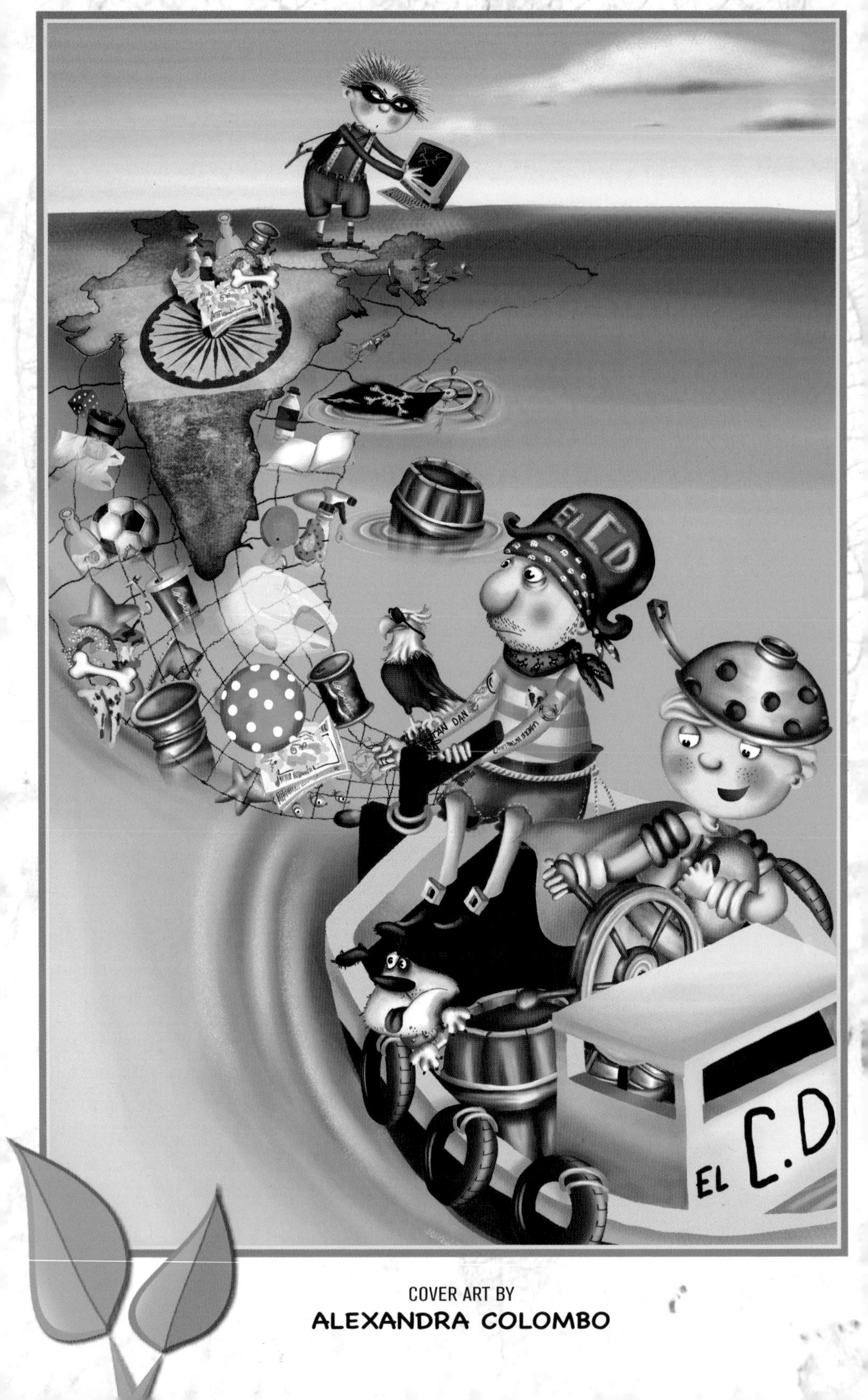
EL C.D
CAPTAIN DAN
EL C.D

COVER ART BY
ALEXANDRA COLOMBO

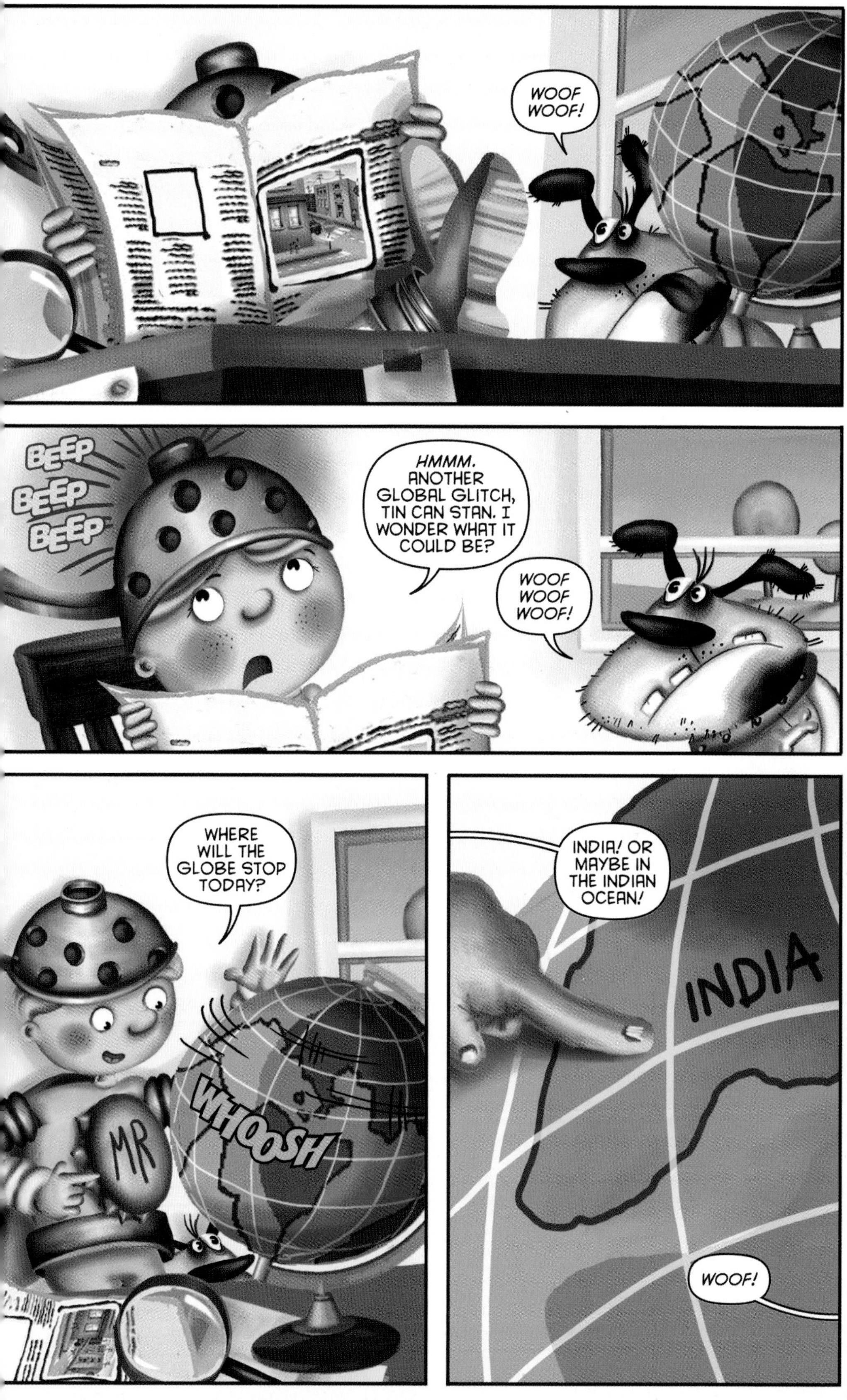
WOOF WOOF!
BEEP
BEEP
BEEP
HMMM. ANOTHER GLOBAL GLITCH, TIN CAN STAN. I WONDER WHAT IT COULD BE?
WOOF WOOF WOOF!
WHERE WILL THE GLOBE STOP TODAY?
MR
WHOOSH
INDIA! OR MAYBE IN THE INDIAN OCEAN!
INDIA
WOOF!

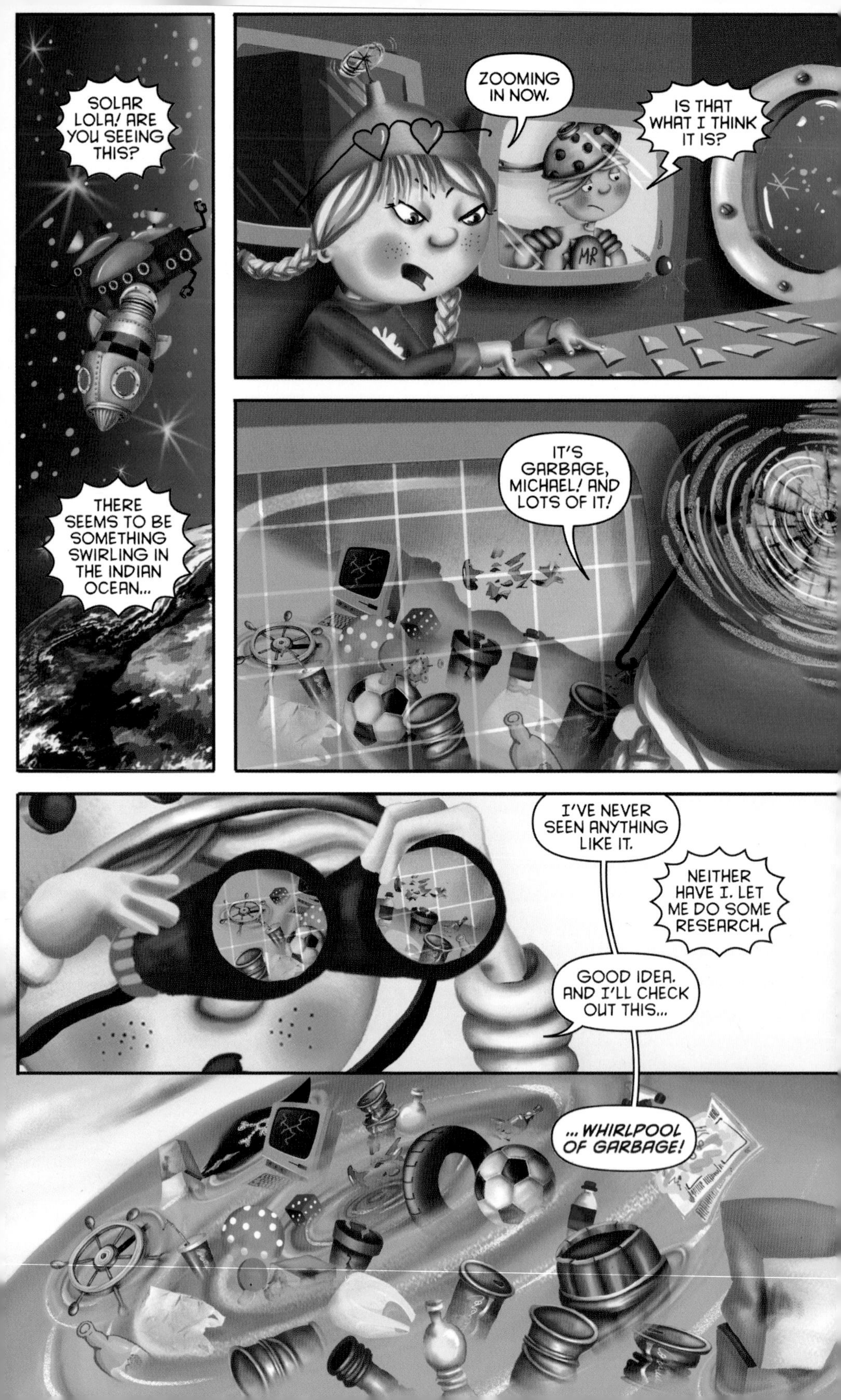

SOLAR LOLA! ARE YOU SEEING THIS?
THERE SEEMS TO BE SOMETHING SWIRLING IN THE INDIAN OCEAN...
ZOOMING IN NOW.
IS THAT WHAT I THINK IT IS?
MR
IT'S GARBAGE, MICHAEL! AND LOTS OF IT!
I'VE NEVER SEEN ANYTHING LIKE IT.
NEITHER HAVE I. LET ME DO SOME RESEARCH.
GOOD IDEA. AND I'LL CHECK OUT THIS...
...WHIRLPOOL OF GARBAGE!

COME ON, STAN! IT'S TIME FOR ANOTHER ADVENTURE! AND THIS ONE SMELLS LIKE TROUBLE...

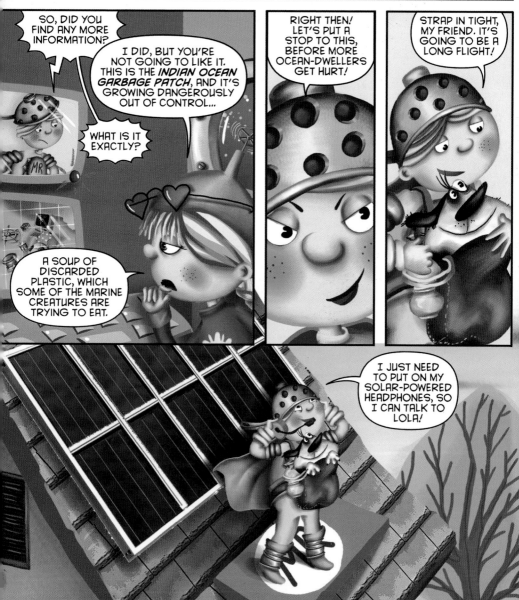

SO, DID YOU FIND ANY MORE INFORMATION?

I DID, BUT YOU'RE NOT GOING TO LIKE IT. THIS IS THE *INDIAN OCEAN GARBAGE PATCH*, AND IT'S GROWING DANGEROUSLY OUT OF CONTROL...

WHAT IS IT EXACTLY?

A SOUP OF DISCARDED PLASTIC, WHICH SOME OF THE MARINE CREATURES ARE TRYING TO EAT.

RIGHT THEN! LET'S PUT A STOP TO THIS, BEFORE MORE OCEAN-DWELLERS GET HURT!

STRAP IN TIGHT, MY FRIEND. IT'S GOING TO BE A LONG FLIGHT!

I JUST NEED TO PUT ON MY SOLAR-POWERED HEADPHONES, SO I CAN TALK TO LOLA!

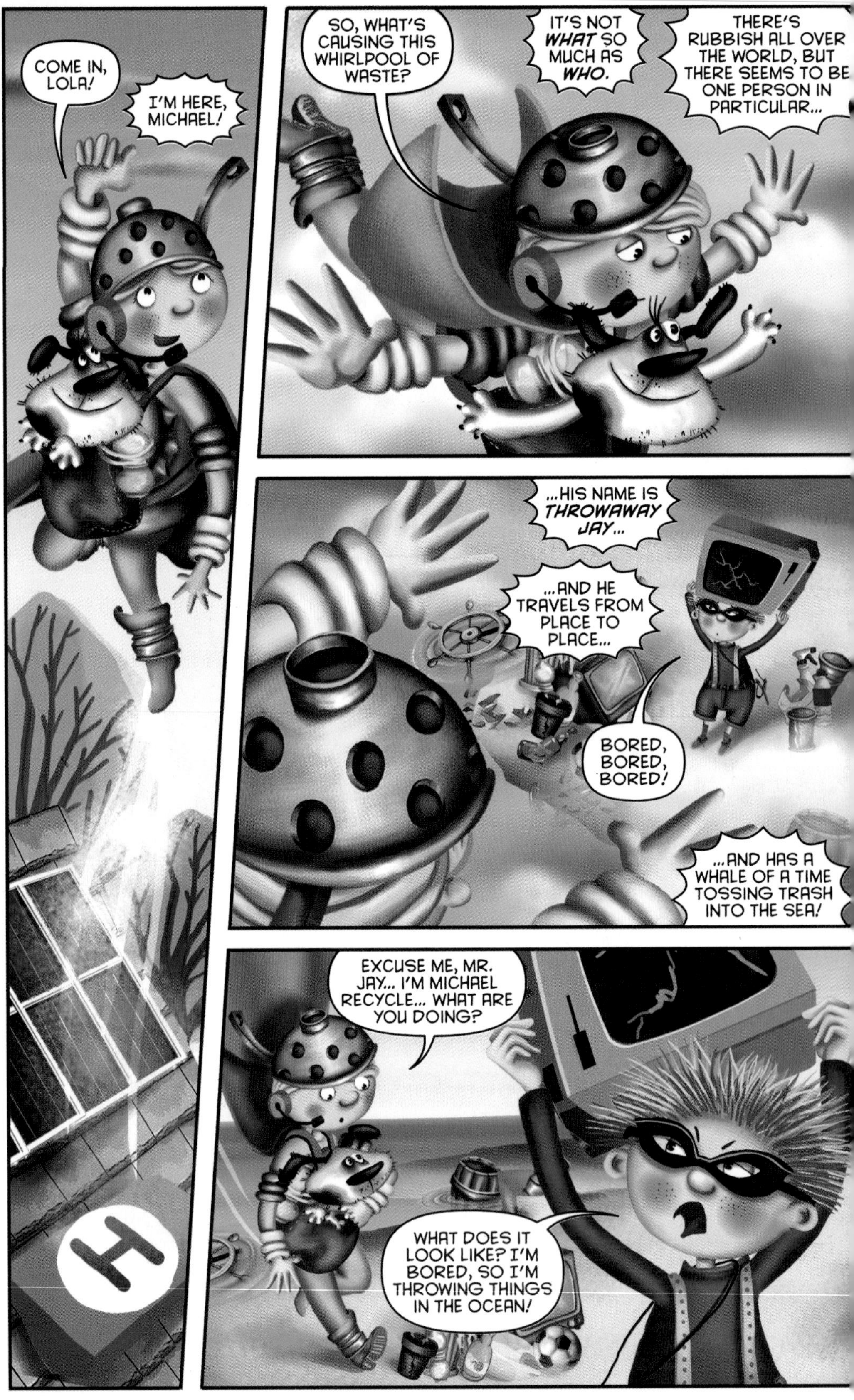
COME IN, LOLA!
I'M HERE, MICHAEL!
SO, WHAT'S CAUSING THIS WHIRLPOOL OF WASTE?
IT'S NOT WHAT SO MUCH AS WHO.
THERE'S RUBBISH ALL OVER THE WORLD, BUT THERE SEEMS TO BE ONE PERSON IN PARTICULAR...
...HIS NAME IS THROWAWAY JAY...
...AND HE TRAVELS FROM PLACE TO PLACE...
BORED, BORED, BORED!
...AND HAS A WHALE OF A TIME TOSSING TRASH INTO THE SEA!
EXCUSE ME, MR. JAY... I'M MICHAEL RECYCLE... WHAT ARE YOU DOING?
WHAT DOES IT LOOK LIKE? I'M BORED, SO I'M THROWING THINGS IN THE OCEAN!

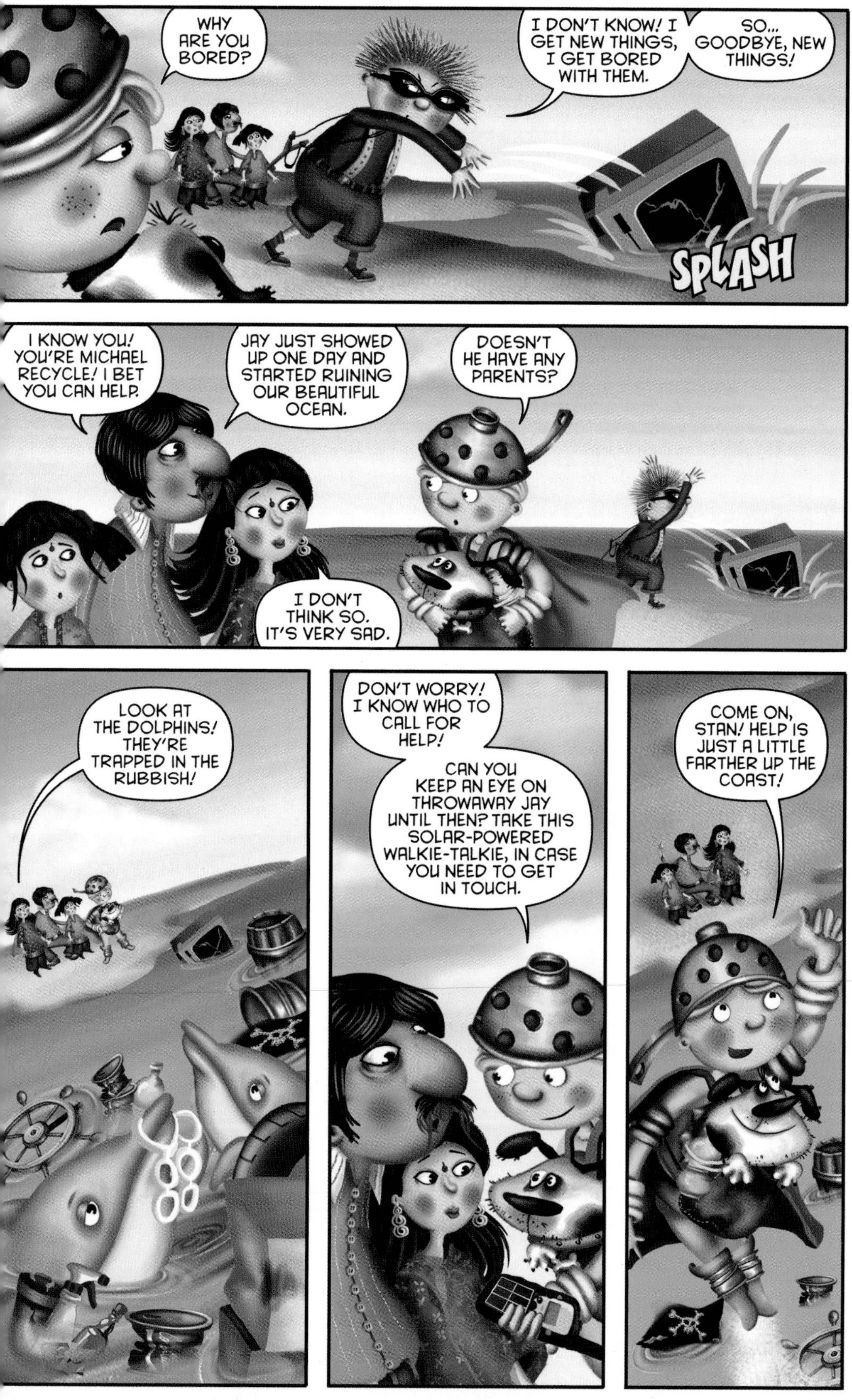
WHY ARE YOU BORED?
I DON'T KNOW! I GET NEW THINGS, I GET BORED WITH THEM.
SO... GOODBYE, NEW THINGS!
SPLASH
I KNOW YOU! YOU'RE MICHAEL RECYCLE! I BET YOU CAN HELP.
JAY JUST SHOWED UP ONE DAY AND STARTED RUINING OUR BEAUTIFUL OCEAN.
DOESN'T HE HAVE ANY PARENTS?
I DON'T THINK SO. IT'S VERY SAD.
LOOK AT THE DOLPHINS! THEY'RE TRAPPED IN THE RUBBISH!
DON'T WORRY! I KNOW WHO TO CALL FOR HELP!
CAN YOU KEEP AN EYE ON THROWAWAY JAY UNTIL THEN? TAKE THIS SOLAR-POWERED WALKIE-TALKIE, IN CASE YOU NEED TO GET IN TOUCH.
COME ON, STAN! HELP IS JUST A LITTLE FARTHER UP THE COAST!

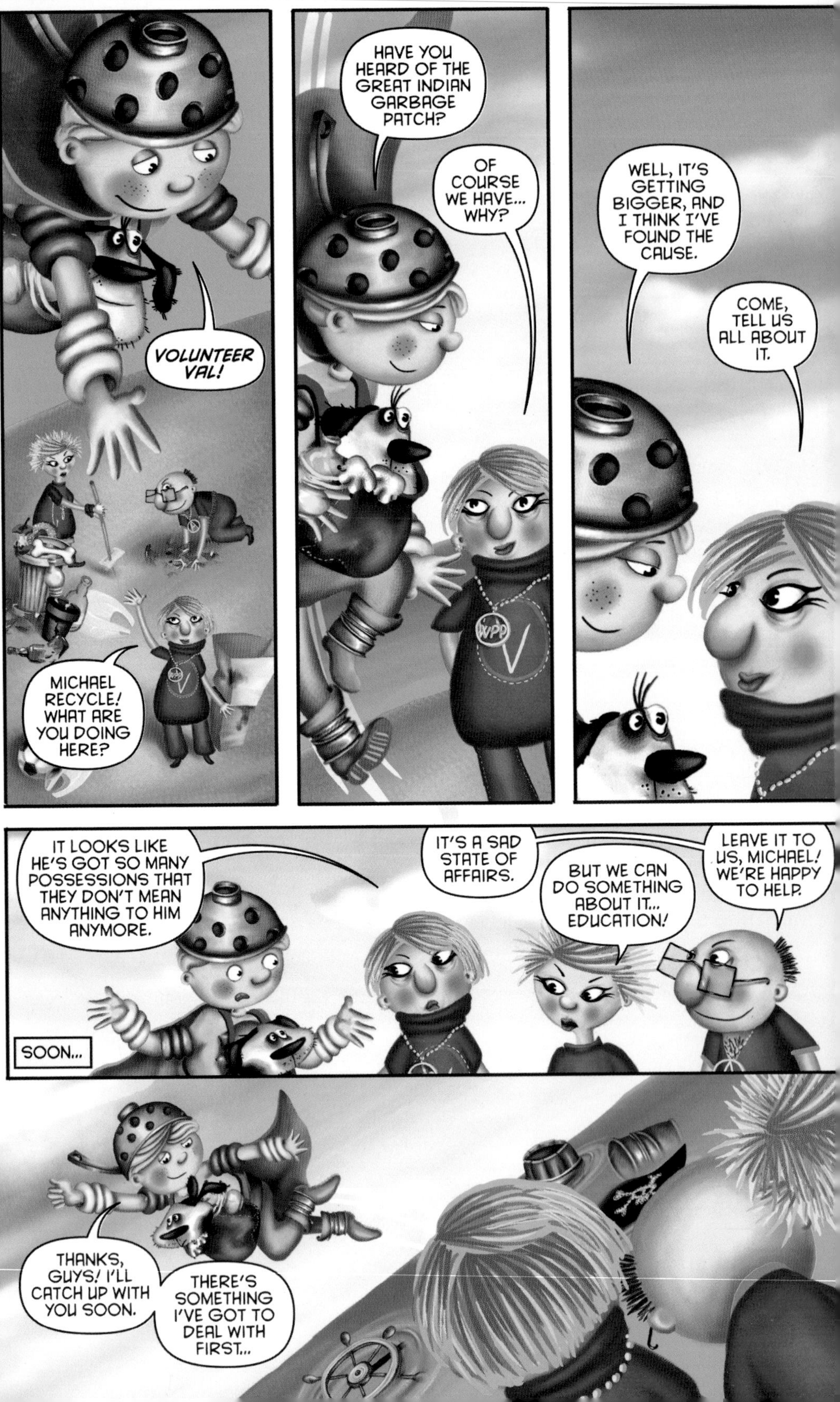
VOLUNTEER VAL!
MICHAEL RECYCLE! WHAT ARE YOU DOING HERE?
HAVE YOU HEARD OF THE GREAT INDIAN GARBAGE PATCH?
OF COURSE WE HAVE... WHY?
WELL, IT'S GETTING BIGGER, AND I THINK I'VE FOUND THE CAUSE.
COME, TELL US ALL ABOUT IT.
SOON...
IT LOOKS LIKE HE'S GOT SO MANY POSSESSIONS THAT THEY DON'T MEAN ANYTHING TO HIM ANYMORE.
IT'S A SAD STATE OF AFFAIRS.
BUT WE CAN DO SOMETHING ABOUT IT... EDUCATION!
LEAVE IT TO US, MICHAEL! WE'RE HAPPY TO HELP.
THANKS, GUYS! I'LL CATCH UP WITH YOU SOON.
THERE'S SOMETHING I'VE GOT TO DEAL WITH FIRST...

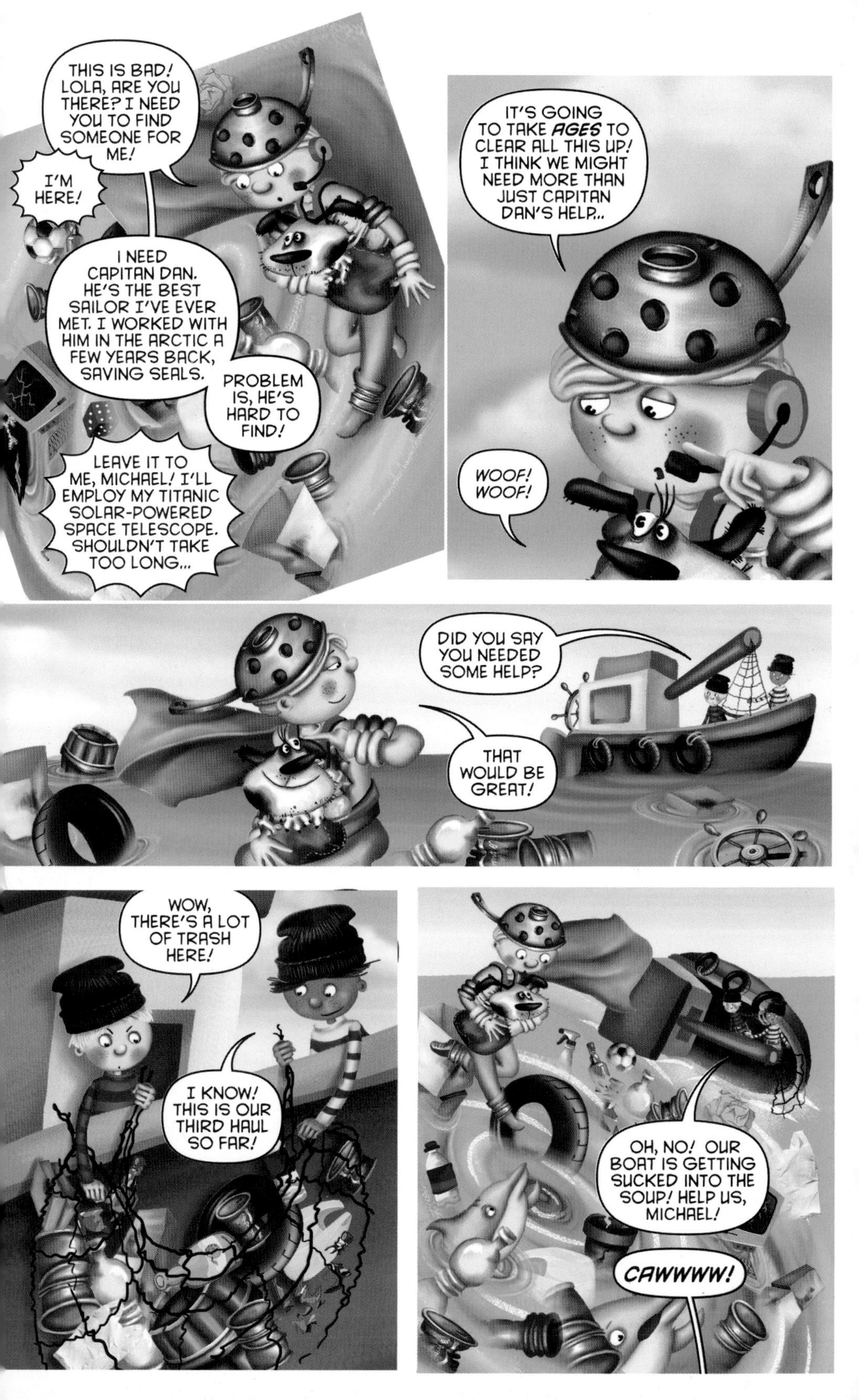
THIS IS BAD! LOLA, ARE YOU THERE? I NEED YOU TO FIND SOMEONE FOR ME!
I'M HERE!
I NEED CAPITAN DAN. HE'S THE BEST SAILOR I'VE EVER MET. I WORKED WITH HIM IN THE ARCTIC A FEW YEARS BACK, SAVING SEALS.
PROBLEM IS, HE'S HARD TO FIND!
LEAVE IT TO ME, MICHAEL! I'LL EMPLOY MY TITANIC SOLAR-POWERED SPACE TELESCOPE. SHOULDN'T TAKE TOO LONG...
IT'S GOING TO TAKE AGES TO CLEAR ALL THIS UP! I THINK WE MIGHT NEED MORE THAN JUST CAPITAN DAN'S HELP...
WOOF! WOOF!
DID YOU SAY YOU NEEDED SOME HELP?
THAT WOULD BE GREAT!
WOW, THERE'S A LOT OF TRASH HERE!
I KNOW! THIS IS OUR THIRD HAUL SO FAR!
OH, NO! OUR BOAT IS GETTING SUCKED INTO THE SOUP! HELP US, MICHAEL!
CAWWWW!

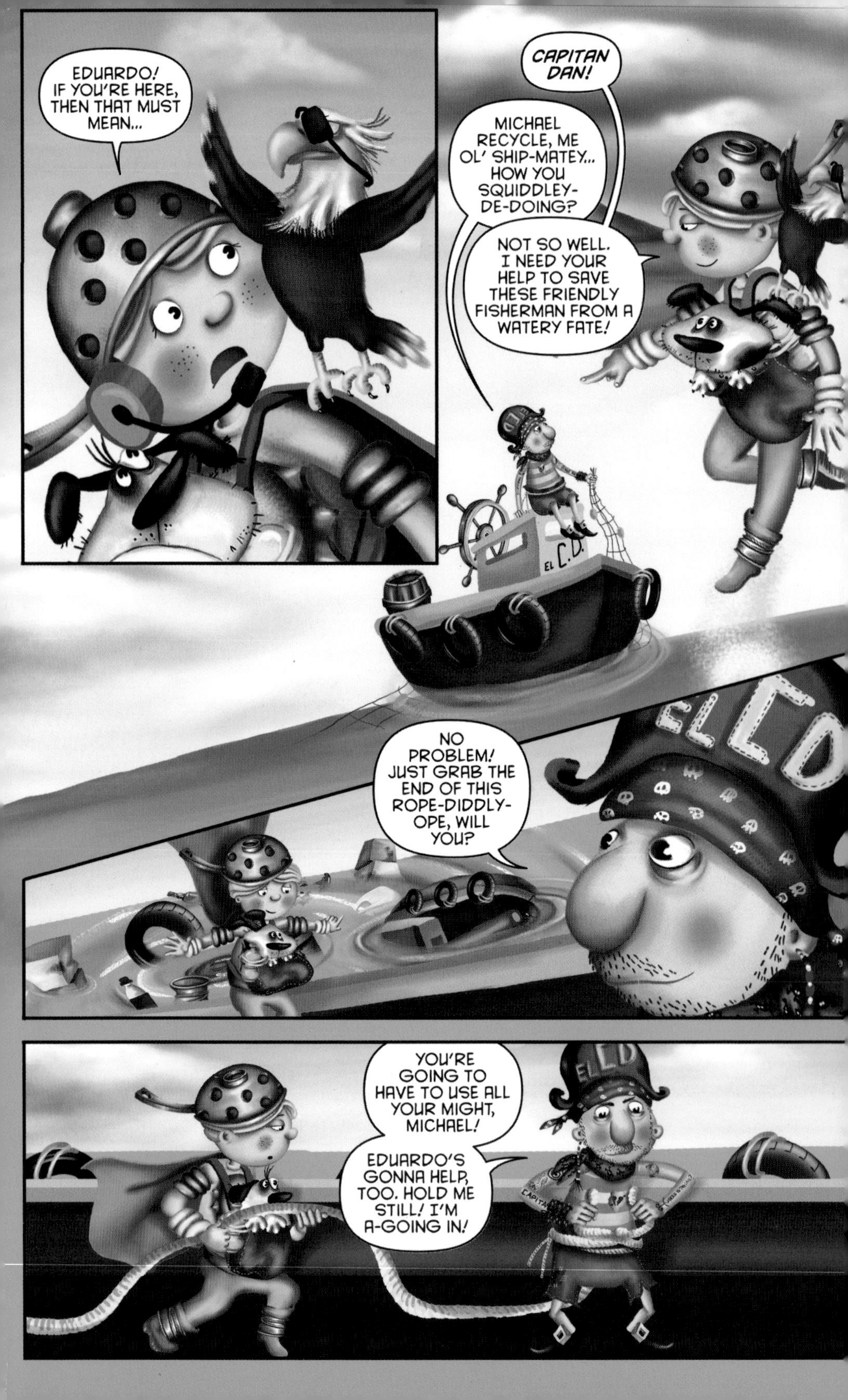
EDUARDO! IF YOU'RE HERE, THEN THAT MUST MEAN...
CAPITAN DAN!
MICHAEL RECYCLE, ME OL' SHIP-MATEY... HOW YOU SQUIDDLEY-DE-DOING?
NOT SO WELL. I NEED YOUR HELP TO SAVE THESE FRIENDLY FISHERMAN FROM A WATERY FATE!
EL C.D.
NO PROBLEM! JUST GRAB THE END OF THIS ROPE-DIDDLY-OPE, WILL YOU?
YOU'RE GOING TO HAVE TO USE ALL YOUR MIGHT, MICHAEL!
EDUARDO'S GONNA HELP, TOO. HOLD ME STILL! I'M A-GOING IN!

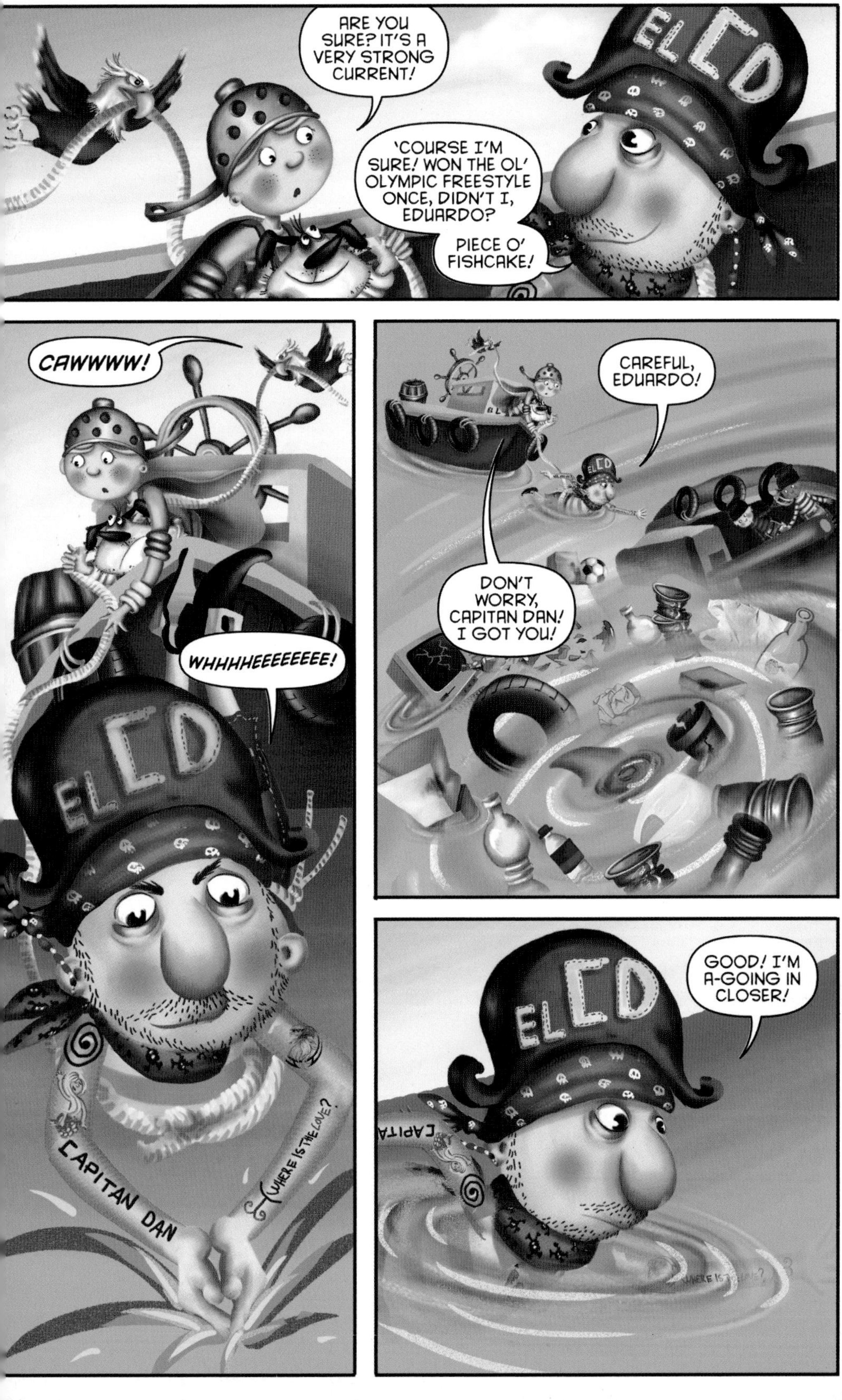
ARE YOU SURE? IT'S A VERY STRONG CURRENT!
'COURSE I'M SURE! WON THE OL' OLYMPIC FREESTYLE ONCE, DIDN'T I, EDUARDO?
PIECE O' FISHCAKE!
CAWWWW!
WHHHHEEEEEEEE!
CAREFUL, EDUARDO!
DON'T WORRY, CAPITAN DAN! I GOT YOU!
GOOD! I'M A-GOING IN CLOSER!

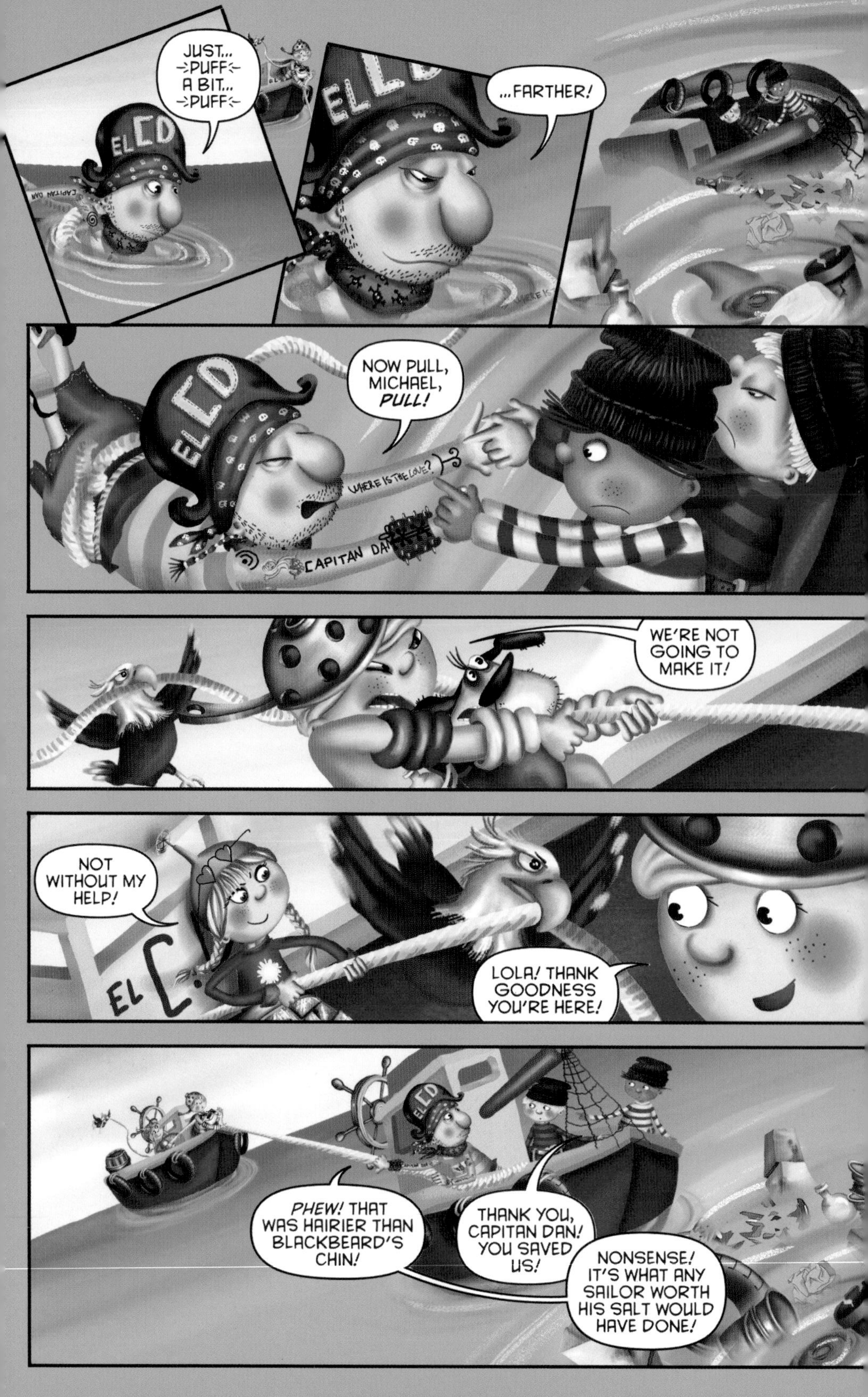
JUST... -PUFF- A BIT... -PUFF-
...FARTHER!
NOW PULL, MICHAEL, PULL!
WHERE IS THE LOVE?
CAPITAN DAN
WE'RE NOT GOING TO MAKE IT!
NOT WITHOUT MY HELP!
LOLA! THANK GOODNESS YOU'RE HERE!
PHEW! THAT WAS HAIRIER THAN BLACKBEARD'S CHIN!
THANK YOU, CAPITAN DAN! YOU SAVED US!
NONSENSE! IT'S WHAT ANY SAILOR WORTH HIS SALT WOULD HAVE DONE!

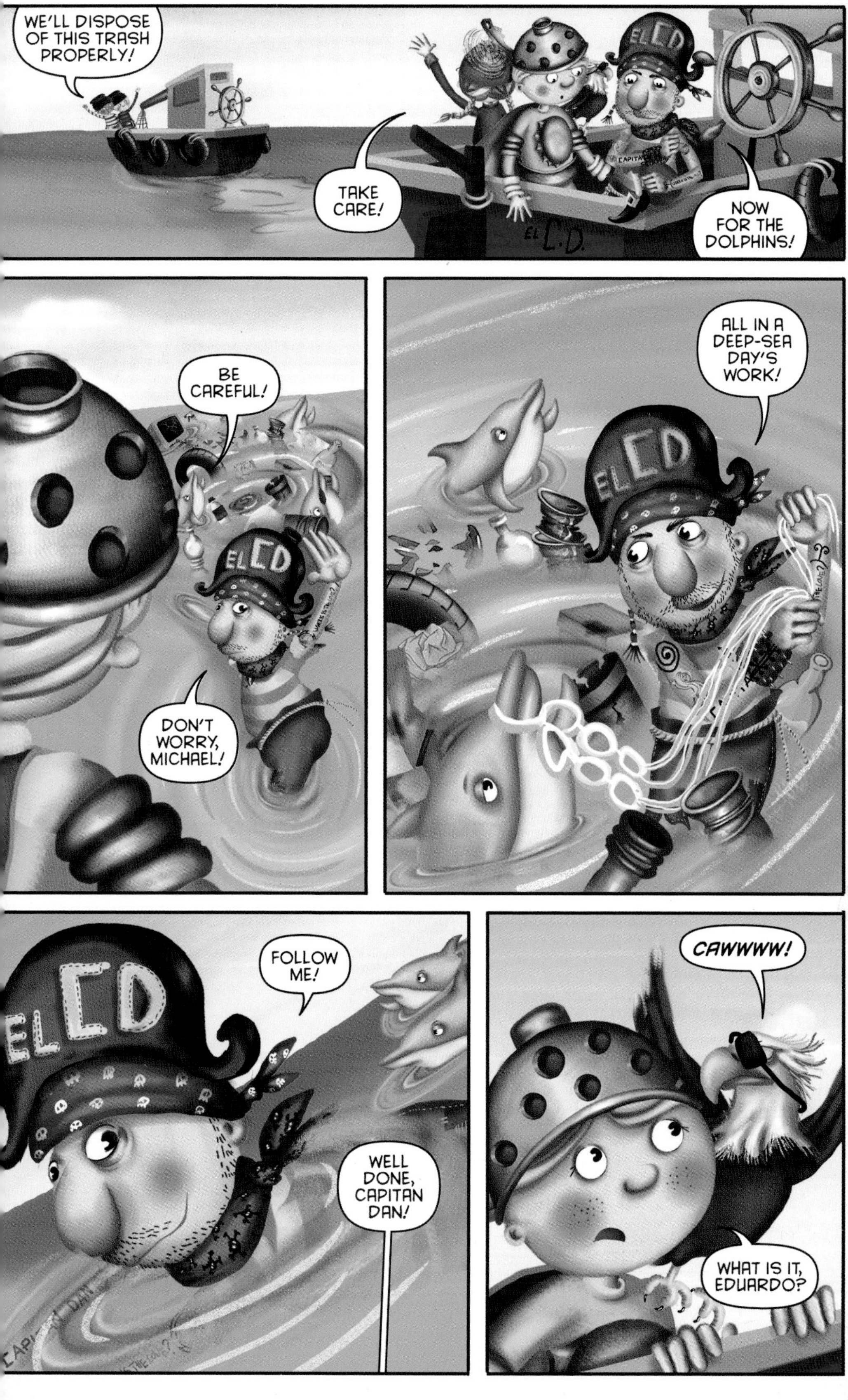
WE'LL DISPOSE OF THIS TRASH PROPERLY!
TAKE CARE!
NOW FOR THE DOLPHINS!
BE CAREFUL!
DON'T WORRY, MICHAEL!
ALL IN A DEEP-SEA DAY'S WORK!
FOLLOW ME!
WELL DONE, CAPITAN DAN!
CAWWWW!
WHAT IS IT, EDUARDO?

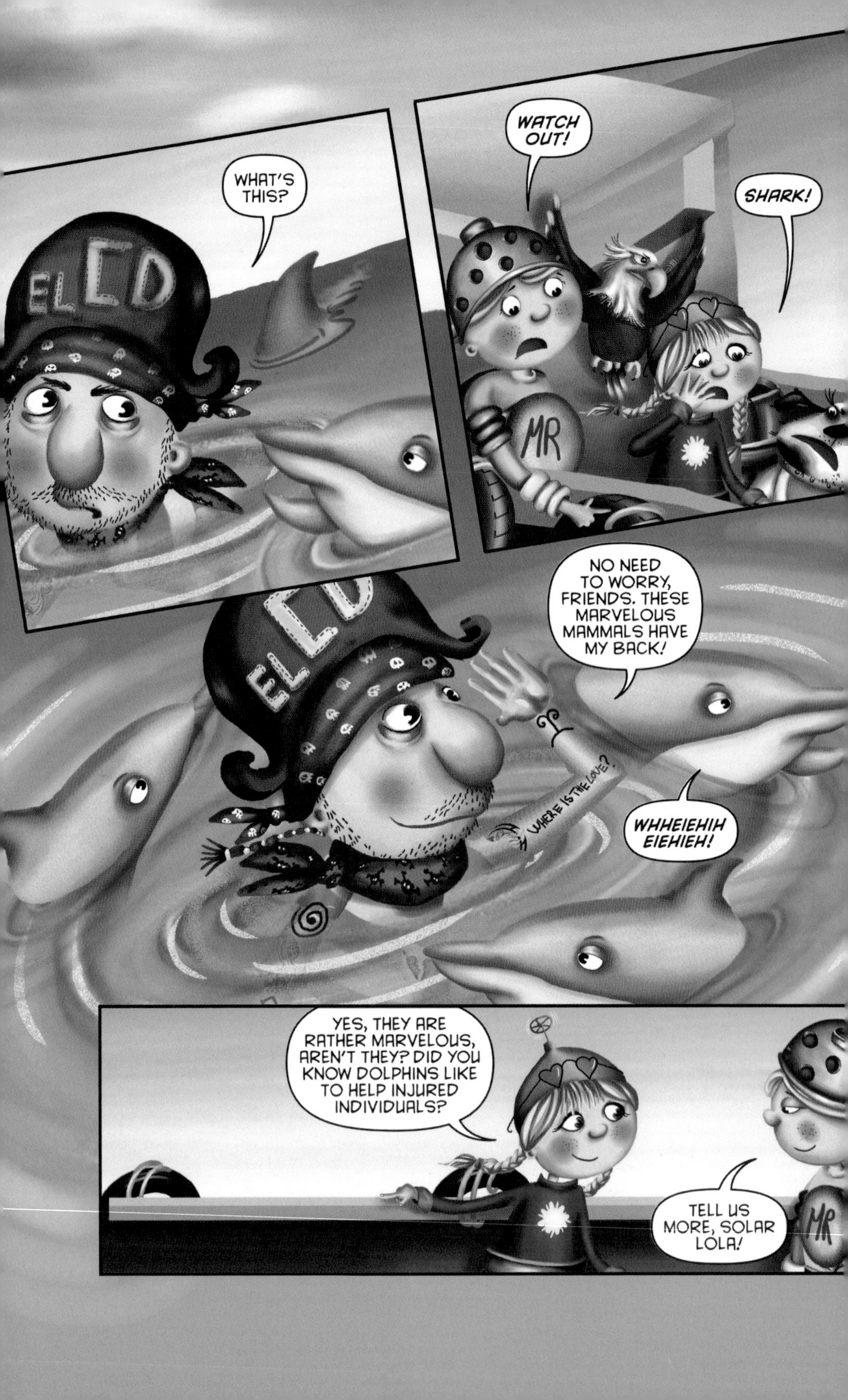

WHAT'S THIS?
WATCH OUT!
SHARK!
NO NEED TO WORRY, FRIENDS. THESE MARVELOUS MAMMALS HAVE MY BACK!
WHERE IS THE LOVE?
WHHEIEHIH EIEHIEH!
YES, THEY ARE RATHER MARVELOUS, AREN'T THEY? DID YOU KNOW DOLPHINS LIKE TO HELP INJURED INDIVIDUALS?
TELL US MORE, SOLAR LOLA!

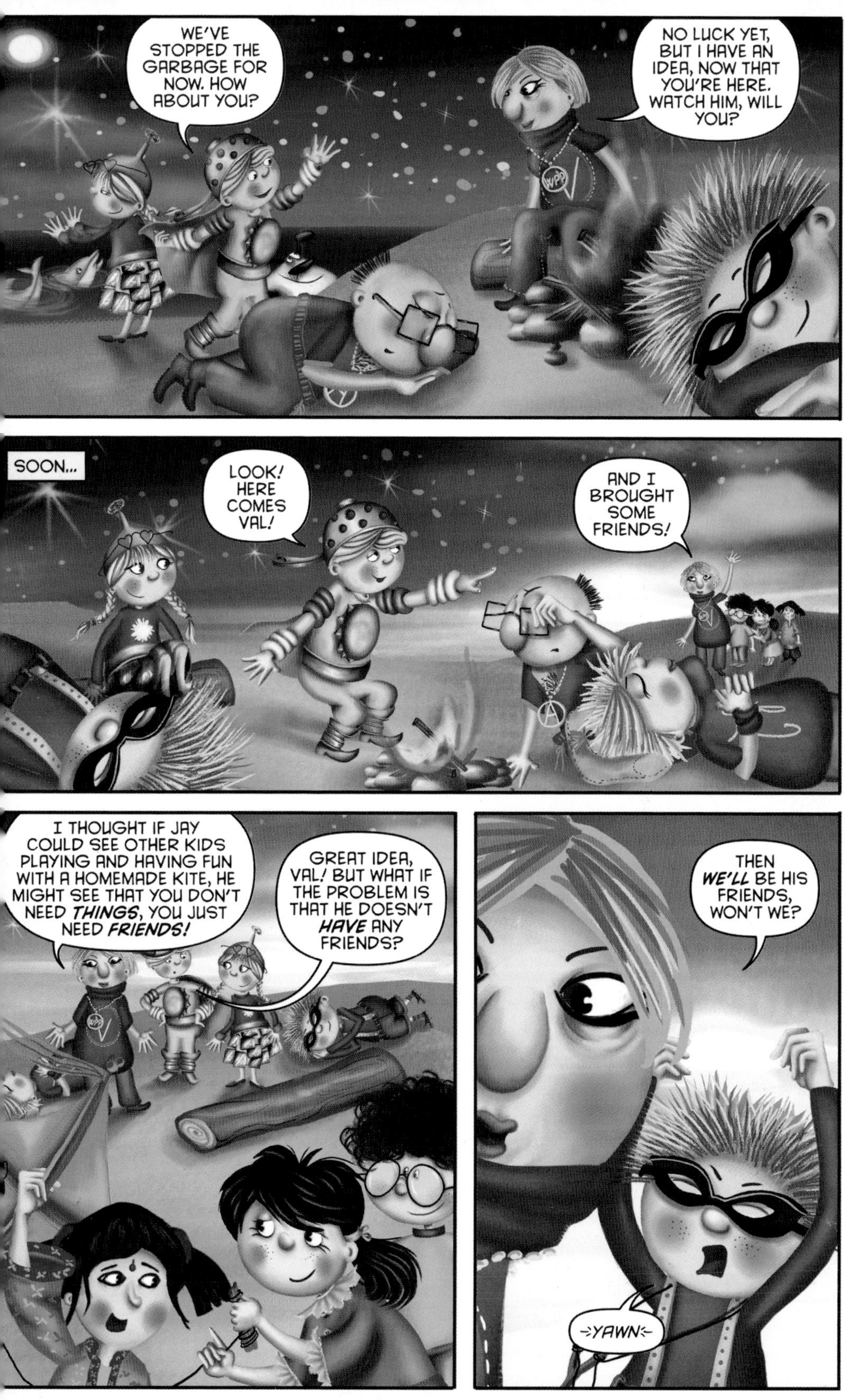
WE'VE STOPPED THE GARBAGE FOR NOW. HOW ABOUT YOU?
NO LUCK YET, BUT I HAVE AN IDEA, NOW THAT YOU'RE HERE. WATCH HIM, WILL YOU?
SOON...
LOOK! HERE COMES VAL!
AND I BROUGHT SOME FRIENDS!
I THOUGHT IF JAY COULD SEE OTHER KIDS PLAYING AND HAVING FUN WITH A HOMEMADE KITE, HE MIGHT SEE THAT YOU DON'T NEED *THINGS*, YOU JUST NEED *FRIENDS!*
GREAT IDEA, VAL! BUT WHAT IF THE PROBLEM IS THAT HE DOESN'T *HAVE* ANY FRIENDS?
THEN *WE'LL* BE HIS FRIENDS, WON'T WE?
YAWN

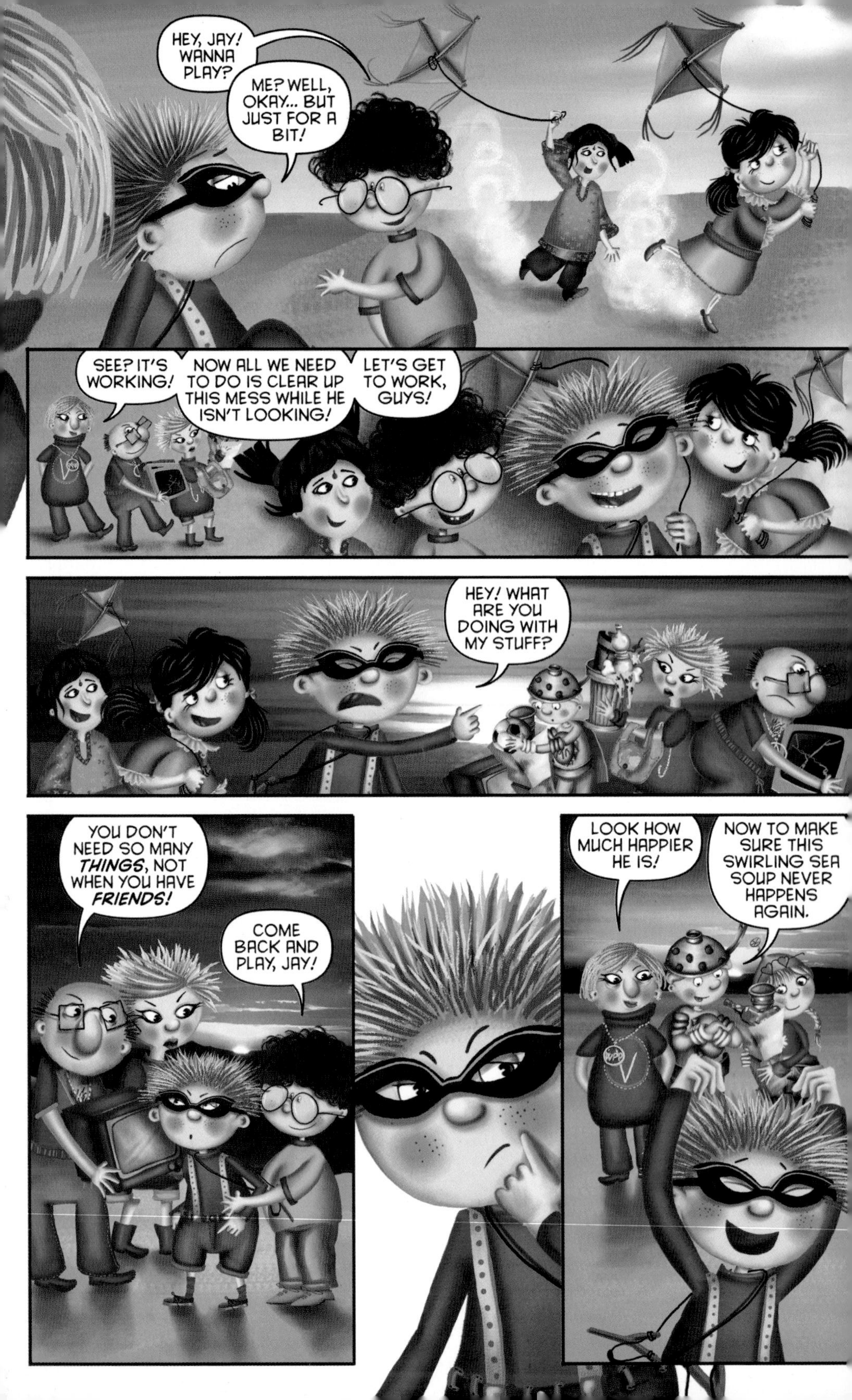
HEY, JAY! WANNA PLAY?
ME? WELL, OKAY... BUT JUST FOR A BIT!
SEE? IT'S WORKING!
NOW ALL WE NEED TO DO IS CLEAR UP THIS MESS WHILE HE ISN'T LOOKING!
LET'S GET TO WORK, GUYS!
HEY! WHAT ARE YOU DOING WITH MY STUFF?
YOU DON'T NEED SO MANY THINGS, NOT WHEN YOU HAVE FRIENDS!
COME BACK AND PLAY, JAY!
LOOK HOW MUCH HAPPIER HE IS!
NOW TO MAKE SURE THIS SWIRLING SEA SOUP NEVER HAPPENS AGAIN.

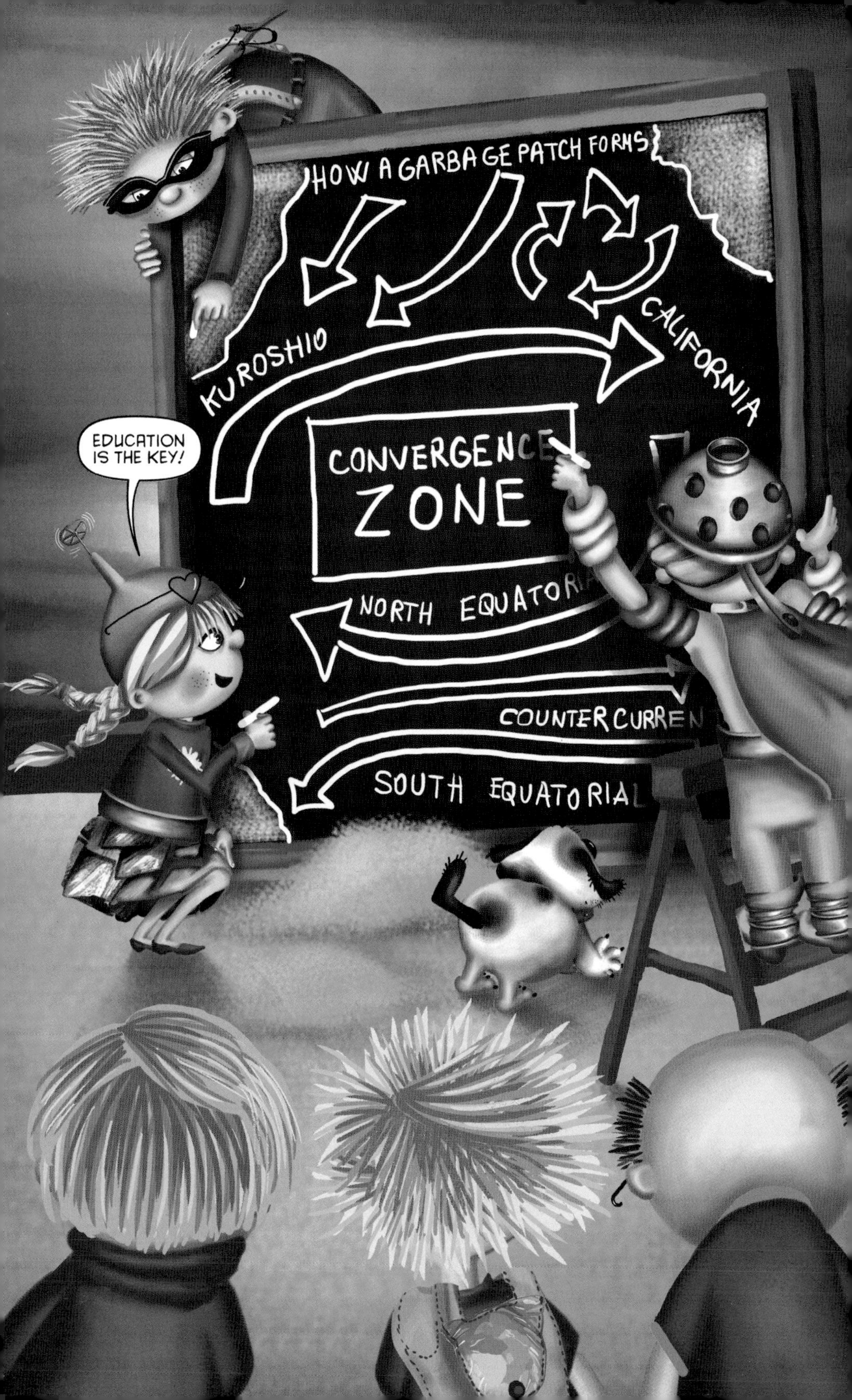

HOW A GARBAGE PATCH FORMS
KUROSHIO
CALIFORNIA
CONVERGENCE ZONE
NORTH EQUATORIAL
COUNTER CURRENT
SOUTH EQUATORIAL
EDUCATION IS THE KEY!

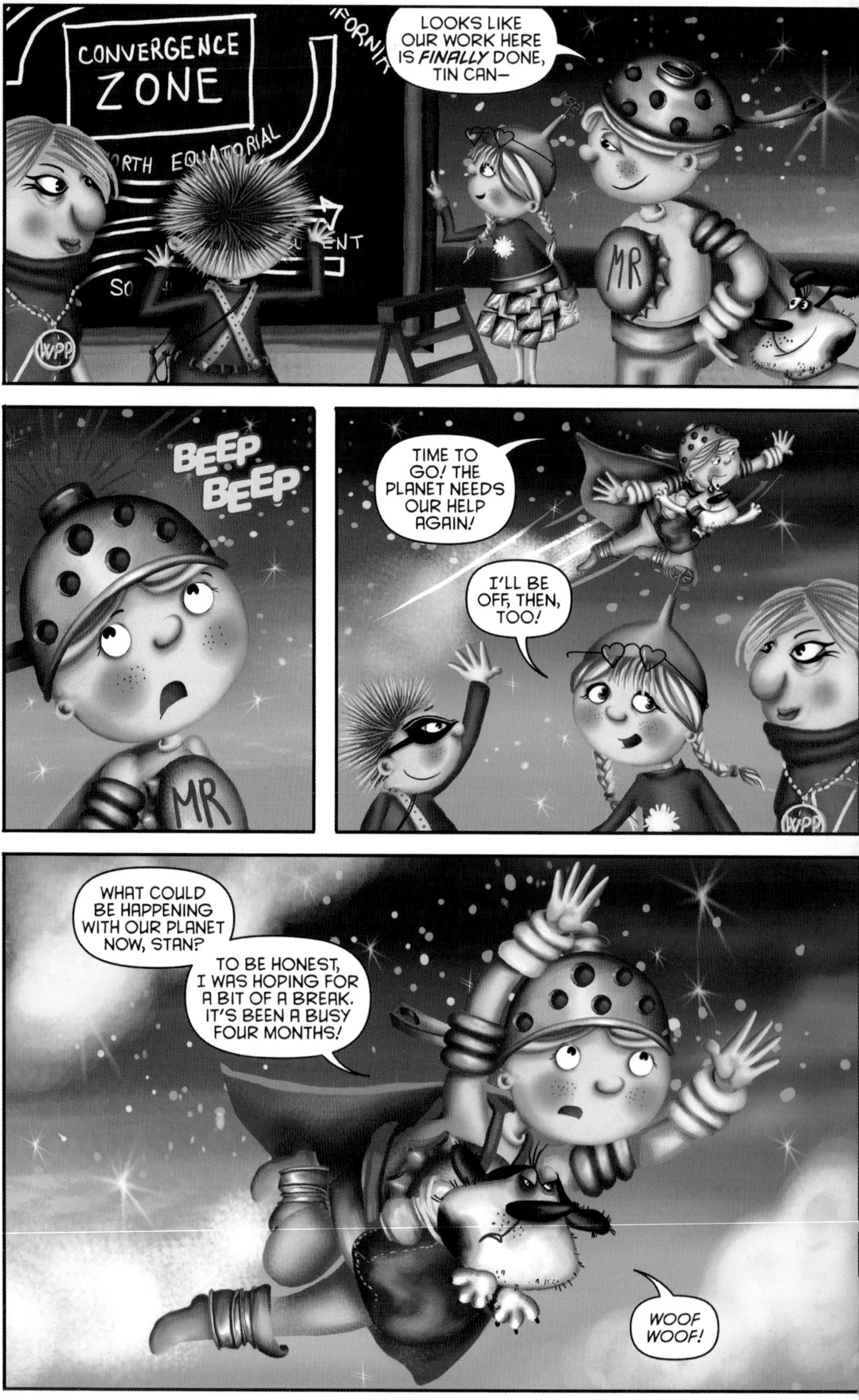
CONVERGENCE ZONE
LOOKS LIKE OUR WORK HERE IS *FINALLY* DONE, TIN CAN—
BEEP BEEP
TIME TO GO! THE PLANET NEEDS OUR HELP AGAIN!
I'LL BE OFF, THEN, TOO!
WHAT COULD BE HAPPENING WITH OUR PLANET NOW, STAN?
TO BE HONEST, I WAS HOPING FOR A BIT OF A BREAK. IT'S BEEN A BUSY FOUR MONTHS!
WOOF WOOF!

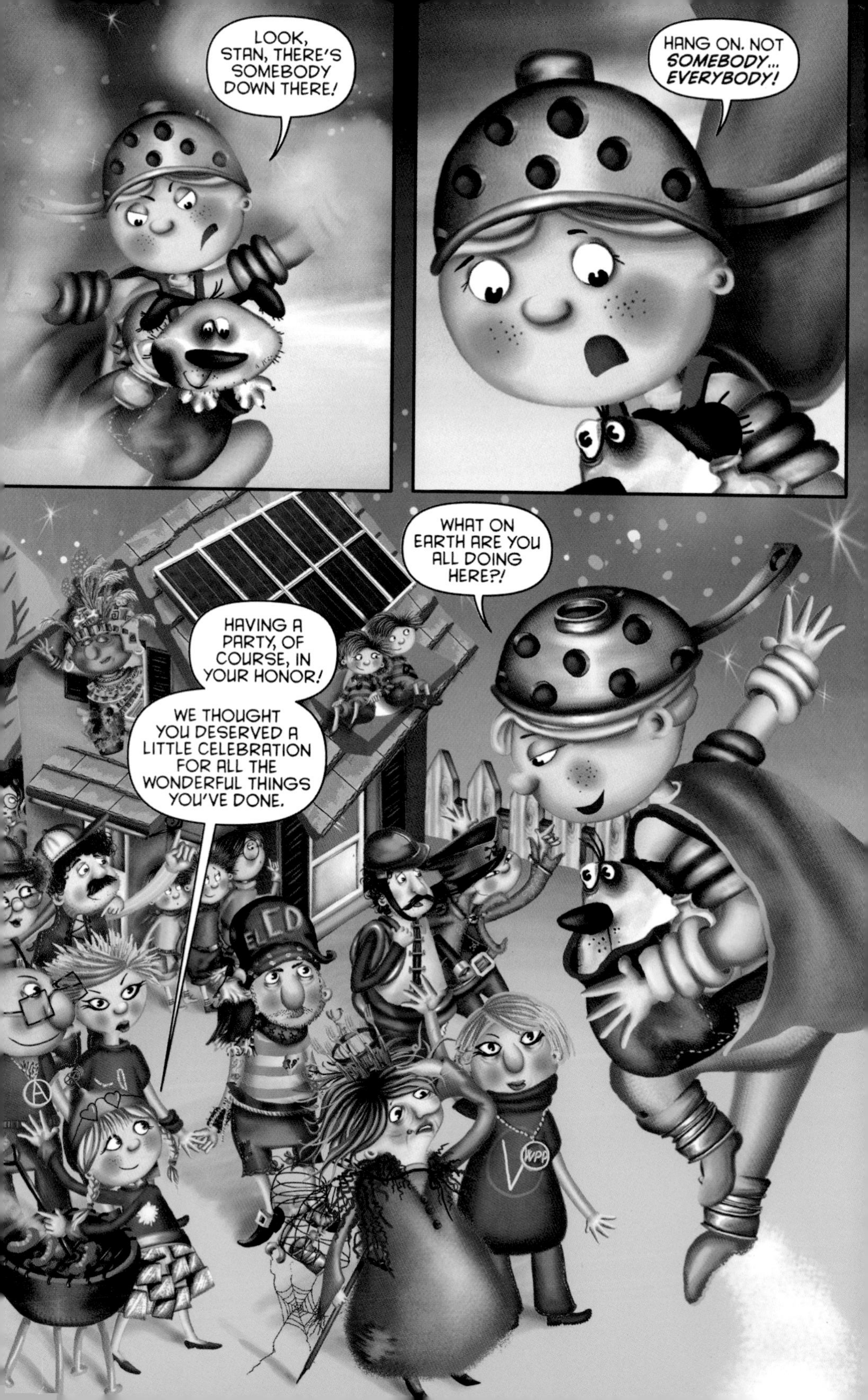
LOOK, STAN, THERE'S SOMEBODY DOWN THERE!
HANG ON. NOT *SOMEBODY... EVERYBODY!*
WHAT ON EARTH ARE YOU ALL DOING HERE?!
HAVING A PARTY, OF COURSE, IN YOUR HONOR!
WE THOUGHT YOU DESERVED A LITTLE CELEBRATION FOR ALL THE WONDERFUL THINGS YOU'VE DONE.
WPP

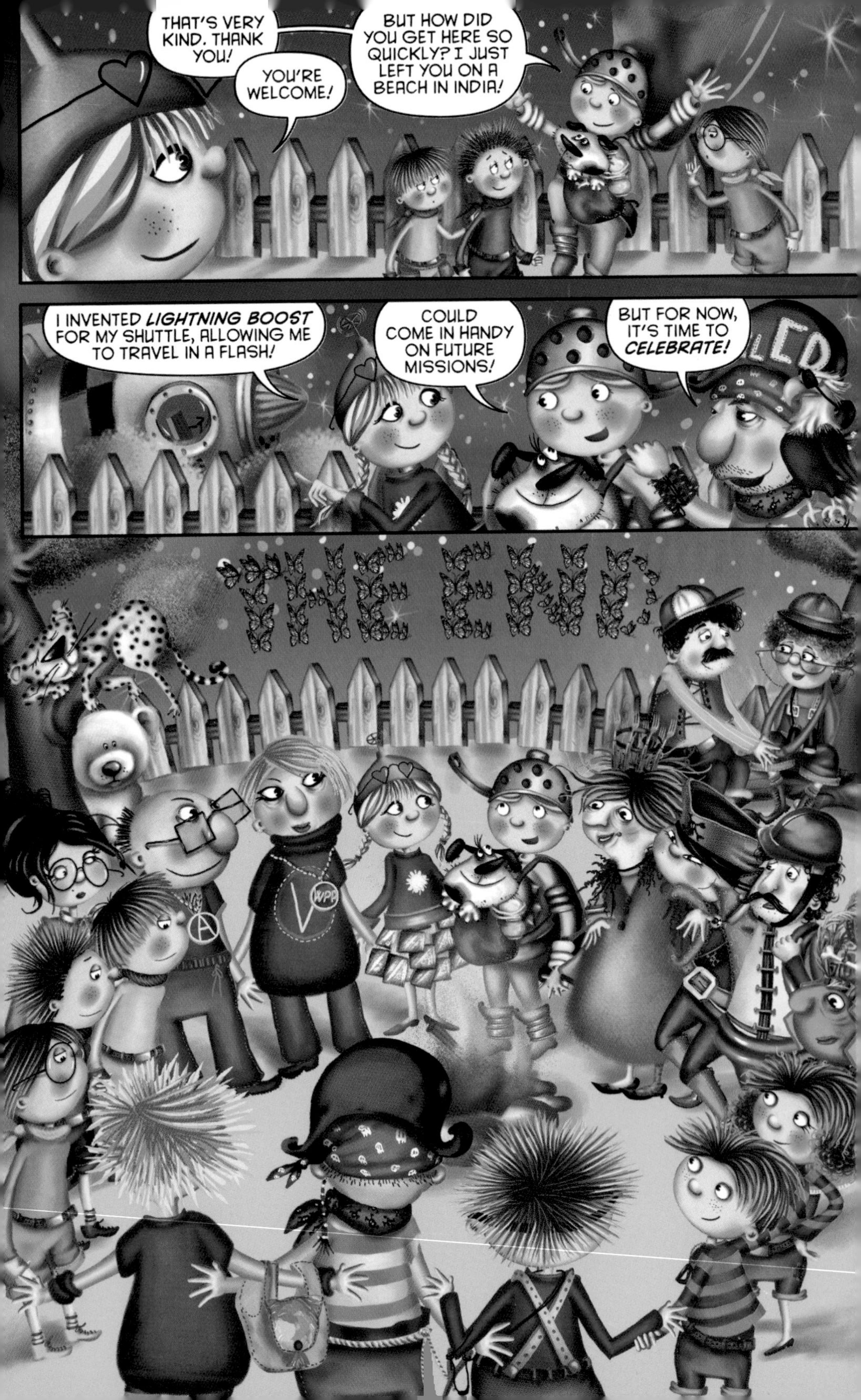
THAT'S VERY KIND. THANK YOU!
YOU'RE WELCOME!
BUT HOW DID YOU GET HERE SO QUICKLY? I JUST LEFT YOU ON A BEACH IN INDIA!
I INVENTED *LIGHTNING BOOST* FOR MY SHUTTLE, ALLOWING ME TO TRAVEL IN A FLASH!
COULD COME IN HANDY ON FUTURE MISSIONS!
BUT FOR NOW, IT'S TIME TO *CELEBRATE!*
THE END

DID YOU KN☀W?

By RANDALL LOTOWYCZ

SOLAR ENERGY

Solar is the Latin word for sun. The sun isn't just bright and hot, it is also a powerful source of energy. The sunlight that shines down on us in a single hour could supply the world with enough energy to last a year.

A LIGHT THAT NEVER GOES OUT!

Solar energy is a "renewable energy" because it never runs out. Renewable energy also does not cause harm to the environment or produce carbon dioxide and other air pollutants. Other sources of renewable energy are wind, hydropower (water), geothermal (heat from the earth), and biomass (natural materials like wood).

UNDER THE SUN!

We've been using solar energy for thousands of years for heating, cooking, and other daily activities. If you've ever hung wet clothing out to dry in the sun or used a magnifying class to melt something, you were harnessing solar power.

SOLAR PANELS BIG AND SMALL!

To collect a useful amount of solar energy, a large surface area is needed. You'll find the world's largest solar power plant in Kamuthi, India, which covers nearly 2,500 acres. But, even if you don't have a lot of space, you and your family can reduce your electricity bills by installing solar panels on your home.

OLD AND DIRTY ENERGY!

More than 80% of the United States' energy use comes from fossil fuels: coal, oil, and natural gas. They were formed over hundreds of millions of years, before the dinosaurs roamed the earth, which is why they're known as "fossil" fuels. They are nonrenewable, so we cannot make more of them. Fossil fuels can also be harmful. When burned to create energy, they release greenhouse gases (gases that can trap heat) into the atmosphere.

EARTH'S BLANKET!

If you've ever been in a greenhouse, you know it's good for growing plants because it holds in heat year-round. The

Earth itself wouldn't be warm enough for us to live if it wasn't for the phenomenon known as the greenhouse effect, in which our atmosphere contains heat-absorbing greenhouse gases.

GETTING TOO WARM!

Global warming is the gradual increase in the Earth's temperature. Of all the greenhouse gases, carbon dioxide is the biggest contributor to global warming and the greenhouse gas most produced by our activities (such as burning fossil fuels). If the Earth gets warmer, it could cause problems for the planet and all the people, plants, and animals that live on it.

POLAR BEARS NEED ICE!

Polar bears are in danger of becoming extinct as the arctic ice where they live and hunt for food melts away. In 2008, polar bears were the first vertebrate species (an animal with a backbone, like us humans!) to be listed by the U.S. Endangered Species Act as threatened by extinction due to global warming. There are an estimated 22,000-31,000 polar bears in the world today but one recent study predicts that population could decrease by 30% by 2050 as the ice continues to melt.

WHAT A WASTE!

The United States produces more than 250 million tons of trash every year. If you arranged all that trash in a straight line, it would be long enough to reach the moon and back 25 times. That garbage has to go somewhere. The trash we produce goes to landfills, places specifically designed to prevent harmful substances in the trash from polluting the surrounding environment. Because we throw so much away, landfills are filling up, and there are only so many places we can build more. Until we make a better effort to reduce the trash we produce, recycling is the best way to avoid filling up those landfills.

RECYCLING = REMAKING

Recycling is the process in which things like cans, bottles, paper, and cardboard are remade into either the same kind of thing or new products. Plastic is melted down and reshaped into other things. So, all your plastic bags and milk jugs get turned into fun stuff like playground equipment!

BENEFITS OF RECYCLING

Every ton of paper that's recycled saves 17 trees. And aluminum soda cans, which are recycled more than any other object in the U.S., use 95% less energy and produce 95% percent less greenhouse gases when made with recycled aluminum instead of new aluminum.

BUILD YOUR OWN RECYCLING CENTER!

Recycling starts at home, and you can build your own recycling center easily. Gather up a few bins and boxes with your parents and label them for cardboard and paper, glass, plastics, and metal. If you're running low on space, then glass, plastics, and metal can all go in one bin. Use paint, markers, crayons, or even stickers to decorate each bin.

RECIPE FOR REACTIONS

A chemical reaction is when two substances are mixed together to make something new. If you've ever created a homemade volcano eruption for school by mixing baking soda and vinegar, you've caused a chemical reaction.

UP IN FLAMES

Combustion is a chemical reaction that produces heat and light. If you've ever watched your parents strike a match or gone to a fireworks show, you've seen combustion in action. Most forms of combustion occur when the gas oxygen interacts with another substance, like when oxygen in the air joins carbon in wood to cause the wood to burn in your fireplace. An important part of fire safety is properly storing and disposing of flammable materials to avoid fires.

FREQUENT FLYER MILES

Throughout North America, monarch butterflies are known for their epic yearly trips from their summer breeding grounds in the north to parts of California and Mexico, where they spend their winters. Their journey can span hundreds to thousands of miles.

JOURNEY OF A LIFETIME

Monarchs born in late summer and fall can live up to eight months. They make the entire journey south for winter over two months. But the monarchs born in spring and early summer only live a few weeks. It takes multiple generations of monarchs to make the trip back home over four months. In other words, the monarchs that reach the north again are the great-grandchildren and great-greatgrandchildren of the monarchs who left Mexico. Population began to decline in the 1990s as an estimated 500 million monarchs made the flight from the northern United States and Canada to the forests in Mexico's Sierra Madre. Today, that number is around 50 million, which is an alarming decline.

HOMELESS MONARCHS

Habitat loss is the most significant cause of decline in butterfly populations. It can happen naturally, but when the habitat loss is caused by humans, the change is usually very quick and local species, like the monarch butterflies, do not have time to adapt.

POISONED FOOD

Agriculture, which is the practice of farming, has also had a significant effect on monarch butterflies. Chemicals known as herbicides are sprayed on crops such as corn and soy to stop the growth of weeds. Unfortunately these herbicides kill milkweed plants, which are the primary source of food for monarchs.

HOMEGROWN

In addition to eating milkweed plants, monarchs also lay their eggs on them. The baby caterpillars that hatch from the eggs eat nothing but the milkweed before making a chrysalis and beginning their transformation into butterflies.

GROW LOCAL

Many people like to plant tropical milkweed because it produces prettier flowers and continues to grow into the fall. But tropical milkweed can confuse monarchs, causing them to lay eggs outside their breeding season and disrupt their migration cycle.

WHERE NO FISH ROAM

Dead zones are areas of the sea where a great number of phytoplankton—super tiny, microscopic underwater organisms—die from pollution. As they're decomposed by bacteria, all the oxygen in the water is used up. This state is known as hypoxia. Fish and other marine life in the area cannot survive hypoxia, and die out as well.

POISONED FOOD CHAIN

Two of the deadliest pollutants found in the ocean are mercury and polychlorinated biphenyls (PCBs, for short). Small fish wind up eating these pollutants. Bigger fish then eat the small fish, and lots of them, so now the bigger fish have a higher concentration of the pollutants in their systems. This makes the larger fish more dangerous for other animals, including humans, to eat.

SOUPY PLASTIC ISLANDS

Plastic doesn't break down easily the way organic material like paper does, so whatever is thrown into the ocean stays there. These partially broken-down plastic particles resemble confetti, and spread throughout the ocean. You'll find large concentrations of it in areas where ocean currents meet, forming plastic "islands." They're not sturdy enough to walk on, however. The largest of these patches is the Great Pacific Garbage Patch, which is found in the Pacific

Ocean between Japan and the United States. Estimates of its size vary, with some saying it's the size of Texas, and others saying it's nearly twice the size of the whole United States. That's a lot of garbage!

THE INDIAN OCEAN GARBAGE PATCH DISCOVERED IN 2010

The Indian Ocean Garbage Patch is the third largest in the world, and is made up of plastic and chemical sludge. It is believed to be 3.86 MILLION square miles in size. An estimated 1 trillion pieces of plastic are floating in that patch.

BEACH CLEANING

One of the simplest ways to keep plastic out of the ocean is to pick up any garbage you find at the beach and throw it out before the ocean tide takes it back into the sea. So, while you're hunting for seashells, bring an extra bag along and collect whatever trash you find. The fish will thank you.

YOUNG BRAINS

A massive effort to remove all plastic from the ocean is underway, thanks to the crowdfunded Ocean Cleanup Project. The founder of the organization, Boyan Slat, was just 18 years old when he proposed new technology to clean up the ocean. After a successful test last year, Slat and the Ocean Cleanup Project will soon be launching their first pilot operation off the coast of Japan. It takes young minds to change the world. What great ideas do YOU have?